TRANSCENDENT GARDENING

ED FALCO

C&R Press
Conscious & Responsible

First Edition
1 2 3 4 5 6 7 8 9

Cover art by xyz

ISBN 978-1-949540-33-8
LCCN 2022942175

C&R Press
Conscious & Responsible
crpress.org

For special discounted bulk purchases, please contact:
C&R Press sales@crpress.org
Contact info@crpress.org to book events, readings and author signings.

For

Those on that day who gathered
in my backyard over a bottle of
good bourbon

I say it once into the darkness.
Come on all you ghosts,
Try to make me forget you.

. . .

Come on all you ghosts,

I know you can hear me,
I know you are here,
I have heard you cough

and sigh when I pretend
I do not believe
I have to say something important.

--Matthew Zapruder "Come On All You Ghosts"

TRANSCENDENT GARDENING

ED FALCO

Falling Trees

Angel considered the shattered windshield of his car. A tree from his neighbor's yard had come down after a long night of wind and rain, the trajectory of its descent demolishing his chain link fence before the trunk settled high on the hood of his car with a ground-rattling thunk that woke him from a comatose sleep. He took in this scene of destruction from a kitchen window that looked out over a covered porch. It was early, a little after 7 a.m. on a wet spring morning in Georgia, Anno Domini 2016. Several of his neighbor's goats had already found their way over the crushed fence and were busily devouring two neat rows of ornamental grasses that lined a pair of gardens bracketing his blacktop driveway. Across the road, Frankie, the half pest, half pet groundhog who had a burrow under Angel's porch, peeked out from a culvert pipe.

Angel went back to bed and pulled a quilt over his face. A moment later, Shelly wrapped her arms around his chest, kissed the back of his head, and rested her sleep-warm cheek on his shoulder.

"Go back to sleep, sweetheart," she said. "It's still early."

Angel's breath went shallow. He *felt* Shelly's cheek against his neck. He felt her arms around his chest. She had yet to manifest visually: If he opened his eyes, he'd be alone. In the dark, though, warm under quilts, she was a physical presence, an animate being with a mind and will of her own. He didn't know what she would say next. He didn't know what she would do.

It hadn't always been like this. In the beginning, she was a simple fantasy. On lazy mornings he'd dream up an attractive woman of his acquaintance. All he wanted was the pleasure of a woman in his bed—and what was so wrong with that? In time, though, over the course of the last few years, those fantasy women evolved.

He understood that he was conjuring these figures. Of course they weren't real. Except...somewhere along the way, not too long in the past, he'd quit dreaming up students or secretaries or the hot bank teller at his local Wells Fargo office, and the woman—women—who shared his bed became a single woman, a shape shifter who one morning whispered her own name—*Tell Shelly what you're thinking, sweetheart*—and then listened attentively while he responded. Warm in his bed, under a comfy quilt, he told her what he was thinking before the fantasy progressed along its usual route of undressing her (he liked the ritual of unbuttoning and unclasping, the slow revealing of breasts and belly and thighs), of touch and entry, the urgent bodily dance that led to release and the moments afterward of quiet and peace, his head comfortable on a down pillow, alone in his bed, the familiar hum of his house the only sound.

That first morning when Shelly revealed her name, he understood that she was a dream, a woman conjured out of his own consciousness. Still. She spoke to him, and there was no sense that he was controlling the conversation. That was different, and it scared him a little, but it also provided such sweet company and comfort that he went along with it, arguing with another part of his mind, the part that objected, arguing that he knew he was dreaming. In fact, there was a term for it—*lucid dreaming*—and a branch of scientific inquiry built around it. He was dreaming while aware of the dream. It frightened him a bit at first when he found himself engaged in conversations with someone who wasn't, literally, present, or didn't, literally, exist. But that was the thing. Those mornings, she did exist. She had a name: Shelly. She changed shapes from visit to visit, sometimes young, sometimes his own age, sometimes thin, sometimes full-bodied, but always the same caring, comforting, loving woman under the skin. Shelly. She spoke to him. She gave him pleasure. She provided comfort. He saw no reason to give her up. When he wanted her company, he got into bed, closed his eyes, and did this thing in his mind that was like sinking down under fathoms of dark water until she was there with him, by his side. And now he could feel her, her hands around his chest, her kiss on the back of his neck as real as his own heartbeat. He was afraid to open his eyes—but he didn't know if he was afraid that he'd see her or afraid he wouldn't.

Pressed against his back, she felt older, a woman perhaps close to his own age. He never knew what he was getting with Shelly. Sometimes she was young. Often she was far too young. But she could also be more age appropriate—he was forty-one—and this morning she felt like a woman in her forties, soft and full-bodied and of course beautiful. She was always beautiful.

Angel said, "I think it's time I had a talk with my neighbor."

"But you don't even know his name," Shelly said. "And he's dangerous. Go back to sleep." She combed a few strands of hair that had fallen over his eyes back off his forehead and kissed him on the ear.

"I should know his name." Ten years Angel had lived in his simple clapboard house near the bottom of Price's Mountain, surrounded by a few families who had lived in the area since the Great Depression. They were families that kept to themselves, which was okay with Angel. Still, in all these years, he should have at least figured out the guy's first name.

"Besides," Shelly added, "between his dogs and the shooting range with that shotgun going off who knows when, it's dangerous. You'd have to climb over the fence, first of all, since he keeps it chained. Once you're on his property God knows what might happen."

"Maybe I could call him." Angel turned over under the quilts to get a look at Shelly. He was right. She appeared to be in her late thirties or early forties, a redhead with bright green eyes and a light field of freckles across her face. She wore a silky blue pajama top that clung to her shoulders and breasts. Her lips were painted bright red and glossy.

"You tried that the last time his goats got out," she said, her breath warm and minty. "His number's unlisted."

A year or so ago, Angel had stepped out of his house to get the newspaper and been confronted by a black and white billy goat staring at him with a contemptuous glare. Behind the billy goat, a half dozen more goats were munching on his poor hostas. When Angel tried to shoo the billy goat away, it lowered its head and butted him in the knee, sending a shock of pain along his spinal column to the back of his neck. He'd grabbed the goat by the horns only to be amazed at the strength of the creature. After wrestling with it briefly, he gave up and limped back to his house. From his kitchen window, he'd watched the goats devour his gorgeous, carefully cultivated hostas. When he tried to call his neighbor—he knew his last name from the mailbox beside the property's front gate—he could find no number listed for the name and address.

"Maybe you should shoot a few of his goats," Shelly said, "or his dogs. Send him a message."

"I don't own a gun. I'm opposed to gun ownership." Angel snuggled up against Shelly, his lips against her neck, under her chin. He went about unbuttoning her pajama top as she ran her fingers through his hair.

"Or you could just kill the dumb cracker," Shelly purred. "Take that confederate flag he flies on top of his dog kennel and shove it up his ass."

"That's not me." Angel paused in his erotic wandering over Shelly's body, given the conversation's turn, which worried him. "I don't believe in violence."

Shelly laughed and stroked his head. Her eyes glittered. "How can you not believe in violence, Sweetie? Do you read the papers? Do you watch the news?"

"You know what I mean." Angel pushed Shelly onto her back and pulled off her pajama bottoms. "My god," he said, his eyes closed tight. "You're gorgeous."

Shelly took Angel's head in her hands. "Go ahead," she crooned. "Go ahead, Darlin'."

"You're perfect," Angel answered, violence and goats, fallen trees and idiot neighbors and shattered windshields—all of it swiftly falling away.

A Conversation

"Tell me this," Cranston Wade III asked, the tone of his voice making it immediately clear he was going to say something stupid.

Cranston Wade III was the principal of the high school where Angel picked up a little extra money—very little—by teaching a once-a-week poetry workshop via the auspices of the Poets in the Schools Program.

Angel wasn't a poet.

Angel had, however, taken a poetry workshop as an undergraduate at the University of Iowa. When he'd told the Poets in the Schools coordinator that he had gone to Iowa, she'd assumed he'd meant the famous graduate creative writing program and had hired him immediately. Once Angel figured out there would be no bothersome dealing with official credentials, that he was about to be hired on the basis of a casual conversation, he chose not to correct the misimpression.

This all happened—Angel first getting hired—a little more than a year earlier, some eight years after Dolores left.

A week after that initial interview, when the coordinator asked to see some of his poems, Angel searched the Internet for a poet who had graduated from the University of Iowa's MFA program, and who had published only a handful of poems in little-known, online literary journals that were most likely read by almost no one. Also, there could be no author's picture available or defining biographical information. The bio had to be a) unavailable or b) say something simple, like "X has previously published poems in X journals. He or she is a graduate of the University of Iowa."

He found several!

Angel chose X.J. Williamson, downloaded his/her poems, and delivered them to the coordinator, explaining that he published under the degenderized pseudonym for its perfect anonymity, which allowed him to write freely, without fear of offending anyone who might turn up in his poems, and also to publish without the onus of gender bias making his publication as a male more likely. He asked her not to share his pseudonym with others.

"Tell me this," Cranston Wade III asked, "isn't Angel a woman's name?"

Cranston was a big guy who'd lost an eye playing ice hockey when he was kid. He wore crazy, brightly colored eye patches that slipped over the right lens of his wire rim glasses. The kids loved him. Today he was wearing a red Spiderman eye patch.

They were standing outside the teacher's lounge. A throng of teenagers sporting multi-hued backpacks chattered and shouted as they hurried along the tiled corridor. A tenth grader in the early weeks of pregnancy had thrown up in her locker earlier that morning and the corridor still smelled of bleach.

"Angel di Maria, Angel Rangel, Angel Renya, Angel Martinez, Angel Gaston Diaz." Angel offered Cranston his standard reply to the isn't-that-a-girl's-name question.

"Who?" Cranston appeared befuddled.

"You don't follow soccer," Angel noted. "How about baseball? Angel Pagen: The San Francisco Giants; Angel Chavez: again, the Giants; Angel Hernandez."

"Oh, yeah," Cranston said. "Angel Cordero Jr.," he added, playing along, "the great jockey. Who's Angel Hernandez?"

"2006 *Sports Illustrated* Third Worst Umpire in Major League Baseball."

"Those are all Puerto Rican names," Cranston pressed. "I thought you were Italian."

"Angel Vivaldi," Angel countered. "Italian, from New Jersey, guitar player for 40 Below Summer."

"If you say so." Cranston slapped Angel on the shoulder and started off down the hall to his office but stopped after only a few steps. "By the way," he said, "Ginny showed me one of your poems." Ginny was the Poets in the Schools coordinator. "You have to explain it to me sometime when you have a minute." He whispered, with a smile, the corridor now empty of students, *"I have no idea what the hell it's about."*

"Sure thing," Angel said, and headed off into the teacher's lounge.

That was a conversation he'd be sure to avoid, since he had no idea what the hell X.J. Williamson's poems were about either.

More Trees and Critters

Every rainy night reminded Angel of that night nine years in the past when a line of thunderstorms had blown through North Georgia, bringing with them waterfalls of rain that rolled down the hillside and into the depression that formed a large portion of his neighbor's land, briefly transforming the farm slash animal menagerie slash shooting range into a muddy pond. Several trees, their roots soaked, had fallen, and Angel awakened in the depth of night to goats and miniature horses and a pair of donkeys gorging themselves on his back yard's elaborate gardens, two fallen trees having sliced through his then new fence. He'd awakened to the nickering of miniature horses and the thudding splash of hooves on sodden ground.

Dolores had already moved out of the master bedroom by then and made a place for herself in the study, sleeping on the convertible sofa formerly reserved for guests.

When he went to look in on her, he found the study empty.

On the Greenway

Claire Maso power walks briskly along the riverside Greenway trail in black Brooks Women's Addiction Walkers, black Under Armour, ultra-tight, skin fit leggings, and a royal blue, sleeveless, graphic T-shirt that reads, "CARPE THE _____ OUT OF THIS DIEM!"

Claire, a twenty-two-year-old social media multimillionaire. This morning, the river to her right flowing fast and high after a wild night of storms. Claire's worried about her father and Kenny and her mother and…fuck. She's worried about everyone. "Why can't anybody, I mean *anybody* I know keep it together!" She's talking to Linni, her walking companion and 24-7 assistant, a six-foot-tall Norwegian goddess of a woman, a former model almost twice Claire's age. And six inches taller.

Linni knows Claire well enough not to attempt a reply. She listens, which is a substantial part of her work.

"My father's still living out in the boondocks. Will he let me buy him a place in town? A nice condo, maybe? Of course not. That makes too much sense. Plus…." Claire starts to tell Linni more and then pulls up. She doesn't want Linni thinking her father's a lunatic. "And Kenny," she switches subjects, "what have we done to that boy? We took this sweet, angelic-looking, golden-haired blue-eyed Momma's boy grocery clerk still living in his mother's house, and now look at him. How many girls can he fuck? Is there no limit to the amount of drugs he can do? Seriously, we've got to get him in rehab."

"In such a way," Linni says, softly but firmly, "that no one knows about it."

"Absolutely," Claire says. "He'll be back clerking groceries in a year if this gets out."

"Is something up with Doll?" Linni asks.

Claire grunts by way of an answer, or by way of saying she doesn't want to answer. God how it irks her hearing her mother called Doll. The woman's name is Dolores. What kind of a name for an adult is

Doll? *Dolores* was perfectly fine all the years Claire was growing up with her—then she's out the door goggle-eyed over Gloria, an idiot twenty-one-year-old local girl and all of a sudden she's a gay woman named Doll. WTF? I was thirteen! Did she even think about that?

Claire picks up her pace. The trail, strewn with branches and leaves wind-ripped to the ground in green clumps, curves closer to the river until they're walking on the bank, rushing water brown with churned up mud and silt roiling alongside them, sloshing over the banks, puddling onto blacktop.

Thirteen. My mother has a girlfriend....

Claire in middle school, a skinny awkward bespectacled kid living with her father who is clueless but tries.

Claire in high school, living with her cell phone, the gadget never out of reach. On Facebook, Twitter, Pinterest, Google Plus+, You Tube, Tumbler, Instagram, Flicker, Vine. What else? Tagged, Meetme, Classmates....

Not MySpace. No one is on MySpace.

Claire skips college. She develops a YouTube channel, a blog, an online fashion site, an e-store. She finds and manages social media celebrities, especially on Vine—jackpot! She travels the world finding talent. She discovers Kenny right here in town bagging groceries. A middle school girl posted his picture on Facebook: *Kenny from Kroger.* Hundreds shared. Claire swooped.

At twenty-two Claire owns a beach house in South Carolina, a condo in Manhattan, a McMansion/office here in Redvale, town of her birth and upraising, such as it was, and here she is on a rainy spring morning power walking alongside a swollen river, and it's like it so often is in this town where she grew up: a familiar place, a few innocuous words, a clicked-on memory, and she's thrown back in time into a place where she was small and powerless.

I'm thirteen and my mother has a girlfriend and now it's just me and dad, me and dad, me and dad.

Linni rephrases her question. "Is Doll still liking it on the Board?

Something going on there?"

"My mother's fine." Claire glances at the rushing muddy water, the ordinary liveliness gone out of her face. "She's concerned about Gloria not reaching her potential." She turns to face Linni for the first time since they started their morning walk. "That's what she talks to me about, how worried she is that Gloria won't reach her potential."

"Ah," Linni's first thought is *What potential?*, which she suppresses. Instead, she appeals to Claire's better nature. "She makes Doll happy. I know you want your mother to be happy."

"Right." Claire picks up her pace, swinging her arms, fists clenched. "We've got the UTA conference call this afternoon. Everything in place?"

"Everything's spectacular, it's perfect, it's huge," Linni says, deadpan, mocking the effusiveness of personalities in the entertainment industry.

Claire smiles and then laughs. She glances down at her Apple watch and checks the data on the health and fitness app before pulling her iPhone out from the waistband of her leggings and navigating to Calm, *the simple guided meditation & mindfulness* app she has only recently downloaded. She puts her ear buds in and a moment later she's listening to the sounds of a Summer Meadow. She closes her eyes and reboots. *I'm thinking of nothing at all*, she thinks, and continues walking at a more relaxed pace. She still has several hours before the UTA—

I'm thinking of nothing at all.

If Gloria were anymore empty-headed the girl would be comatose.

Nothing at all, nothing at all.

Dad, really? The mumbling, the talking to yourself, come on—

Nothing, nothing nothing, nothing, nothing….

Kenny.

Nothing.

Kenny. Kenny from Kroger. The boy's smile….

Nothing.

Alongside the muddy river, on the Greenway, Claire smiling, Linni lost in thought, the two of them at the start of the day, on their morning walk.

Angel's Lullaby

Outside, wind picks up again, twigs and branches hit the gable roof, clatter over shingles.

Outside, a small sinkhole fills with rainwater, expands.

Outside, bombs explode in war zones.

Outside, demagogues lean over lecterns and exhale curses.

Outside, bombs explode in markets.

Outside, the world judges and makes demands.

Outside, the Predator B drone, the MQ-9 Reaper.

Outside, fallen trees, insurance adjusters, rental car companies, collision repair services, body shops.

Inside, Angel spent, warm and sleepy, his head resting comfortably on a pillow, the familiar hum of his house a kind of lullaby, a restful song.

Where Am I?

Kenny hopes he remembered to make them sign the contracts. He'd check his pockets, but he doesn't have any pockets at the moment.

He sits up in bed. He has no idea where he is.

No cell phones, no pictures or videos, no tweets, no Facebook postings, no gossip sheets, no blogs, etc. It's all in the contract.

The girls are both sleeping. Gingerly, he climbs over the tall one. Dude, she has a great ass! His jeans, draped neatly over the back of a stuffed chair. He's in a bedroom that's bigger than the living room in his mother's house, where he lived from birth until his twenty-first birthday two months to the day from this morning when he doesn't know where he is.

The bedroom: gleaming hardwood floors. Sliding glass doors that look out to a balcony and beyond to mountains in the distance, the day overcast and wet from a rainy night. Polished dark wood furniture. Cherry? He thinks so. Probably. A long dresser with a mirror in which he sees his reflection and the sleigh bed and the sleeping girls. The mess of his curly blond hair. He combs it with his fingers, shakes it into place. Dude, this bedroom is huge! He could throw a party in here! A 60-inch flat screen mounted on the wall. A turntable on an entertainment unit, over about a bazillion albums. Someone's into vinyl big time! He checks out a couple of album jackets. John Coltrane? Sonny Rollins? He shrugs and slides them back in place.

Damn, his pants pockets are empty. No contracts. He checks the pockets of his sleek leather jacket hung over the chair back, a jacket that cost several times more than he paid for his first car. Nothing in the jacket pockets. He falls back into the stuffed chair and holds his head. He's screwed if they didn't sign the contracts.

In bed, the short one turns over and pulls the comforter to her chin. She's pretty: shoulder length silver blond hair, eyebrows angled like a bird's wings in flight over blue eyes.

The jigsaw puzzle pieces of the previous night snap back into place: Willies, a crowded dance floor, with Amayr and Bobby before the girls and the parking lot, getting high in the back of a yellow Hummer, then to their house, the girls' house—they're sisters! Willow and Aspen, the tree family girls. Birch, their younger brother, is with their parents in St. Thomas. It all comes back to Kenny now. The pieces jaggedly fall in place: the boys, the bar, the girls, the Hummer, this ballroom-size bedroom.…

But not the contracts. He can't remember whether he made them sign the contracts.

Kenny checks the nightstand next to Willow, the tall one with the great ass. On the tabletop, an opaque globe that might be some kind of art or might do something when you touch it, like light up or play music. He doesn't touch it. He opens the night table drawer, where he finds a silver coke bullet, two sleek gold mushroom snorters, and a mirror dusted with coke. He checks his reflection in the mirror, combs his fingers through his hair again, shakes it out again.

He glances out the sliding glass doors and guesses the time, noon or so. There are no clocks around, no phones. But if no cell phones, then he explained the conditions, and if he explained the conditions, he would have apologized and pulled the contracts from his pocket and gone on about his own contract, and, sorry, but, like, that's the deal.

But also…they were high even before the Hummer and so he can't be sure.

Kenny is getting that pulled down feeling that comes over him after a big night. He looks out the window toward the mountains and remembers it's Sunday and that he told his mom he'd go to church with her.

Shit.

But she wouldn't have waited. Probably, she never expected he'd show up. He hadn't been good like that for a long time, keeping his word, doing whatever it is he'd said he'd do. Somehow they'd slipped into this place where he just said things and made promises that they both knew he didn't mean and wouldn't keep but they both went along, with Kenny saying whatever was needed to make her happy, his mother happy in the moment, both of them knowing it meant nothing at all.

Kenny closes the night table drawer. He finds his underwear inside his jeans and is about to pull on his boxers when Aspen sits up in bed. "Kenny," she says, her high-pitched voice still thick with sleep, "you're not leaving, are you?" She sounds a little like Minnie Mouse from those old cartoons.

Kenny takes a good look at Aspen and for the first time wonders about her age. They met at Willies, where you have to show ID to get in, but damn she looks young.

"I just remembered," Kenny says, his boxers dangling from one ankle, "I promised my mom I'd take her to church this morning."

Willow, on the opposite side of the bed, a single lane of emptiness between her and Aspen, opens her eyes and touches the mysterious globe on her night table. It lights up with the time: 1:45 PM. "It's too late for church," she says, with the same Minnie Mouse voice as her sister. It's kind of funny.

Together, in sisterly synchronization, the girls pat the empty space between them.

Kenny thinks about it, realizes a) he doesn't have his car and b) he doesn't know where he is. "Well, shit," he says, and he flashes them the smile that's making him rich, all white teeth and boyish under glittering blue eyes. "Guess I'll have to miss church then," he adds, and he crawls up onto the bed, moving like a cat as the girls reach out for him.

Weird Shit Happens

Angel dreamed about an uncle he hadn't seen since he was a child. Uncle Augustino, an old-school dock yard laborer with just enough English to get by. The stereotype *I'm a gonna give you a slap across a da face!* Italian patriarch off the boat from Napoli when he was fifteen, a job on the docks a week later where he worked until he suffered a slight heart attack in his sixties while swinging a cargo hook at the head of a Ukrainian kid who had said something he didn't like. Eleven children. Nine boys, two girls. Every summer for two weeks Angel and his brother Tony would spend Fourth of July week with Uncle Augustino and Aunt Mary and all the cousins in Canarsie and on the Fourth they'd cram on board Uncle Augustino's fishing boat to watch fireworks in the harbor, the colorful explosions draped over the Statue of Liberty. Fat Uncle Augie in his grease-stained coveralls and yellowing T-shirt, a thick, foul-smelling stogie stuck in his mouth, a face like a gargoyle: sharp nose, big eyes, ugly as roadkill.

In the dream, Uncle Augie was dressed like Colonel Sanders: white suit, black bow tie, black suit pocket square, gold wristwatch, a wood crookneck walking cane. Impeccably groomed. No stogie. They're in Angel's basement rec room. Uncle Augie stands in front of a recliner, blocking Angel's view of a ball game on TV. Angel says, "Uncle Augie, I'm trying to watch the game," and Uncle Augie replies, in perfect English, with a hint of a British accent, "Don't you know who she is, Angel? Open your eyes!" Angel has no idea what Uncle Augie is talking about. He looks him over, the white suit, the crookneck walking cane, the British accent. "Uncle Augie," he says, "What the hell happened to you?" but before his uncle can answer the question, Angel's bedside phone rings and wakes him from the dream.

And who's on the phone? His brother Tony.

And why has Tony called? To tell Angel that their Uncle Augie died a few hours earlier.

Angel shouted, "Get the fuck out of here!"

"What?" Tony shouted back. "The guy was 96 years old! You're shocked he died?"

Angel considered telling Tony about the dream and decided no. Tony already thought Angel was a flake. Tony with his CPA business in Manhattan, his television-producer wife, his two boys graduated from Cornell. Angel with his gardening slash landscaping business in the boondocks of North Georgia, his lesbian ex-wife, his daughter who didn't even go to college and is still somehow making a fortune doing mysterious things with social media that Angel himself didn't understand well enough to fully explain. Tony had consequently gotten it into his head that Claire was really a drug dealer. The social media stuff had to be a cover. He had repeated this theory to Angel several times. Thus, they weren't currently getting along.

"Look, I just called to tell you about Uncle Augie," Tony said. "I thought you'd want to know."

"Thanks," Angel managed, and after another few seconds of bullshit hung up and pulled on a pair of jeans and a faded blue sweatshirt with his business logo—a blossoming yellow rose—under the business's name, *Transcendent Gardening*. Yes, he knew it was a stupid name for a gardening slash landscaping business, but he had loved it—until the sweatshirts and t-shirts and business cards and phone book ads and internet site were all delivered and posted and then it just looked stupid but then it was also too late to change. So now he's Angel Maso, *Transcendent Gardening*.

He was already in the kitchen before he remembered the fallen tree and the shattered windshield and crumpled hood of his car. On the porch step under the kitchen window, Frankie sniffed the air as he lazily gazed out over his domain. Critter looked like a mix between a squirrel and a small dog, with a dog's soulful eyes. The rain had mostly stopped, nothing more than a light drizzle. A low roof of clouds, dreary day.

Angel knocked on the window and Frankie, startled, leapt off the porch and waddled speedily over grass and down into the culvert pipe.

Behind Angel, Shelly said, "Honey, face it. You simply have to do something about your neighbor."

This was something new. This was weird.

Not that he hadn't heard Shelly's voice in his head on numerous previous occasions and even held mumbled conversations with her, if out in public, and full on out loud conversations at home—but she had never before stepped out of her dream space to join him in the kitchen. He heard her voice as if seated at the kitchen table. She seemed to be not a voice in his head but in the room, approximately seven feet behind him, at the faux marble kitchen table with its hand-crafted, wooden bowl full of unopened mail, and its black and white ceramic dueling Gandalf and Saruman salt and pepper shakers, a gift from Claire during that brief period in her life when she was in love with kitsch.

"Are you even listening to me, Angel?" Shelly's voice urgent, maybe annoyed. On the edge of angry. "You're letting that sorry son of a bitch walk all over you. Have you not sent him a letter by certified mail demanding he cut down or prune back the several trees in danger of falling onto your property? Now look at this! Your car's a disaster!"

This was also something new, the angry tone of voice.

"I'm only thinking of you," Shelly cooed, all sweetness once again. "Have you not also tried to speak to him on at least two occasions?"

"The one time," Angel said, "I waited for him at his gate, and he completely ignored me."

"That was after those foul-smelling goats destroyed your beautiful hostas."

"Right," Angel said. "He got out of his truck, unchained the gate, and acted like I wasn't right there, talking to him. He unchained the damn gate, ignored me, and drove off."

"And the other time?"

"I tried shouting to him over the fence."

"Ignored you again."

"Exactly."

"Now look," Shelly said, and then she was a step behind him.

"Look at that mess: the car's a wreck, the goats have eaten all your pink cotton candy grass, the fence is crushed…. Where are you even going to start?"

"Call Oline, I guess." Oline was Angel's auto insurance agent.

"She's not going to be happy. She wanted you to sue him last time."

Angel turned to look at Shelly—and there she was. Same voice, new body. The sight of her calmed him. He put her age at twenty, twenty-one max, far too young for him, but who cared? It's not like she was real. Well, really real. Here with him in his kitchen she was real enough. Barefoot in blue jeans and a black V-neck cashmere sweater cut low, she nuzzled into him as he pressed his cheek against cascading waves of rich blue-black hair, her head against his chest.

"Really," Shelly whispered, "we can't let him keep disrespecting you like this." She cuddled closer, kissed his chest. "We need," she cooed, "to think seriously about killing the redneck, shit-for-brains, half-wit, confederate-flag-waving, inbred son of a bitch."

"Shsssh," Angel said, still stroking her hair. "I don't think like that. I'm not a violent man."

"I know you don't," she murmured, voice like a second-grade teacher consoling a little boy, "but we need to seriously consider crucifying the bastard: tying him spread eagle to the fence and then, I don't know, maybe shoving that shotgun of his down his throat and pulling the trigger. Maybe cutting off his balls. Maybe we could say something like 'Try ignoring me now, shithead! Are you ignoring me now?' You know, something like that."

"Sweetheart," Angel said, "you're talking crazy." He put his arm around her waist and led her back to the bedroom. "Come on," he said, "I've got a better idea."

Vocabulary for Achievement

Doll arranged herself standing sideways in front of a full-length mirror. In the bedroom of her two-story, mountain-ridge home with a panoramic view of the valley. Black slacks, black jacket, simple white blouse accented by a thick silver wheat chain necklace. *You're getting fat,* she said to herself as she pulled a brush over still dark, still lustrous shoulder-length hair. *You're not fat. You're middle-aged, a little thick around the waist and in the thighs. Okay, so, a belly. Big deal.* "How do I look?" she asked Gloria.

Gloria, who turned 30 a few days earlier, can't buy beer without getting carded, can't get into a bar without showing ID, can't even get a glass of wine in a restaurant without flashing her driver's license. Still in bed. Sitting up, faded blue cotton sleep shirt clinging to her shoulders, sandy blond hair cut boy-short. Big brown eyes, petite body, full breasts, sleek skinned, an anime girl come to life, lounging in Doll's bed, watching Doll dress for work.

Go back ten years. Doll is Dolores Maso, née Kostopoulos. She's just been elected County Clerk. Into the clerk's office walks a beautiful child. She looks sixteen, maybe. Dolores is thirty-two. The child's name is Gloria Tiller. She's filing divorce papers. Twenty-one, married while still a senior in high school, twice issued restraining orders against her ex. *That's all over now,* she says to Dolores. *I'm done with men.* She offers up a smile that works on Dolores like a power outage: in an instant, the light changes, the atmosphere shifts. Everything is altered. Is it possible for a smile to change the molecular makeup of a human body? That's what it feels like. Dolores isn't Dolores. She's changed. She might as well have been floating several inches off the ground.

"You look hardass," Gloria said. "You look...," searching for the word, perplexed smile, "formidable." Having found the right word, her face lit up. She was proud of herself. She'd been working on her vocabulary for years, ever since she started up with Doll. It made her insecure, all the big words Doll knew that she didn't. Soon after they'd gotten together, she'd bought *Vocabulary for Achievement* and *SAT Vocabulary Building Flashcards*. She'd kept them hidden ever since, working on her vocabulary in secret.

This overcast and rainy morning, Doll was on her way to a Redvale County Board of Supervisors meeting, where she was serving her first term as a board member. She looked herself over one more time, straightened out her jacket, and then sat on the edge of the bed and tugged at Gloria's ankle under the comforter. "Are you going to talk to Mikala today? I've been singing your praises to her. I'm almost positive she'll hire you. You just have to go in and talk to her."

Gloria frowned elaborately. "Not today. I'm getting my hair cut and I have a mani pedi this afternoon."

"Gloria...," Doll's stern voice. Her serious face.

"I don't know why you want me to work all of a sudden." Gloria snatched a pillow and hugged it to her chest. "It never bothered you before that I didn't work. You used to be fine with it. In fact," she added, leaning forward, "you told me any number of times that I didn't have to work. That you liked taking care of me."

"I do like taking care of you," Doll said, "and you don't *have to* work. I just think it would be good for you to get out of the house more, expand your social circle, interact with more people. Really, Gloria, do you want to spend the rest of your life getting mani pedis and massages?"

"Yes!" Gloria howled. "I do!"

Doll glowered, unwilling to be amused.

"Okay, okay," Gloria said, "but not today."

"I'm thinking of you," Doll said. "I swear. I only want what's best for you."

"I know," Gloria said. "You want me to have a more capacious social circle."

Doll covered her face with both hands to hide the smile that threatened to turn into laughter. She rubbed her eyes and struggled to look as if she were yawning. "Exactly," she said once she regained control. "I think you'd be happier with a more capacious social circle." She pushed the comforter aside and lifted Gloria's foot by the heel. "What are you going for this time?"

"Aruba blue with a flower design." Gloria wiggled her wine-red-with-a-thin-stripe-of-gold-glitter toenails. "It'll look gorgeous," she said, "with the yellow gold toe ring you got me for my twenty-fifth birthday."

It was endearing the way Gloria remembered every single gift Doll had ever given her, both the gift and the occasion. It was more than endearing; it made something glow inside Doll. She kissed Gloria's ankle. "I've got to get to work."

"Love you." Gloria slipped down under the comforter. "I'm going to sleep in a bit." She snuggled her head into a pillow.

"Love you, too." Doll, on her way out of the bedroom, sneaked a last look at Gloria before closing the door gently.

Lazy, selfish, sweet, beautiful Gloria.

Doll adored her.

The Man with an Ugly Heart

Angel began the day, every day, by reading *The New York Times*. But this day was slipping away from him. Noon, and here's Angel trudging out of his bedroom in the same ragged, yellowing white terry cloth robe that's been hanging on the back of one bedroom door or another since Dolores swiped it from the Spirit Lake hotel where they'd spent their weekend honeymoon.

Iowa. She was already twelve weeks pregnant.

Angel paused his start-of-day routine coffee making and breakfast preparation and newspaper reading. He took a seat at the kitchen table and fingered his scalp gently, as if massaging memories.

They'd been dating since freshman year, after meeting in Intro to Playwriting. In class, the professor—a strange man with a bald, alien-big head and crazed, pop-out eyes—had the students arrange table readings of their original plays, and Dolores had asked Angel to read the role of a child-molesting Catholic priest. It was sweet. (The gesture of asking him to read the role was sweet, not the role itself, which was a horror show.) Child-molesting Catholic priests had been in the news at the time in Iowa City, and Dolores' play was, as the professor explained, mockingly, *ripped from the headlines*. He didn't think it was a good idea to rip plays from headlines. Admittedly, it wasn't a very good play. The priest talked to God a lot and said things like *I know I'm a bad man! But you made me this way, God! You made me such as I am!* A lot. And every time the priest explained how bad he was and how God made him that way, the professor's eyes looked like they might detonate and blast across the room. But Dolores had asked Angel to read the big role in her play, and Angel had been pleased. He was just starting to have a crush on her then. Cute girl, dark hair, a line of three small red stars tattooed on the web between thumb and forefinger. Excellent posture. An almost military demeanor. He had also just started writing his own play, *The Man with an Ugly Heart*, which he had been trying to complete, on and off, ever since.

Angel roused himself from his kitchen table stupor and went

about putting up a pot of coffee. Outside, goats roamed the yard, munching on his grass and devouring his plants. They'd be there until the neighbor came and herded them back to their barn—or until he called Animal Control, which he didn't want to do. Angel's father had been a lunatic who fought bloody battles with all his neighbors, and Angel had grown up caught in the middle of those endless lawsuits and police cruisers parked in his driveway and screaming adults raving like men on fire. All his life he had striven not to be like his father, and that very much included not getting into squabbles with his neighbors. He understood how those squabbles could escalate into life-threatening events, like the night his father pulled a baseball bat out of the garage, crossed the yard between his suburban home and his neighbors, and went about smashing every window in the neighbor's house while screaming curses so vile Angel cringed even now at the memory. "May you die with a prick through your heart!" That was one of them, a curse lodged frighteningly in some bright undying spot in Angel's consciousness. His father had spent a weekend in jail after that, and there had been serious talk of civil commitment.

Did Angel love his father? Was he terrified of the man? Yes, and absolutely. Had anyone been there in the car with them on a Saturday morning trip to the mall, they'd understand. A quiet weekend morning on suburban Long Island. Angel in the back seat of one of the unending line of Buicks his father drove. His older brother Tony in the front. Someone on the road does something of which his father disapproves, and off he goes, screaming out the window, shaking his fist. A short, brawny man, bulky and muscled from hauling steel beams and girders, an ironworker. His face turns red. Veins bulge in his neck and temples. Tears of fury well up in his eyes, and when the car that has so offended him stops at a light, Angel's father steps on the gas and crashes into it. Then he backs up and does it again. Then he's out of the car and suddenly he's fighting with multiple men, three or four at least, the details go fuzzy before Angel's glazed eyes. Other men emerge from other cars. One of them is wearing a bright orange, tufted vest. It's cold. They have his father pinned to the hood of the Buick. Tony is out there, too. He's on the hood. He kicks one of the men in the face, a solid blow that catches him between nose and eye. The man backhands Tony, who's maybe nine years old, and knocks him to the ground. Now there are women out of their cars and everybody, everybody is screaming. At some point the police must have come. At some point order must have been restored. Angel doesn't remember. Just the screaming and Tony tumbling to the ground and the gathering crowd, while he's huddled in the back seat, curled up into himself, his own arms wrapped around his own shoulders, as if he's both the protector and the child in need of protection.

While the coffee brewed, Angel dropped two eggs in a pot of water, placed it securely in the center of an electric burner on the stove, turned the heat up high, and set the timer for fifteen minutes. First, coffee and breakfast. Then he'd deal with the mess outside. Meanwhile, he carried his iPad from the study and sat down with it at the kitchen table. While coffee brewed, while eggs boiled, while goats wandered over his property, while Frankie snuggled in his burrow, Angel read the news. A boat carrying migrants sinks in the Mediterranean, 500 lost. A bomb explodes in an Iraqi market. Kalashnikovs. Ak-47s. ISIL. Magnitude 7.8 earthquake in Ecuador, 650 dead. ISIS treatment of Christians and Yazidi declared genocide. The primaries, the candidates for president, riots at rallies. Another Boko Haram massacre in Nigeria. Climate Change. The extinction of species. The coming plague. Terrorist, terrorism.

Terrorists

Terrorism

Terrorists

Terrorism

The usual for a weekday morning, spring 2016.

Angel gets lost in the reading.

The world around him fades.

"The Crossing"

Cranston harbored suspicions. Late afternoon of a dreary spring day and he's thinking about Esther Price, sweet little Esther who played a hummingbird in the second-grade Thanksgiving play back when he was teaching English and Math to seven-year-olds, sweet little Esther Price vomiting such copious amounts of green bile infused with strings of what looked like bright red Ramen noodles into the depths of her hallway locker that a stinking stream of the stuff spilled out into the corridor and threatened to pollute the entire city with its noxious odor. Then the nurse and her parents and that asshat, Ricky Mulvaney, who God help us all was on his way to being a father at sixteen.

Cranston sighed like a thousand-year-old man as he picked himself up from his wobbly desk chair with one perpetually stuck roller and carried the ever-increasing bulk of his body to the office window where he looked out to the now nearly empty parking lot. Forty-seven. Married with four children, all girls. It was almost five o'clock.

On Principal Cranston's desk, the sleek, 27" iMac computer screen lit up with a poem by X.J. Williamson.

The Crossing

You can hurl
your heart into his brazen
shoes if you want to
do what you always do

What you always do bright songstress shattered
chalcedony

On simmering pavement

Broken promontory

If I swish through the ballroom will you dance
with the party queen

and her entourage of exquisite dreamers

An apologue
Depends from my cervix

A skirring in fields of diazepam

Your slender fingers under a shattered red dress

Cranston had read the poem so many times he had it nearly by memory. He couldn't for the life of him figure out what the hell it might mean, but he knew what a cervix was and he knew Angel didn't have one. He might not understand the poem, but it still sounded awfully girlie to him, with its bright songstress and somebody's slender fingers under someone's red dress. The poem troubled him.

Last time he spoke to Angel, he had almost gathered up the nerve to confront him with his questions but wound up instead asking if *Angel* wasn't really a girl's name. What the hell was that about? What were you thinking, Cranston…that Angel was secretly a woman and that's why he wrote poems with cervixes in them? Cranston slapped himself in the head. He wasn't the brightest bulb on the string, but he wasn't stupid either, though, admittedly, stupid things did flash out of him often enough that he'd learned to keep his mouth shut as much as possible. But this poem had troubled him ever since Ginny texted him the URL under *Read Angel's poem! It's brilliant!*

Cranston checked his wristwatch, and in doing so magically summoned Ginny, who careened into the parking lot driving her falling-apart junker as if it were a Formula I race car. She took a corner fast and tight enough that the rear of the car spun out before she screeched across the lot and came to a halt alongside his Honda Civic, where she parked taking up two spaces. Was she drunk? Hadn't he spoken to her on multiple occasions about slowing down on school property? Cranston's face reddened and his shoulders with a will of their own hunched up as his head sunk down into his chest. His wife called it the turtle thing he did when he was angry, his head retreating into his chest with a scowl, his neck disappearing. He moved around to the front of his desk, leaned back against it striking a casual pose. When Ginny came through his office door, he said, "Ms. Diaz. I've asked you before to drive cautiously on school grounds." He pointed out the window. "I just observed you speeding through the parking lot at a dangerous...speed. I know," he added, backing off a little, "that the parking lot is empty. However, I have to insist that you drive cautiously on school grounds regardless of the time of day or the circumstances."

Ginny threw up her hands in surrender. "My bad," she said. "I won't do it again. Promise!" She flashed Cranston a smile, put her hands on her hips and cocked her head, waiting for forgiveness.

Cranston sighed, another thousand-year-old man exhalation. "Okay," he said, "but I'm serious."

"I know. Truly," meaning she truly understood that he was serious. She wrapped her arms around his wide chest and gave him a loud smooch of a kiss on the cheek. "You're a darling!" she laughed and fell back into the tufted leather chair waiting in front of Cranston's desk. "Love the Spider Man," she said, nodding to his eye patch. "What did you want to see me about?"

Cranston pulled his office chair around to the front of the desk and sat across from her. She was an odd-looking young woman. He knew that she had just turned thirty a few weeks earlier, but she looked older. Or her face and her demeanor made her appear older. She was skinny, with red, blotchy skin: a persistent case of Rosacea if he had to guess, her cheeks almost bright red, and she wore unflattering, squarish, black frame glasses with thick lenses. She dressed, though, like a teenager, currently in black spiked high heels, red jeggings, and a black T-shirt with *Paramore* in big white chalky letters across the front and *Still Into You* in smaller letters under that. A band T-shirt, he assumed. Then there was her chin-length hair, always a startling array of colors, currently predominantly blue, with greenish streaks and a swatch of yellow in the middle. Looked enough like his Italian grandmother's spumoni to make him hungry.

"It's Angel Maso's poem that you sent me." Cranston arranged himself in his seat, his back upright, his hands gripping the armrests. "It concerns me."

"What about it?" Ginny asked, surprise written large across her face. "'The Crossing'?"

"Well, first...," Cranston twisted around and retrieved a printed copy of the poem from his desktop. He handed it to Ginny. "Do you understand it?" he asked. "Can you tell me what it means?"

"Well, I wouldn't call it a transparent poem," Ginny answered, without looking at the letter-sized sheet of white paper in her hand, "but I don't think it's opaque, either."

Cranston fixed his gaze on Ginny and waited.

"Angel doesn't write transparent, narrative poems. That's pretty much a used-up form in the 21st Century anyway," Ginny went on, "poems that *express* something, putting *the meaning* right out there, like punching you in the face with it."

Cranston waited.

"But it's not an opaque poem, either." Ginny dropped the sheet of paper to her lap and laid her hand on top of it as if swearing on a bible. "It's not a poem that's uninterested in any rational, discernable *meaning*."

"Good," Cranston said. "So what does it mean?"

Ginny squinted, her look playful, amused. "You want me to explicate the poem for you?"

"Yes." Cranston opened his hands, befuddled. "I'm at a loss."

"Okay." Ginny pulled her hair back off her face. "So, the first stanza: 'You can hurl / your heart into his brazen / shoes if you want to / do what you always do.' That's, you know, if you were a woman that would just be so clear—"

"So that's a woman?"

"Who's a woman?"

"The poem."

"Well," Ginny said, "it seems to be written from the perspective of woman, if that's what you mean, yes."

"You can do that?"

"What? A man write in the persona of a woman? Sure."

Ginny's words were saying one thing, her tone another. Cranston wondered if the gender issue was only now occurring to her. "What would be so clear," he asked, "if I were a woman?"

"Well," Ginny said, "hurling your heart into his brazen shoes is like, you know, women always giving themselves up to tough guys, falling in love with the brazen ones, the tough guys who, probably, are just going to shit all over them in the end."

Cranston took the poem back from her and looked it over. "So she's a bright songstress, okay—but what the hell is 'shattered chalcedony' on 'simmering pavement / broken promontory'?"

"I love those lines!" Ginny, perking up, snatched the poem back from Cranston. "When you get stepped on and walked all over by his brazen shoes, you're like the crushed crystalline stone, the *chalcedony*, you see shimmering in the pavement sometimes; you're a *broken promontory*, i.e. your heights have been blasted away. Then," she continued, excited, glancing down at the poem, "she thinks, 'if I swish through the ballroom will you dance with the party queen / and her entourage of exquisite dreamers,'" meaning, if I make myself like all the other dumb, look-good-for-your-guy kind of empty-headed girls full of pretty dreams about getting married and having kids, etcetera, then will you be good to me, i.e., 'dance with the party queen'?"

Cranston snatched the poem back. "And the apologue depending from her cervix?"

"That's perfect!" Ginny nearly shouted. "Did you look up *apologue*?"

"A story with a moral." Of course he looked it up. Did she think he was an idiot?

"So it's like, inside my, you know," Ginny lowered her voice, "sex, place of sex, there's a bunch of little moral stories telling you who to love, or, who to make love with." Her eyes flashed. "This is so, like, every woman would get this."

"But Angel wrote the poem?"

Ginny let the question pass. "Then it's like," she said, "after you make love with this jerk, after you let him step all over you, there's this *skirring*, this annoying, grating sound, like you just got wrecked on some serious downers."

"Downers," Cranston repeated. "That would be the 'skirring in fields of diazepam'." The line had been stuck in his head for days. Meaningless, but stuck there.

"You bet," Ginny said, "and the asshole's still reaching up under your dress, even though your passion—the red dress—has been shattered. Really," she added, "it's a brilliant poem. It's published in *Pumice*, which is this little, tiny online literary journal, but it could absolutely be in *The New Yorker*. I wouldn't be surprised at all to find this poem in *The New Yorker*. I think it's one of the most exciting poems I've read all year. Really."

"Huh." Cranston looked over the poem. Maybe it did make sense after all. "Still," he said, sliding the sheet of paper back onto his desk, "doesn't it strike you as odd that Angel wrote a poem like this, apparently from the perspective of a young woman who's fed up with dating jerks? I mean, if Esther Price wrote this poem about that shithead Rickey Mulvaney, I'd be, sure, I'd understand that. But Angel Maso? Doesn't that strike you as more than a little strange?"

Ginny gazed out the office window as if looking for someone. "Angel is such a sweetheart," she said. "I've always found him to be a really super nice, really smart guy."

"I like him, too," Cranston said, raising his voice a little. "That's not the thing. The thing is that this sounds like a woman wrote this poem. Have you talked to him about the poem? Does he have anything to say about it?"

"He won't talk about his poetry," Ginny said. "Nada. He says talking about his poetry interferes with the writing process."

"Great." Cranston left his seat across from Ginny and retreated behind his desk. "Look," he said, "I agree that Angel is a sweet guy, and that he's a smart guy, but, look," he snatched the poem from his desk, the sheet of paper now pretty crumpled from all that snatching, "this troubles me." For reasons of which he had not the slightest comprehension, he began folding the poem into a paper airplane.

Ginny silently watched him, fascinated.

"Given that Angel Maso is publishing under a name other than Angel Maso, and that the poem sounds like it's written by a woman, and Angel is not a woman…." Cranston went silent again for a second or two. His thoughts were as blank as an untouched sheet of paper, though at some deeper level he must have been trying to pull words together. You'd think, right? But apparently not. "Look," he said finally, giving up. "He's around my students. I have to be concerned. If he's not who he says he is—"

"Oh, I can't believe that," Ginny said, her face collapsing into a cartoonish frown.

"I'm not saying that's the case." Cranston dropped down into his desk chair. He didn't want to believe it, either. He genuinely did like Angel Maso. He was quiet, sure. But he was a nice guy, gentle with the kids, encouraging them all the time, caring about them. He knew a lot about poetry. Cranston didn't want to think that Angel Maso was a fraud. Even though he did have that thing he did where some of the kids had seen him mumbling to himself, and he could get awfully awfully quiet and distant. But still, no, he was a good guy and Cranston didn't want to think of him as a liar and some kind of lunatic who'd pretend to be someone he wasn't. "Look," he said to Ginny, "he's around my students.

I have to be concerned."

"I understand." Ginny crossed her arms on the edge of Cranston's desk and laid her head on them as if she wanted to take a little nap. "I have a friend—I mean, not really a friend. I haven't talked to the guy since grad school. But I know him well enough to give him a call, if I can locate his number, or, I think he's on Facebook. Anyway, he used to go out with the editor of *Pumice*, so maybe I can make a connection through him. Quietly, you know, discreetly, and see what they know about X.J. Williamson. If they know it's Angel's pseudonym or what." She closed her eyes for a second before sitting back and shaking off the need to sleep that had momentarily overwhelmed her.

"Or you could just talk to Angel," Cranston said.

"And say what?" Ginny stood up and straightened out her T shirt. "Excuse me Angel, but are you a lying piece of shit?"

"Surely there are more politic ways to phrase the question."

"I'm not good at politics." Ginny, unable to muster up a departing smile, offered Cranston a little wave of the hand on her way out the door. "I'm on it," she said, and disappeared.

"Wait a second!" Cranston followed Ginny out into the hallway, where she stopped and turned, hands on hips, waiting, a bright flash of color—the red pants, the spumoni hair—in a drab cinder block corridor. "Did you know *paramour* is misspelled on your T-shirt?"

Ginny glanced down at the white chalk letters on her black T. "It's a band name," she said. "That's what you ran out here for?"

"No." Cranston had hoped to be amusing—but apparently not. "What does the title of the poem mean, 'The Crossing'?"

"It suggests both being crossed by a lover," Ginny said after a long moment's hesitation, "or star crossed—as well as a crossing point, a place where the speaker is finally changing." She smiled slightly and pushed her hair back off her face.

"Ah," Cranston said, "I see." After an awkward little wave, he returned to his office and waited until he heard an outer exit open and close before he picked up the paper-airplane poem from his desk, considered it, and flew it out the door, where it took a long slow graceful curve and followed Ginny out of sight.

"Here's How to Know if You're Masturbating Too Much"

Claire said, "My father's driving me crazy," as Linni expertly kneaded her tight trapezius muscle, pushing knuckles down the length of it from the occipital bone to the lower thoracic vertebrae and across the width of it to the scapulae. Claire, gazing down through the u-shaped opening in the massage table's face pillow to the bright geometrical patterns of a hand-knotted oriental rug. Her thoughts drifting sleepily through images, memories, places, concerns, as she slides irresistibly toward sleep before pulling herself back to wakefulness by casting out a sleepy sentence in Linni's direction. One moment she's wondering if it's still politically acceptable to call the lovely work of art she's gazing down at an *oriental* rug, or if *oriental* has only specifically been banned when referencing Asians. The next moment she's remembering a few days earlier when she hit the space bar on the computer in her father's study and watched the celestial screen saver disappear to be replaced by a Buzzfeed piece on the dangers of excessive masturbation, titled in bold: "Here's How to Know if You're Masturbating Too Much." Which was not one of the past week's better moments and led her to blurting out *my father's driving me crazy*.

"Try to relax." Linni, dressed for a workout in black spandex, moved up from the trapezius to the tight muscles of Claire's neck and shoulders. She is not employed to be Claire's massage therapist, but it is one of her many talents. "You're even more tense than usual."

"Really?" Claire lifted her head out of the face pillow and glanced back at Linni. "I'm half asleep."

"Still, you're tense." Linni guided Claire's head back into resting position.

Looking down from one of the treetops surrounding Claire's bronzed solarium on three sides (the fourth side opening onto a long hardwood deck): a slate tile floor, a room tastefully but sparsely furnished with white cushioned lounge chairs, a few tables, a wet bar, some counter space upon which brightly colored magazines, books, and CDs are neatly arranged. In the center of the room, awash in daylight, a massage table upon which Claire's petite and superbly fit twenty-two-year-old body is stretched out unclothed, the bright flesh tones almost pink against a slim dark mat. Hovering above her, massaging her neck, Linni, barefoot (she likes to be barefoot when giving a massage, explains it helps her *connect* with the subject's body). The scene bespeaks entitlement and luxury, though Claire is no pampered child of wealth, no self-absorbed brat ensconced in the batting of privilege; and Linni is not her attendant, glorified domestic, well-paid servant. No. Claire has earned a great deal of money very quickly and remains at heart a middle-class girl, the child of a county clerk and a man with a landscaping business who prefers to think of himself as a master gardener and an artist, a writer who keeps whatever it is he's writing entirely to himself. No. Claire thinks of Linni as a dear friend and associate, an older woman upon whom she depends for advice and counseling, personal and professional. And Linni thinks of Claire as a wunderkind, an extraordinary and complex girl toward whom she feels great love, but of the maternal kind, the nurturing kind. She's proud to be Claire's associate and confidant. Though she has only been in Claire's employ for a little more than two years, she would, without hesitation, as the American cliché goes, take a bullet for her.

Claire considered telling Linni about the Buzzfeed web page. In typical Buzzfeed fashion, the tone is breezy and amused, and, of course, the article is arranged as a list—in this instance, with funny little GIFs under each heading. Claire had wandered into her father's study while waiting for him to get ready. She had stopped by unannounced to take him out to lunch. At first, when the screen saver morphed into the web page, she thought, embarrassed, that she had caught her father on a porn site. The GIF pictured a fully clothed woman with one hand busy out of sight below the frame, the other hand on her belly, and her mouth open and face absorbed in sexual pleasure. Then she read the header: *And finally, if masturbation is interfering with your daily functioning, your relationship, or your sex life, that's a problem,* and realized that she was looking at a Buzzfeed listicle answering the question, "Can you actually masturbate too much?" At that, she put the computer back to sleep and hurried off to the kitchen, where she gazed out the window at a couple of goats and a donkey on the asshole neighbor's land.

On the one hand, she wanted to confide in Linni, to hear what she might have to say about Angel viewing such a page after Googling, as she had noted on his browser, *excessive masturbation.* On the other hand, she really really didn't want to think about her father masturbating, though of course, she knew, intellectually, that everybody masturbated, still…. But *excessively?* Her own sex life was entirely relegated to masturbation and had been since a four-month fling, more than a year earlier, with a thirty-year-old (if even that was true) real estate developer from Manhattan who turned out—and how she didn't figure this out sooner still baffled and infuriated her—to be married. Still, she didn't think of her own fairly regular indulgence in private sexual satisfaction as *excessive.* How often was excessive? Was it different for a man? Of his age? Should she even be thinking about this? No, probably not. Definitely not. And yet, she worried about her father. It had been nearly a decade since the divorce, and he had not, that she knew of, been out on as much as a date. Never. Certainly not while she was growing up and living with him. And not that he had mentioned since then. That was not normal! And now lately with the mumbling and his landscaping business nonexistent and his hardly ever leaving the house unless she went over and dragged him out for a meal. Thank God for that Poets in the Schools gig, though hell if he had ever mentioned to her that he was a poet.

"Will you please, please try to relax?" Linni urged.

Claire considered once again telling Linni about the Buzzfeed thing and decided no, she didn't want to talk about it, even with Linni. Then she thought maybe she could tell her about the latest mumbling incident, when, though she couldn't make out most of the words, she had definitely heard her father talking to someone behind his closed bedroom door. This was a few weeks earlier. She had shown up in the morning to take him out to breakfast at Mama's Palace, a local eatery that served a great breakfast, where he used to take her every Sunday for brunch when she was a teenager. She had used her own key to come in the front door. In the moments before she could call out his name, she heard him talking to someone. Once she realized he was in his bedroom and the door was closed, she assumed he was with a woman—and her face lit up. She took one more quiet step closer to the bedroom, listened, clearly heard him say "do you really think that's a good idea?" and then waited for the response. When she heard nothing until her father mumbled something else she couldn't discern, she slipped quietly out of the house, locked the door behind her, and drove around for a half hour before returning in the hope of meeting her father's lover. And yes she was baffled when she returned to find her father alone at the kitchen table, and yes she was upset when he told her that yes of course he was alone, why would she think otherwise? No, she didn't confront him. He had been talking to himself behind the closed bedroom door. That was what she had overheard. She had caught him before talking to himself. Yes, she was disappointed. Yes, she was worried.

"What are you thinking about?" Linni asked. "Your muscles are positively knotting up under my fingers."

"Kenny," Claire said.

"Kenny? What about him?"

"I'm worried about that boy."

"That *boy*," Linni said, "is not even a full year younger than you." She stepped away from Claire and the massage table to flip through a line of CDs on a countertop. "I'll put on some music," she said. "Maybe that will help."

"I'm relaxed," Claire said. "Hurry and finish me up, though. We've got a busy day. Are we all set for the UTA conference call?"

"Stop worrying about Kenny." Linni ignored her. "I personally think you're crushing on him."

"Please."

"So you say. Here," Linni pulled a CD out of the stack—*Detaching the World Vol 1: Ambient Music for Massage/Relaxation/Meditation*—removed it from its jewel case and slid it into the adjacent CD player. "He is hot, the little darling," she said, as the solarium filled with the calming patter of a soft rain accompanied by deep comforting rumbles of thunder and a mellow organ-ish, flute-ish, melodic wave of sound.

Claire thought about saying *I'll admit he's awfully good looking* but then Linni's hands were moving gently over her back as the words drifted off, lost in transit between head and tongue, and her body seemed to slide down a slick warm tube into oncoming fog and, okay, she'd admit it she would, there was a gentleness in his eyes a sweetness if, okay, she'd admit it too, that no he wasn't all that bright but a kind of gentleness, a sweetness and vulnerability, and what had she done making him a heartthrob, an object of preteen infatuation a boy band model cut-out figure for the mountains of cash, but the girls and the drugs, on her list now to do something, to do something, he was though, she'd admit, she would, she'd admit...damn, dad, Buzzfeed? Really? She'd admit...like trying to climb up through mud...is it raining? Okay so she would, she'd admit it she would....

Feargasm

This happened to Angel. He's on the way home to Georgia from a visit to family in New York and someplace in the mountains of Pennsylvania the snow starts coming down heavy. It's been snowing all along, the highway slick with a slushy mix of snow and ice, but navigable, not a big deal, just take it slow—though the big sixteen-wheelers aren't interested in slow. They pound through the wintry gunk, a spray of mess thrown up behind them as they rush past in the left lane. Been like this for hours. Angel doing 55 in the right lane; the truckers and the reckless doing 75, 80 in the left. It's late afternoon, a low roof of dark clouds, dreary winter light.

In Pennsylvania, in the mountains, the snow switches gears. Coming down so hard it's like driving through a tunnel, fresh snow rushing up to the window and swirling around the body of the car. Angel at the wheel feels like he's in the cockpit of some ocean-diving vessel, swirling snow like the sea all around him. When it starts coming down so thick and hard he can't see more than a few feet of the road, he slows down to 40. He doesn't want to go too slow lest someone crash into him from behind and he's afraid to go too fast. Now he can't see a damn thing until he's on top of it, and then he passes the first tractor trailer on its side in a ditch, and then another one jackknifed taking up most of the road and he has to drive on the shoulder to get past it—and now, and this is the crazy thing, Angel recognizes a sexual urgency rising up from the familiar depths of his groin. He's simultaneously frightened and sexually excited.

He doesn't have time to think about this. He's busy trying to avoid the now dozen or so cars and trucks that have spun off the road. He's concentrating on driving, trying not to get himself killed by crashing into or getting crashed into, straining to see what's in front of him what's behind him. And then, before it's over, before he finds an exit and gets off the highway, while he's still in the most danger—he comes. Frightened, concentrating on trying to navigate danger—he has an orgasm.

Has such a thing ever happened to anyone else? Angel will never find out because he will never tell anyone. Too weird. Too strange. When he remembers the moment, that combination of intense fear and sexual pleasure, he's bewildered. He thinks *Was there ever a man more a mystery to himself than me?*

Who has feargasms, Angel? Who?

Come to think of it, you often feel fear as a twinge in your testes, don't you? What's that about, Angel? Is it like that for other men, this twisted intimacy of sex and fear? Who in the world has an orgasm when facing danger? Who's ever heard of such a thing?

You, Angel. Only you.

Kenny, At Home, Opens His Eyes to Shadows

It's late afternoon by the time Kenny rolls into his mom's driveway washed out and dragging, snug in the cockpit of his glistening adrenaline red Viper.

The day has gone dull.

A dark sheet of clouds shrink-wraps a cluster of low flung ranches.

His mom's house the mirror image of Mrs. Jennings' house across the street and Mrs. Shoup's next door.

A cluster of single moms, two divorcées and one widow. His dad, brain cancer, when Kenny was nine.

Soon after her marriage, his mom found religion. A Baptist, she outraged the family by converting to Catholicism. There are aunts and uncles who still won't speak to her. It's the confession, she told Kenny, the priest an emissary of Almighty God who can hear your sins and forgive. The quiet of the confessional booth. The shadow of a priest's face behind the screen.

Kenny in Catholic school, where he was baptized in the faith, received first holy communion, later confirmed. At age ten, an altar boy. Father Sardinia taught him the Latin mass. He sang *Dominus vobiscum*. Father sang *Et cum spiritu tuo*.

Sixteen before he broke her heart and quit going to church with her on Sundays. She still holds out hope. She still prays.

Kenny placates her now and then by attending services, as he had promised to do on this very particular Sunday. And failed. And now he steps out of the comfort of a blood red Viper and into the dull atmosphere of an overcast day on a dreary suburban street of ranch houses with green lawns and perfunctory minimal landscaping. He looks around, at his house, at the old neighborhood. A little shimmer of relief vibrates through him as if he's once again arrived, safe, at home.

Hidden in the shadows of her living room, Mrs. Jennings across the street is watching Kenny. She's only in her mid-fifties, but a combination of osteoporosis and a ruptured disk have relegated her to a wheelchair and a walker. Otherwise, she's a youthful, attractive woman. From where she sits in her living room recliner, a glass of sweet tea spiked with vodka and lemonade in hand, she admires Kenny, as she has been admiring him since he was a toddler out playing on his front lawn. He was a beautiful boy then and he's a gorgeous young man now, maybe a touch too pretty for some women's tastes, the curly blond hair a shade too long, the cool blue eyes too vulnerable. But not for Mrs. Jennings' tastes. She saw him and thought of Michelangelo's David stepped down from his stone pedestal. She watches him leaning against a wet red race car in tight blue jeans and thin leather jacket and if it weren't for her damn back she'd be outside on whatever excuse she could come up with just to get a chance to say hi and get a hug, which he's always generous with, the hugs—and she'd try to not be obvious about the pleasure of putting her arms around that young hard body. But Mrs. Jenning's back is bad today, and so she watches him from the shadows and sips her spiked tea until Kenny shakes himself off like a wet dog, as if trying to wake up or switch into a new and brighter personality, before going to the front door of his mother's house, unlocking it with his own key, and disappearing from sight, leaving the day once again drab and uninteresting, except of course for the bright red car, like a signal fire announcing his presence in the neighborhood.

Inside, Kenny shouts for his mom and gets no answer. The house smells of lemons, and there on the polished wood mantel over the living room fireplace, the bright yellow spray canister of lemon Pledge next to a brass tchotchke of a spinning girl in a tall hat. He shouts again for his mother before checking the kitchen and then trotting up the stairs, taking them two at a time, to the upstairs bedrooms. The door to his mom's bedroom is open. The double bed with its old fashioned, brightly colored quilt, neatly made. The bedroom's bathroom door is closed, and behind it the muffled watery sound of a running shower. It occurs to Kenny—a quick flash of inconsequential thought that he thoughtlessly disregards—that it's odd for Mom to be taking a shower *after* church. He closes her bedroom door and descends the stairs to the living room where he hurls himself onto the chaise end of a beige sofa and pulls a red throw up to his chin. His own condo in town is filled with ridiculously expensive ergonomically designed Swedish furniture, which is, as he likes to tell everyone, crazy comfortable—but it can't touch the comfort of crashing on his mom's sofa, snuggling under a throw. He closes his eyes as sleep deliciously seeps into his limbs and shoulders. His body merges into the cushions.

Kenny's thoughts settle on Willow and Aspen. He is not thinking, though, of the fun stuff, the sexual gymnastics, the visual delight. Rather, he's troubled. This was not his first time with two girls. Girls seemed to like being with him in pairs. In the last year, his second time? No, third, counting Japan, where they had crowded around him backstage to get their paid-for-in-advance hugs and selfies, after he'd spent ten minutes on stage lip-syncing songs no one could hear over all the screams and howls. Some of the girls in that audience couldn't even have been half his age, and this was before he'd turned twenty-one. Later, at his hotel, he'd found two young women—not children, he had made them show ID—waiting outside his room. That night, and another, and last night with Willow and Aspen, Kenny had been troubled, even in the midst of it, by a sense of unreality he couldn't quite comprehend. It was almost as if it wasn't him in the bed, it wasn't Kenny under their hands and lips and bodies. Not the Kenny of suburban Redvale, Georgia, the boy raised by his mother after cancer buried his father, not the altar boy attendant to his mom's every wish, not the aimless young man living in his mom's basement, smoking too much weed, bagging groceries at the local Kroger. Not that Kenny Walker.

Hours later, the house is dark and quiet. Kenny opens his eyes to shadows and waits while the familiar shapes of the living room coalesce and emerge: the old-fashioned, hulking television in the corner, the nearby coffee table with its centerpiece wicker basket filled with fake fruit and multicolored flowers amid green plastic leaves. He sits up and listens. He's not thinking anything at all, not on the surface, not con- sciously. He's awakened from the sleep of the dead, dreamless and blank as the abyss, to a sudden hyper-awareness of his surroundings. He's in his mom's house and something is wrong. Why is the house dark? Where is his mom? He sits up and calls out. He gets to his feet, flips the wall switch and the overhead light shocks the room back to life. He calls out again and then climbs the stairs and he's not halfway up when he hears the shower running. He doesn't know what to make of that. He can't figure it out. At his mom's bedroom door, he knocks and calls to her again. When she doesn't answer, he pushes open the door. The bedroom is dark, only a thin strip of light coming from under the closed bathroom door. He turns on the lights. He knocks on the bathroom door. He calls out again for his mom. He doesn't hear the edge of panic in his voice. He doesn't feel panicky, not consciously. He's befuddled. What exactly is going on? He knocks harder, calls louder. When there is no answer, he turns the knob and opens the door.

In neon yellow and black sneakers, baggy blue jeans and a man's white, short sleeved T shirt, his mom looks younger than her forty plus years. She looks like a college girl, her face pink from where the pulsing stream of the shower has been cascading over it for hours. The T-shirt is soaked through, clinging to and revealing her small breasts. She's flat on her back, one leg draped over the white porcelain rim of the bathtub. Her mouth is open and filled with water, a little pool of water brimming around the oval of her pink lips. A bright green canister of bathtub cleaner, with a dopey picture of a smiling scrub brush, has settled against her right shoulder. Near her thigh, a blue sponge. Kenny kneels beside the tub. He turns off the shower. He seems to have gone numb, an unseen source of pressure, of weight, holds him together. When he touches his mother's face to push a lock of hair off her forehead, he sees that his hands are shaking. Carefully, he turns her head to the side so that the water will spill out of her mouth. If there's a thought anywhere in his head, he's unaware of it. He leaves his mom long enough to call the police from the land line beside her bed. He explains and then hangs up, though a voice has asked him to stay on the line. He's not sure he gave the voice the address. He sits on his mom's bed for only a second before jumping up as if the act of taking a seat had been a terrible, momentary mistake. In her closet, he removes the first blouse he finds off its hanger. It's a cowgirl shirt of heavy cotton fabric, faded red with white pearl buttons.

In the bathroom again, he takes a bath towel down from the rack and lays it over his mother's face and arms and chest to soak up water. Gently, he sits her up and slips her arms into the sleeves of the shirt, pulls it around her and buttons it up. He's crying, but silently, the tears spilling over his cheeks and down his chin. Once she's covered up, he lays her down gently. He dries his hands and arms, puts the towel back neatly on the rack, and looks at his reflection in the mirror over the sink, beside the white commode with its white seat, the seat and top closed, beside the tub and his mother's body, one leg still over the rim, blue jeans and neon yellow and black sneakered foot. He can't see the rest of the body. He's looking at his own face, but it doesn't look like him looking back. He doesn't recognize the face in the mirror. When he hears sirens approaching, he descends the stairs and meets the police and the ambulance attendants at the front door.

He shows them up to the bathroom.

He explains as best he can.

Later, he'll regret watching as they dropped her into a black plastic bag and zipped it closed. He's sorry that's the image he's stuck with, the pink of her face disappearing under the zipper of a black plastic bag.

And then they leave him, just like that. And he's alone.

Atramentous

Atramentous: of or relating to ink, inky, black: as night atramentous erases day, as light retreats and dark emerges atramental and trees and grass and houses, all the things of this world, each in turn fade until what remains is sheathed, voided, tenantless, a black surround: *atramentous*.

The Only Thing That Can Stop a Bad Guy With a Gun Is a Good Guy With a Gun

Doll had ambitions. The only woman on the five-member Board of Supervisors, she was accorded a patronizing, though well-intentioned, gentlemanliness by Hansen and LeDoux, who, luckily, sat on either side of her behind a red oak judge's bench with a computer screen and a mic for each board member. The two men in cheap suits with matching power-red ties seated on either end of the bench, Williamson and BeDouchian (was there ever a more perfect name?), despised her: a pair of evangelical Christians, they considered her very presence an affront to decency and her lifestyle an abomination. She didn't like them either. LeDoux, the longest-serving member of the board, was an ex-alcoholic who had given up whiskey for prescription drugs and showed up for most meetings at least a little stoned.

From the parking lot: The Redvale County Administrative Center, a rectangle, a long fat box, two strips of concrete top and bottom frame a four-story wall of glass, windows looking in on various county offices. Rainy day, on and off, overcast. Flag poles outside the main entrance. Inside, corridors, entrance ways, tile floors. Follow the concrete path to the front doors, enter into the stale air of a controlled environment, take the elevator to the fourth floor. Step out, turn right, at the end of the hall, the Board of Supervisors' Meeting Room. Done up lavishly in Institutional Despair: buzzing fluorescent lights, drab carpeting, bare mustard yellow walls, red oak judge's bench, several rows of bolted-down auditorium chairs in the center of the room, facing a lectern, also red oak. You've found Doll.

Judd Hansen, a skinny socialist radical in his youth, moderate Democratic in middle-age, a bald and precisely bearded, wiry, nervous looking character, stood opposite Doll in the empty meeting room, beside the lectern, the Board meeting wrapped up a half hour earlier. He leaned forward, hands in his pocket. His forehead close to Doll's, his attention appeared to be focused on the silver wheat chain just above the neckline of her blouse. While he talked intently, nodding at key words for emphasis, Doll listened with her head turned slightly toward the door, as if keeping an eye out should someone enter the room. The subject of Judd Hansen's disquisition? He wanted the Board of Supervisors to propose a policy banning the open carry of semi-automatic weapons in the city of Redvale. Attempting such a policy proposal, they both knew, would be political death. And Doll wasn't sure they could legally institute such a ban, given possible constitutional challenges.

Hansen brushed off any such concerns. He ticked off a list of cities with bans already in place. Lips locked together grimly, he admonished Doll with a quick look into her eyes for bringing up the irrelevant question of a successful legal challenge. "In Redvale, though," he went on, his face turning red with barely contained outrage, "you can walk into a supermarket with an assault weapon dangling from your neck, a shotgun in hand, and a Glock 19 with a 33 round mag strapped to your hip—and it's perfectly legal."

Hansen had been angling for a way to get gun control measures passed since Sandy Hook. An easy crier, he couldn't talk about the 20 children slaughtered that day by a boy with an assault rifle without his eyes welling up with tears and his voice choking with emotion. When arguing gun control policy, though, he was a machine ticking off statistics: gun deaths in the U.S. vs. every other country in the world, deaths by handgun, deaths by semi-automatic, mass shooting in the U.S., one per day on average so far in 2016. None of his facts, figures, statistics, comparisons, or carefully presented arguments, however, had any effect on Williamson or BeDouchian, who believed whole-heartedly and repeated ad nauseum, with a passion impervious to reason, that the only thing that could stop a bad guy with a gun was a good guy with a gun. Thus their answer to every mass shooting was more proposals to make it easier for the citizens of Redvale to purchase and carry guns, the bigger the better. If they could have legalized surface-to-air missiles for ownership by individuals, they would have it so.

"Listen," Hansen said, and Doll pretty much stopped listening. She knew where he was going. A few weeks earlier, a local guy who had been unemployed for the past two years, put on his best camo, stole his ex-wife's car, drove to the downtown market, and shot up several businesses with a semi-automatic assault rifle. Somehow, no one was injured, though there were people in every shop, behind every shattered storefront window.

"This is the right time." Hansen took a step back and put his hands on his hips. "We have an opportunity now that we may not get again."

"And LeDoux?" Doll said. "He's not crazy. He won't back an open carry ban—"

"And buy-back program," Hansen added.

"You're out of your mind, Judd. Have you forgotten where you live? This is Redvale, Georgia. This is Governor Guns-Everywhere country."

"Where a maniac with an AR-15 just went on a rampage in the downtown market!" Hansen lunged at Doll and grasped her by the shoulders before instantly remembering himself and stepping back. "Sorry," he said, and his eyes filled with tears. "This issue makes me crazy." He shoved his hands deep into his pockets. "Sorry, really."

"Even if I supported an open carry ban on semi-automatics," Doll said, lowering her voice and glancing out the open door into the empty hallway, "—and forget about the buy-back program; that's not happening—but even if I went in with you on the open carry ban, again, what about LeDoux? Without him, no chance."

"It's a moral issue, Doll." Hansen pulled a hand from his pocket long enough to wipe away the wetness from his eyes. "People are dying. Children are dying," he said, and the words weren't fully articulated before tears were once again brimming and he had to cover his eyes with his hands.

Doll had a fantastic urge to punch him in the face. "Look," she said, "I'll think about it," but even as she said it she knew the notion of an open carry ban in Redvale was crazy. The local political currents were running in exactly the opposite direction. A policy requiring every schoolteacher in the county to carry a Colt 45 strapped to his or her hip?

That might have a chance of passing.

"If you think about it," Hansen said, mopping at his face with a crumpled cloth handkerchief, not the least embarrassed by his tears, "you'll do the right thing."

"Okay, got to go now." Doll watched Hansen neatly fold up his handkerchief and put it back in his pocket. They were probably about the same age, but he seemed to be of another, much older, generation. Who the hell carried a cloth handkerchief anymore?

"Let me deal with LeDoux," Hansen said, and he suddenly brightened, as if plugging into a hidden reserve of optimism. "If you'll come on board, I think we can get this done!"

"Good," Doll said, curtly, the desire to punch him in the face replaced with a much weirder urge to bite him on the lips.

"We can do this," Hansen said to Doll's back as she headed out the door.

Doll thought there was no way in hell they could get it done, moral issue or no moral issue. Plus, she had ambitions. Elections were still a long way away, but not long enough, she calculated easily, to survive a boneheaded, certainly doomed gun control measure. Not even banning the open carry of semi-automatics after someone had just raked the downtown mall with semi-automatic fire. This was still Redvale, Georgia. This was still the South.

And Doll wanted to be Redvale's next mayor.

Look at this Clown!

Angel at the kitchen table, engrossed in a news brief about a man in Malaysia who hurled a Molotov cocktail at an ATM after being unable to make a withdrawal, startled at the sudden monstrous growl of a chain saw. His head jerked back, his arms flew up, and he turned halfway toward the side door and the source of the noise as if ready to defend himself against a grizzly crashing through the wall. Then he cursed, a common profanity referencing mothers and sex. At the window in his tawdry old robe over black silk pajamas with vertical white stripes that made him look like a cross between a prison inmate and a rich Mafioso, he watched as his neighbor deftly sliced through the fallen tree, a clinquant shower of yellow pulp flying up into the man's safety goggles. Though the rain had quit, the day remained soggy and dull. A low, logy, exhausted sky pressed close to the crowns of newly budded trees.

Neighbor had apparently just returned from biking, which was weird. Here he was, a camo, shotgun, turkey-hunter, blaze orange hunting dog Ford 250 kind of guy dressed in neon blue Lycra compression shorts and a lime green, form-fitting cycling jersey—Rural South meets Urban Cyclist. Weird. Even weirder with the chain saw and safety goggles. Angel observed as the severed tree trunk tumbled off his car, further crumpling the sloping hood and knocking the front bumper askew. The goats had been rounded up and herded back into wherever the hell he kept the little shits. Having separated the trunk of the fallen tree, which was on his property, from the remainder on Angel's property, his neighbor silenced the chain saw, dropped it to the ground, and pushed the safety goggles back to look over what he had accomplished.

He was a fairly big guy, Neighbor. Angel estimated six-foot, maybe six-one, built solid, a tight gut, bulging biceps, a muscular chest. In his late thirties, maybe early forties, but with a haircut that harkened back to the middle of the last century, a ducktail, Elvis-Presley-Johnny Cash-ish style, with the whole piled up pompadour thing in front. And long sideburns. Weird. A flat face and crooked teeth, the front incisors angled out just enough that it looked like eating might cause him to pinch his bottom lip. Weird looking but big, a solid five or six inches taller than Angel, who was, like his father, short and bulky, but, unlike his father, not an ironworker and thus without the brawn and muscle. Angel was built something like a duckpin, which might be difficult to visualize since is there even such a thing as duckpin bowling anymore? Picture a bowling pin squashed down a few inches and thus wider around and harder to knock down. Angel was built like that: short and wide, looked like he'd be a difficult man to knock off his feet, though there wasn't much muscle involved, just bulk. Solid bulk. Women didn't find him unattractive, though no one ever told him he could be in the movies. He had a pleasant, unremarkable face, except maybe for the cleft in his chin, which was deep and pronounced.

Dolores said it was his eyes that made her fall in love with him. They were vulnerable, she said. Sensitive eyes.

"Fuck that," Shelly said. "Obviously they weren't vulnerable and sensitive enough to keep her from running off with Gloria."

"Point." Angel turned to find a girl sitting on the lip of the kitchen sink, one leg crossed over the other. In a red plaid reform school dress that came down maybe to mid-thigh, with black stockings held up by garters; long, shapely legs; black, shiny spiked heels; and a black halter top that tied in front, leaving a substantial portion of her substantial breasts revealed. She looked fifteen. Maybe.

Angel turned his eyes away from her, embarrassed. He looked out the window at Neighbor, who was busy patching up the fence with cage wire. "For God's sake," he said. "Shelly…."

"What?" Shelly hopped down from the sink, wrapped her arms around his neck, and pressed herself against his back, her chin resting on his shoulder.

"You can't be dressed like this," he said. "How old are you? Really, what the hell is wrong with me?"

"Oh, come on," she answered, full of the petulance and sulk of a teenage girl. "Do you have to overthink everything? I mean, why not?

It's not like we're hurting anyone." She kissed him on the cheek, and her voice shifted to coy and sexy. "And you know," she said, "that you like it."

"If you must be so young," Angel said, under his breath, barely audible, "do you have to be wearing such a ridiculously porny outfit? It's humiliating."

"You're the one dressing me," she said, sulky again. "Obviously I'm in that sick brain of yours somewhere."

"Well, go back."

"Go back where?"

"Wherever you came from in my humiliating brain. Go back there."

"Can't. You need me." She wrapped her arms around his waist and gave him a hug.

Angel sighed the kind of sigh he used to hear his mother issue now and then, usually when she thought she was all alone, a deep, mournful sigh of resignation. He did feel better with Shelly's arms around him. He didn't want her to go. What he wanted to do was turn around, take her by the hand, and lead her back to the bedroom. That would make three times so far today. He shook off the desire as best he could, though his body was already up for it.

"Look at this clown," Shelly said, peering over Angel's shoulder. "Check out his package in those cycling shorts! He might as well be wearing a codpiece."

"Stop it," Angel said. "I don't want to be noticing this idiot's codpiece."

"I bet you he's not even going to apologize. I bet you he's not even going to have the common decency to come over here and say he's sorry that *his* tree on *his* property fell over onto *your* car. I bet you he doesn't even bother to come over to talk to you."

"Give him a chance," Angel said. "Let him finish patching up the fence."

"I'm telling you," Shelly cooed, and as she did so she raised herself up on her toes and kind of slid down his back, grinding her body into his, her hands moving down his belly to his thighs. "I'm telling you," she sang, "time to grow some balls. He's not coming."

Angel, at the window, in a paralyzing state of confusion: Shelly's seductive movements, her sexy voice, her hands on his body vs. *time to grow some balls*. Did she just challenge him, insultingly, to grow some balls, while simultaneously sexually arousing him? What the hell did that mean?

He wanted to take her back to the bedroom. He wanted to defend himself.

He needed a nap. He needed some self-respect.

He said, "My father threw a pan of boiling water at my dog."

"What?"

"My dog. My father threw a pan of boiling water at her."

"Oh my God." Shelly kissed him, a tender peck on the cheek. "Did he hurt her?"

"Killed her."

Shelly wrapped her arms around Angel so tightly he could feel his chest constricting. "That's so ugly," she said. "Poor puppy. Poor Angel."

Angel shrugged. "It was a long time ago."

Shelly was quiet a moment, then asked, "So why are we talking about this now?"

"Don't know."

"Huh." Shelly kissed him on the cheek again, as if to put an end to the subject. "Your father was insane."

"Most likely."

"He was a lunatic."

"I've spent my whole life trying not to be like him."

"Did he at least mellow out as he got older?"

"Not at all," Angel said. "The opposite. Got worse as he got older."

"Oh my God," Shelly said. "Worse than boiling your dog?"

"He got crazier and more violent every year until he keeled over from a heart attack in his fifties—in the middle of breaking the good China, screaming at Mom. He'd throw a plate at the wall, scream something, then hurl another one." Angel closed his eyes, remembering. "Then, in mid-pitch—I was in the living room, watching from under a chair—he cocked his arm, another plate in hand, ready to toss it, and suddenly hesitated. Froze, kind of. Just a second, maybe two, as if he had remembered something important. He froze, his eyes went out of focus, and he fell like one of the twin towers collapsing, crumpled to the ground.

"That's so sad," Shelly said.

"Not really." Angel paused, recollecting. "I think we were all relieved to finally be rid of him."

"You need comforting." Shelly kissed him on the back of the neck.

"I've worked all my life not to be like him. To be a *rational* man. To be a *decent* man."

"Well, yes," Shelly said, a bit of wickedness in her eyes, "but look at me. You're not all that decent."

"I'm not looking at you. That's the point. I may want to look at you—but I'm not."

"You're not looking at me, but what's this? Huh?" Her hands moved lower on his body until she found what she was looking for and squeezed. "Someone's excited," she whispered in his ear.

"Oh, come on! I don't believe it!" Angel backed away from the window, nearly knocking Shelly over. His hands flew to his hips with indignation. Outside, at the fence, Neighbor was gathering up his gear, clearly getting ready to leave.

Shelly stepped in front of Angel and gripped the windowsill with both hands.

Good God, she was gorgeous! Those creamy curves and silky skin under the crisp pleated fabric of a barely-there skirt! Those legs—and the way the spiked heels tilted her ass, that angle—

Shelly spun around, undid the belt of Angel's robe, and yanked it off his shoulders and to the ground. "You're not going to let him get away with this again," she said, her voice so husky with rage she sounded like a middle-aged man. "Go out there and confront him," she said. "Be a man!"

And then Angel was out the door, in his luxury black silk prison pajamas with the vertical white stripes, hustling down the steps and around the fallen tree to the patched-up wire fence, which he grabbed with two hands, leaned over, and yelled, "Excuse me! Excuse me!"

Neighbor in his spandex cycling outfit, hauling a chain saw, a coil of cage wire, and a toolbox, safety goggles on his forehead, turned around to face Angel.

And what is it that Neighbor must have seen? Yes. Right. Exactly. He saw a short, bulky man in silk pajamas—with an obvious erection. Angel's uncombed, sleep-deformed hair a crazy nimbus shooting off in every direction. His face an unreadable mix of pleading, crazed, and angry.

Angel pointed to his driveway. "Your tree," he sputtered, "fell on my car." Oh, good. Like that was news.

Neighbor stared at Angel, his eyes dropping to Angel's crotch then back up to glare at him—before turning to walk away.

Oh, shit! Angel just leapt the fence like an Olympic athlete, hurdling his cannon ball body over cable wire strung between wooden posts. When his feet hit the ground, they flew out from under him, the dirt field still muddy from the night's hard rain. He landed on his ass, got up, fell, landed on his butt again, got up again, and with what little dignity he had remaining, strode carefully through the mud to Neighbor, who was watching him with a wildly concentrated look of stupefaction, as if he had just seen a pig fly.

"Now look," Angel said, when at last he stood upright, opposite

Neighbor. "I don't want to be whiny about this or anything, but come on, now. I mean," he turned and pointed back to his driveway, "your tree fell on my car!"

Neighbor, still holding the chain saw in one hand and the loop of cable wire and toolbox in the other, said, softly but menacingly, "Get the hell off my property."

"Hey," Angel said, hands to his hips, "come on now. Be reasonable."

Neighbor was unmoved. "I'm going back to my house," he said. "When I get there, if I look out my window and see you still on my property, I'm coming back with a shotgun and blowing your head off. How's that for reasonable, you disgusting little bastard?"

Angel was unable to reply. There were two things going on within him simultaneously that apparently required every iota of his resources, physical and mental. From the outside, he might look simply like a man stunned into paralysis—but Angel was aware of his mind working rapidly. First, Neighbor surprised him. He'd always imagined him to have a thick country accent, full of y'alls and slow, mile-long vowels, but his accent, though apparent, was slight, and though he hardly came off as a great orator, he did seem, even in a couple of sentences, fairly articulate. He didn't, Angel thought, sound dumb in the least. That was the first thing going on in those few seconds though they felt like eons, the way a long fall feels in the last seconds when you've never fallen that far before. First, Angel's quick reappraisal of Neighbor. Then, the other thing…. The other thing was magical and swift, a gurgling, bubbling process of transubstantiation, like Dr. Jekyll might have felt in the wake of downing his transformative concoction.

By the time Angel was able to speak, Neighbor was all the way across the field. "Hey!" Angel shouted, his voice like a shotgun blast. "Fuck you, you redneck, hillbilly, piece of shit!" Arms akimbo, Angel waited for a response—but Neighbor only continued on across the field toward his house.

The transformative thing was this: Angel wasn't in the least bit scared. He was disappointed that Neighbor didn't throw down his chainsaw and cable wire and toolbox and come charging at him across the muddy field in a neon streak of fury. He would have welcomed it. He seemed to want nothing more than to get his hands on Neighbor. He wanted to pummel him until he was reduced to a slick of bloody pulp trickling through mud. And the crazy thing was this: the feeling was elevating. More than elevating, it was ennobling. He recalled Shelly in the kitchen, urging him to be a man, and a deliciously warm smile seeped through his torso and limbs, spreading out from his chest to encompass the whole of him.

Neighbor in his kitchen looked out his window and saw Angel standing where he had left him, arms akimbo, a self-satisfied smile on his face. He went to his open gun safe, pulled out a shotgun, checked to be sure it was loaded, and returned to the window. But Angel was gone. Only muddy fields and a few trees under a dreary sky. He returned the shotgun to the safe and slid it into place between a pair of AR-15s. Standing in front of the five-foot high, 24-gun cabinet, he hesitated. The house was quiet, his wife still at work, the kids out somewhere. He thought it over a bit and then strapped on a hip holster, pulled out a Glock 9mm, checked to be sure it was loaded, nestled it snuggly in place on his hip, and went out to feed the goats.

Angel by then was already back in bed, snuggling under quilts, his eyes closed, busy conjuring Shelly.

He was anxious to talk to her again. He felt like he had so much to say that he wanted, needed her to hear—and he was pretty sure she'd be proud of him. Though he did hope she'd be dressed more sensibly. That last getup was embarrassing.

Proverbs 10:2

Claire holds a phone to her ear with her right hand while her left hand rests on Kenny's knee, giving it a squeeze or a pat now and then as she continues making arrangements for his mother's funeral. Poor Kenny. He moves when he moves like someone who has awakened suddenly with a fever, not feeling well and disoriented, a sick blind man awakening in a strange house with no idea how he got there. When he phoned Claire, minutes after the attendants left with his mother's body, he said, "Hi. Claire. My mom died." Claire came back with a barrage of questions in quick succession. *How? Oh, Kenny . . . What happened? Where are you? Are you handling things? I mean, do you need help? Oh, Kenny . . . I'm so sorry. Where are you now? What's going on? Is anybody with you? Kenny? Kenny?* On the other end of the phone a long silence that was the vast dark cavern of Kenny's blacked out nervous terrain. A long string of synapses refusing to fire. The silence of his mind, a defense system against recognition. Nothing gets through right away. Everything needs to be repeated. *"Kenny? Kenny? Are you okay? What can I do?"* More silence, then, "She had a heart attack. They're pretty sure." Claire: another series of quick questions mixed with occasional sincere condolences. Kenny: silence. Claire: *"I'm coming over."*

When Claire arrived at his mother's house (an easy guess, even though Kenny never said), she found him seated on the living room couch, his hands folded in his lap, a polite boy waiting patiently. Dazed. He said, his voice barely a whisper, "Hi, Claire. I'm really glad you're here." The lights were on in every room, the place lit up like a department store. That was more than an hour earlier. Since then, Claire had made him a cup of decaffeinated pumpkin spice Scripture Tea (found in a kitchen cabinet alongside a box of Apple Cobbler American Hero tea; she went with the scriptures because it was decaf), served him crackers and cheese to go with the tea, turned down lights throughout the house, took a seat alongside him, put one hand on his knee, and went about making the necessary funeral arrangements with a Mr. Joseph P. Riggins at Wellspring Funeral Home and Crematory Services. It had taken forever for Kenny to choose burial over cremation, since he couldn't remember his mother ever having expressed a preference, but other than that, he responded to most questions with a nod or a few words, though she occasionally had to ask the question more than once. After the essentials were completed, the how the where the when, she called Linni and put her on wrapping up the rest of the required responses to a sudden, unexpected death. When she put the phone down finally, placing it on the coffee table, alongside a wicker basket of plastic fruit, the silence of the house rose up and wrapped itself around both of them, seated side by side on the sofa, Claire's hand still on Kenny's knee but now awkwardly. She folded her hands in her lap but then saw herself next to Kenny, as if looking from across the room, the two of them like school children waiting for an adult to tell them what to do, and so she put an arm around his shoulder and kissed him on the cheek and said, the words coming unbidden and unexpected, "You're going to be okay, Kenny. You're going to get through this."

As soon as the kiss was delivered and the words spoken, she feared she might have overstepped the boundaries of their relationship. She was his employer, not a close family friend. She wasn't even sure he considered her a friend, though certainly they were friendly, and they'd spent a good bit of time together over the last year. He made her laugh easily. She did the same for him. They seemed to like being around each other. But it wasn't as if they hung out. It wasn't as if they got meals together, did stuff together. It was a business relationship, and, yet, she was the one he called, no one else, though he had family nearby and friends. He called her. He called Claire. These thoughts bulleted through Claire's mind in the seconds after the kiss and the reassurance, before Kenny laid his head in her lap, wrapped his arms around her waist, and cried like a child, his body heaving with sobs, his head pressed against her thighs. What was it Claire felt then, in that dimly lit room, Kenny's head in her lap, Kenny crying and holding fast to her? Well, not sadness primarily, though she was sad for Kenny and his loss. And for Sandra, his mother, who couldn't have foreseen this possibility, that she would die suddenly from a heart attack while scrubbing the bathtub. Probably, she was young enough, she still had dreams of meeting the right man, someone who would make her life brighter, happier. Probably, her thoughts were full of dreams of travel, and family, of the various pleasures of a good long life. She was sad for Kenny's mother, for her too young death. And she was sad for Kenny, weeping, his arms around her. He was orphaned now, fatherless and motherless. So Claire felt sadness, she did. But there was something else in the moment, something she couldn't name. Comfort, maybe. Peace. She could be of help. She could handle the details and leave Kenny free to grieve. She stroked his hair and let him cry until the sobbing transitioned into breaths long as sighs, and then to stillness and silence.

"Kenny," she said. "Do you want to stay at my place tonight? You probably don't want to be here alone."

Kenny nodded and sat up and wiped his eyes roughly with a forearm. "Could I?"

"Of course. You can have the upstairs bedroom."

Kenny said, "Thank you," but didn't move. He seemed to be waiting for Claire to tell him what to do.

"Let me just clean this up." Claire gathered up the teacup and the plate with the crackers and cheese, which Kenny hadn't touched, and brought them back to the kitchen. She washed the cup and saucer and plate, and put them in the drain, and then carried the tea bag to the trash. The scripture verse on the little tag at the end of the tea bag string read: *Ill-gotten treasures are of no value, but righteousness delivers from death. Proverbs 10:2.*

"Wow," she said aloud, without realizing it, upon reading the verse. "That's weird."

She turned off the kitchen lights and returned to the living room to get Kenny and take him home.

Bright Birds Rising Up

Cranston's oldest daughters, seventeen-year-old Marcy and fourteen-year-old Ellen, were both sexually active. *Sexually active*, a euphemism, sort of, for the things he didn't want to think about them doing. His girls, his babies, in the back seat— No, really, he didn't want to think about it too much, but, Lord God, he worried. Especially Ellen. Fourteen and her mother finds a used condom tangled in the sheets, which means the boy, Jack Neely, also fourteen, a *ninth grader* who was supposed to be her study partner…is that what they called it these days? Studying? But what were they supposed to do beyond what they'd already done: grounded her, lectured her, took away privileges, talked to Jack's idiot parents, who seemed to think it was no big deal as long as they used protection. Really? At fourteen? They seemed proud of the kids—that's how they referred to Ellen and Jack, the kids—proud of them for using protection. *Surely*, the mother had said, *you're a high school principal. You know most fourteen- and fifteen- year-olds these days are* sexually active. I know Esther Price is *sexually active*. I know that moron Ricky Mulvaney is about to be the father of her child. That I know. But did I know about Ellen? Did it even occur to me?

"Cranston?" Ginny Diaz was waiting for him to say something. They were in her studio apartment, where the late afternoon sun came in through a triptych of rectangular windows and passed through a multicolored Tibetan prayer flag suspended in a semicircle from a brass curtain rod. Sun through the prayer flag dotted the room with green, blue, red, yellow patches of light.

Cranston in a big leather recliner, a blur of red light on his chest.

Ginny across from him on a beige couch with tufted cushions, a rectangle of green light across her bare stomach. A coffee table between them with brightly colored magazines and books scattered on the glass tabletop.

As to why Cranston is thinking about his daughters being sexually active…he has no idea. When Ginny told him about Angel, he slumped back into the comfort of the recliner. He didn't know what to say. And then he was thinking about Marcy and Ellen. And now Ginny was waiting for him to say *something*.

Though Ginny had called him at the end of the school day and asked him to come by her apartment, he seemed to have caught her in the midst of house cleaning. She sat across from him casually, her legs tucked under her, barefoot in blue jeans that were awfully tight, though he understood that everybody wore tight jeans, boys and girls, men and women. But, wow, they clung to her body, which was slim and tight. One arm draped over the back of the couch. Looking at him. Waiting. In a rust red chiffon blouse that tied in front, just above her navel, the top two buttons open, exposing enough cleavage to reveal a brightly colored flock of birds wrapped around her left breast and flying up toward her shoulder. His brain seemed to be jammed. He couldn't think of what to say. All the girls were tattooed now, even the cheerleaders. He'd put his foot down with his girls: no tattoos until they were 18 and graduated—though he had a strong suspicion Marcy and Ellen were both tattooed in hidden places, which is what you get these days when you try to establish some boundaries: you force your children to go behind your back because peer pressure, because the culture, it was so much stronger, had so much more influence. These kids with their tattoos and their piercings and their intensely sexualized manner and dress—

"Cranston? Hello? Are you there? Anybody home?" Ginny leaned over the coffee table. More bright birds flying up out of shadows.

"I'm...shocked," Cranston said. "Well, maybe not shocked as much as disappointed. I mean," he said, struggling for the right words, "I had suspicions, obviously. I asked you to look into it. But I don't think I really...expected...or maybe I just didn't want it to be the case. I don't know. But now, I find myself speechless."

"I know. I didn't want to believe it either." Ginny grimaced and squinted, an exaggerated expression of distaste, as if she had just seen something disturbing.

"Are you absolutely sure?"

"X. J. Williamson is a gay black woman who lives in Denver and owns an art gallery. My friend went to school with her at Iowa—which is another lie. There's no record of an Angel Maso graduating from the Iowa Writers Workshop. I checked."

"Damn." Cranston met Ginny's eyes and then, helpless, gazed down at the flock of bright birds rising along their softly curving flight path.

"Cranston?"

"The kids love him," he said. "Matt Romano, who was about the last kid I ever thought would be into poetry, his mother called me just last week amazed, which I can absolutely understand, that Matt was peeling himself away from computer games to *read*. She was shocked. The kid used to be allergic to books, now he's writing poems and reading books of poetry."

"Well, that's the thing about poetry in the schools," Ginny said, "it can open up kids like Matt." She frowned, a big clownish exaggerated frown. "I really like the guy," she said, meaning Angel of course. "This is kind of heartbreaking."

"I don't think he's done any serious harm," Cranston said, wanting to comfort Ginny. "He's just misrepresented himself. Still," he added, and threw open his hands in resignation, "I can't have him around our kids. I'll have to cancel the workshop unless you can find a replacement."

"I'll do it until we can find someone else."

Cranston clapped once, meaning that was that, nothing else to be done. "I don't know what I'm going to tell the class."

"You'll have to talk to Angel and come up with something that works for all parties. It's a shame," Ginny said. "I really do like him." She got up from the couch, sat down again at Cranston's feet, hugged his legs and rested her head on his knee. "You know you want to," she said, without looking up.

Cranston fiddled with his eye patch. His head jammed up again.

Ginny kissed him on the knee. "I figure you'd never make the first move, but I know you want to."

Cranston looked just beyond Ginny, to the flower patterns woven into the velvety lush pile of an area rug that filled the space between the couch and the recliner. The rug soft and cushiony enough to sleep on. "Want to what?" he whispered, as if asking her to share a secret.

Ginny laughed and looked up at him with a smile that hovered somewhere between coy and wicked.

Cranston loved his girls, all five of them, his daughters, his wife…. A therapist friend had once suggested he was over-bonded with his children, whatever the hell that meant. And Theresa, his wife…. They'd been married twenty years, had four children together…. So, sure, you couldn't expect the excitement with each other to last forever, but they had something much deeper. They had commitment. They had a shared life. And, sure, you couldn't expect a youthful body to last forever either. But they had the warmth of their commitment, their connection to each other over twenty years of joys and fears and hard work, the hard work of raising children, of building a life together. He loved Theresa, his wife, his soul mate, the mother of his children, his life partner.

So why was he sliding off the recliner and into Ginny's arms and down in a rush onto the velvety soft pile of a flower pattern rug where patches of color from the last of the sunlight through the window and the prayer flags painted them as their clothes came off shirt by blouse, bra by undershirt, pants by pants until Ginny's brightly colored birds escaped and flew up over his lips and tongue and into his mouth, the two of them silent as their bodies moved like creatures both foreign and intimate?

Cranston had no idea. He had no idea at all.

Be a Man

Angel has arrived back at his house in a rental car. Evening is coming on, sky darkening, a crescent sliver of moon balanced on chimney bricks. He's alone and quiet in his rental, in his driveway, the fallen tree a barrier between him and the side entrance to the house. His battered, tree-crushed car has been hauled away to Collision Specialists in town. Frankie is peeking out from under the porch steps and appears to be watching Angel, waiting for him to get out of the car before he hustles back underground.

Angel settles into the quiet. He has come to like living alone. Perhaps too much. He does worry about that at times.

He hasn't done any gardening in a good long while, and not because the work isn't there, which is what he's told Claire. The work is available, but he's found himself unable to return phone calls or reply to emails. To reestablish old relationships or to establish new ones.

Months earlier, with spring coming on and inquiries coming in, he seemed to have decided to give up Transcendent Gardening. That's what he's thinking about at the moment, because at no point did he consciously make that decision. He only stopped pursuing work. The emails and voice mails are waiting. He can still pull it together.

The thing is, money is running out and he's not about to let Claire support him.

Bills are overdue.

He's behind on the mortgage.

Alone in the car, outside his house, it's like being between two worlds. The world he's built for himself in the comfort of his home. The world outside with all its demands all its chaos.

His father called him stupid, called him ugly. For God's sake, that was thirty years ago. Let it go.

Angel lets nothing go. Every wound every slight is held close to his heart. He remembers forever. Every embarrassment, every humiliation.

Dolores loved him for a time, right up until the end when she didn't. He'd drive home from a job in his pickup, gritty from a day working in dirt, and he'd thank God, say his little prayers, thank God for Dolores, who applied balm to all the old wounds, who believed in him, who encouraged him, who was always there, her arms around him.

A therapist explained it this way. This is a healthy relationship:

Two individuals bonded, holding hands.

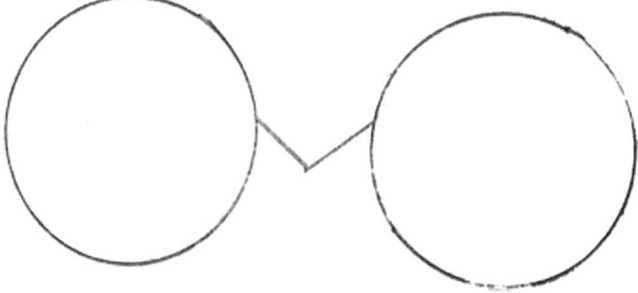

This is an unhealthy relationship:

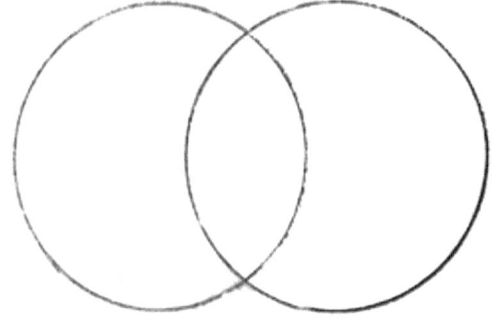

Individuality has been submerged. The submerged one will at some point need to break free, leaving a gaping wound in the other.

Angel is looking out the car window at the fallen tree and his house and the crescent moon, but he's seeing two merged circles and he's inside a stuffy office seated in a comfortable chair as a therapist draws and shows him and explains and he nods as if oh sure, I understand.

Only he doesn't understand. Of course he's merged with

Dolores. Isn't that what love is? Isn't that what happens when you have a child together? When you sleep in the same bed, eat at the same table, work toward the same goals?

Apparently not.

Dolores had apparently never even merged, let alone submerged. That was all him. That was all Angel. Maybe. Maybe not. It still confused him.

For God's sake, get a life. This was nearly ten years ago already.

Dolores had been out all night. When she came home the sun was already up. Claire asleep in her room.

She came through the front door quietly and her face shifted a little when she saw Angel at the kitchen counter, waiting.

It had rained hard all night. It had rained violently, wind slashing at the roof, two trees coming down.

She wasn't wearing her wedding ring.

Angel looked at the strip of lighter skin on her ring finger, looked up into her eyes.

Dolores sat across from him at the counter and peeled apart their lives, chunks of the living room floor falling through to the basement, patches of the ceiling falling in, piece by piece everything comes apart as Angel absorbed the shock waves quietly, saying little, listening.

It was so hard to take in. He never saw it coming. Later, he'd tell others it was like being smacked across the head with a two-by-four.

Gloria, a twenty-one-year-old local girl. A woman.

A woman?

Yes, a woman. I think I've always wanted to be with another woman. I just didn't know it until now.

She put her hands on his cheeks, her face wet with tears, and kissed him on the forehead.

They could work out arrangements later.

She kissed him and left without saying anything more.

Angel went into Claire's room and sat at the foot of her bed.

Ever since, it felt to Angel as if he'd been navigating an impossible maze—and at this particular moment, waiting for nothing in his car as day fades to night, it's making him furious.

Not at Doll, not at anyone but himself.

For God's sake, Angel.

Be a man.

"That's kind of perfect, really."

The last thing Kenny remembered: sitting on the edge of a mattress in Claire's guest bedroom. He didn't remember taking his clothes off, getting under the covers, settling his head on a pillow. None of that. Just, then, sitting on the edge of the mattress, and now, awake in Claire's guest bedroom, lying on his back, looking across the room to a dimly illuminated digital clock on a dresser. 4:15 a.m. Oh, he didn't remember getting undressed because he wasn't. He'd fallen asleep in his clothes, shoes and all.

Warm, he tossed the covers off. The house was quiet. Outside, a breeze through the surrounding trees. Inside, the occasional settling tick or knock. Dark. A hint of must, a stale smell.

With his thumb, he wiped a tear from one eye and then the other. A paralyzing remorse slowed his heart, a weight on his arms and legs, a constriction of his chest. He'd seen his mother's dead body face up in the bathtub, a pool of water in her mouth as if she were a statue, lifelike but unliving, water overflowing her lips, spilling over her chin and down her neck. He'd seen his mother dead. Her small breasts under a soaked T-shirt. He'd lifted her dead body, covered her with a shirt from her closet. These things had happened and still he felt that somehow they had to unhappen, because surely he would go home and find his mother at the door, the way her face always lit up at the sight of him, the way her arms flew open and wrapped around him for a hug and a kiss on the cheek. Always. Every time. Even if he had only been out of the house for a few hours. Surely.

And when in the dark he accepted that no, he would never again return home to find his mother waiting, remorse was tinged with a taste of fear.

They'd carried her body away in a black plastic bag. He'd watched as they zipped it closed, disappearing her moment by moment, until the zipper passed over her face, drawing the black plastic together, and his mother became something carried out of the house and slid into the back of a van and carted away. Not like trash. No, not like trash.

Where was he now? What was he doing?

Remorse not because for the last year and more he largely ignored her, and not because he had repeatedly lied to her about drugs and girls and money, how much he was making, what he was doing with the money, the number and nature of his hook ups, the drugs, but because she knew he was lying. She knew he was lying, and he knew, and they'd fallen into this falseness, into this fake relationship, an acceptance based on lies, and about this he was ashamed. He'd treated his mother with disrespect, though she had always made him feel he was the center of her world, though there was never any doubt that there was nothing she wouldn't do for him, nothing at all, nothing possible she wouldn't forgive, nothing possible that could make her love him less, still he treated her with disrespect. He lied to her. He ignored her. And none of this now would he ever be able to undo.

She knew. She knew he was a liar. And now it couldn't be undone.

Kenny sat up in bed. If he didn't move he might come apart.

He left the guest room and quietly descended a flight of stairs. He followed a hallway overlooking a living room. He'd been to Claire's house many times before, and he knew the bedrooms were off this hallway, though he'd never seen the inside of one. He tried the first door, gripping the knob and turning it slowly. The door opened to a room with a double bed against a cathedral window beyond which the shadows of tree tops wavered like ominous guards. Claire's assistant, Linni, was asleep on her side, a bright shock of blond hair tinted blueish in the light from a digital device on her nightstand. He pulled the door closed soundlessly.

The second door opened onto Claire's bedroom.

Claire, sat up in bed. In a whisper, she asked, "What are you doing, Kenny? Are you all right?"

Claire had awakened at the sound of Kenny descending the stairs. She'd considered the possibility that he might be coming to her bedroom and had quickly calculated several possible scenarios. She was shocked at first and then, surprisingly, indignant, and then briefly furious when he stopped at Linni's bedroom. She might even have felt hurt. That feeling was possibly there.

Kenny asked, "Can I get next to you, Claire?" and without waiting for a reply crossed the room and sat at the foot of her bed.

"Get next to me? What does that mean, Kenny? What are you doing?"

Kenny slipped off his shoes. "I just want to get in bed with you, if that's okay." He hesitated, looked down at his feet, then back up to Claire. He said, apologizing, "But I don't want to sleep with you. I mean, have sex with you. I'm just not," he said, "I mean, because of my mother. I just don't feel like I can. I hope you're not…I hope that doesn't make you feel—"

"Kenny, what are talking about? Is there some reason you think I'd want to have sex with you?"

Kenny's face blanked. He appeared to be at a loss for words. Finally, he managed, "You don't?"

Claire pulled the quilt to her breast and sat up straight. She'd worn a sheer, wrap-around romper to bed. It tied closed on the side and the tie had come loose. "Kenny," she said, "we have a professional relationship, and I hope we've become friends—but that's all. I am truly sorry," she added, "about you mom, and I want to help in any way I can—"

"This is how you can help," Kenny interrupted. "Really, Claire, I'm kind of a wreck." He covered his face as tears erupted.

Claire wrapped the quilt around her and slid down the bed to put a hand on his back and massage there a little as he sobbed. After a while, she laid her head on his shoulder and gave him a hug. She said, "I'm really so sorry about your mom." In the quiet that followed, she wanted to say that she understood what it was like to have a mom one day and then not to have a mom the next, which is how it felt when Dolores first took up with Gloria. For a good six months after that, she'd hardly seen her. Most of that, of course, was because Claire herself refused to see her, but, still. One day she has a mom, the next she doesn't. Though it wasn't like her mom was dead and so she didn't say what she was thinking. She said, "If you want, Kenny, we can get up and I'll make you some coffee and eggs and we can hang out in the kitchen and talk."

Kenny nodded and said, "Please. I'd appreciate that. That's kind of perfect, really."

"Good." Claire gave his shoulders a squeeze. "Go on," she said. "You know where the kitchen is. I'll be down in a minute."

When Kenny turned to face Claire, his eyes were full and his cheeks were wet. He pulled his shirt sleeve across his face and kissed Claire on the lips, a friendly peck of a kiss that nonetheless seemed to surprise both of them.

"I'll be right down," Claire said, and then watched, the quilt clutched to her breast, as Kenny crossed the space between her bed and the door, moving so slowly it felt like it took forever before he was out the door and on the stairs and she was out of bed and at the closet looking for the right thing to wear.

Judd Hansen Preps

AK-47 & AR-15. Chattanooga Military Recruitment Center. 5 Murdered.

DPMS AR-15 & Smith & Wesson M&P AR-15. Inland Regional Center. 14 Murdered.

.223-caliber semi-automatic. Santa Monica College. 5 Murdered.

.223-caliber Bushmaster XM15-E2S semi-automatic. Sandy Hook Elementary School. 27 Murdered. (20 children between 6 and 7)

.223-calibar Smith & Wesson M&P15 semi-automatic. Aurora Theater. 12 Murdered.

AK-47 Romarm Cugir variant automatic & AK-47 Norinco Arms variant automatic. IHOP. 4 Murdered.

AR-15 SWAT semi-automatic. Crandon duplex. 6 Murdered.

.223-caliber Bushmaster XM16. Youth With a Mission. 4 Murdered.

WASR-10 Century Arms semi-automatic. Westroads Mall. 8 Murdered.

AK-47 semi-automatic. Burns International Security. 5 Murdered.

7.62mm AK-47 Chinese variant semi-automatic. Caltrans Maintenance Yard. 4 Murdered.

9mm Israeli Military Industries Uzi Model A carbine semi-auto. San Ysidro McDonalds. 21 Murdered.

MAC 11 assault rife. Jackson fire station. 5 Murdered.

MAK-90 semi-automatic. Fairchild Air Force Base. 4 Murdered.

AK-47 Chinese variant semi-automatic. Cleveland Elementary School. 5 Murdered.

AK-47 Chinese variant semi-automatic. Standard Gravure. 8 Murdered.

Puzzles

Gloria stared at a ginormous jigsaw puzzle while Doll paced the room talking animatedly to the empty space in front of her, a Bluetooth earpiece following the line of her cheek bone. The house otherwise quiet and serene, the way both Dolores and Gloria liked it. A kind of sanctuary, everything in its place, everything neat and tidy. Gloria loved all the nice *stuff*. The sturdy furniture from good manufacturers, the quality mattress on their bed, the thick pile of the area rug under the dining room table, the gleaming hardwood floor in the living room, the slate tile floor in the kitchen. Nice things everywhere throughout the house, tasteful things, and she and Doll comfortable in the little bubble of their home. When Gloria remembered the trailer she grew up in, the mud surrounding it that was supposed to be a yard, their loud drunk neighbor the police finally locked up, thank God, the time her father pissed off at her mother had set the kitchen on fire—when those memories surfaced she only had to look around and see where she lived now, and the anger gave way.

Doll stopped as if she had walked into a wall. "I did not!" she said emphatically. A few seconds later she repeated, "I did not!" before going silent, hands on hips, and continuing her pacing.

Gloria was transfixed by hundreds of black and white and mostly grayish puzzle pieces spread across the dining room table. She knelt on a chair turned with its back to the puzzle, her arms wrapped around the stiles, her chin propped up on the cresting rail. In her eyes, a look of intense concern at that gray sea of indistinguishable puzzle pieces.

This was only a few days after the board meeting when Judd Hansen had tried to enlist Doll's support for a semi-automatic ban in Redvale. Doll had been, at best, noncommittal—and yet here she was fielding the fourth call of the evening asking about her support for a semi-automatic ban and buy-back program. At the moment, she was on the phone with Linni Sorland, Claire's assistant who seemed to know something about everything that went on anywhere in the world. Doll was pretty sure she could ask Linni about the government's negotiations with Iran over their nuclear program and Linni would know someone who knew someone with inside information on their progress. Linni, who had assumed the role of ambassador between the enemy states of Doll and Claire, had called to let Doll know that Kenny from Kroger's mom had died, but the conversation had quickly worked its way around to the semi-auto ban. Linni had heard about it from someone at the *Redvale Times*, which was planning to run a story about the policy proposal in the next day's paper.

"That's just crazy," Doll said. "I in no way committed to support any gun control policy for Redvale whatsoever, not a semi-automatic ban or any other kind of ban—and I sure as hell would not support a buy-back program."

"That's too bad," Linni said on the other end of the line. "Claire was really excited when I told her."

"She was?" Doll had grown so used to Claire's disdain that she was both surprised and curious to learn she could elicit any other kind of response from her daughter. "Why?"

"Well," Linni said, and then hesitated, as if weighing her words. "Well," she repeated, pushing on, "she was proud of you."

"Oh, please," Doll answered, pleading with Linni. "Does Claire understand that any policy attempting to regulate gun ownership in any way whatsoever is a) doomed to fail, and b) certain to rile up the Redvale Gun Club and the NRA, and c) likely to bring in NRA money to be sure any government official supporting such a policy is kicked out of office? Does she understand that supporting a semi-automatic ban and buy-back program would be a political disaster?"

Linni didn't answer for several seconds, and Doll could almost hear her deliberating on the other side of town. Finally, she said, "Yes. I believe she does understand. That's why she was proud of you."

"Oh, please," Doll said again, only this time it came out as a long sigh.

"Anyway," Linni said, and she changed the subject to the goings on in Claire's life over the last few weeks.

Doll listened as best she could while her thoughts were wrapped up with Judd Hansen, the audacity of the guy going around telling people he had her support for a semi-auto ban—and buy-back program!—when she had told him no such thing.

"Claire sends her love," Linni said, before ending the call.

"I'm sure," Doll answered, after slipping the phone back into her purse, which was dangling from a dining room chair.

"Were you listening to any of that," Doll asked Gloria, who seemed to be lost in a trance, her eyes fixed on the puzzle.

Gloria had, actually, fallen into a sleep-like state as she stared at the puzzle pieces. She knew from the box cover that the puzzle pictured a room as if seen from above—well, maybe. It was according to how you looked at it. But a room with a sort of triangular arrangement of staircases with these mummy-like figures walking up and down them—except the picture shifted every time you looked at it from a different angle.

"Gloria? Honey?"

Gloria shook herself awake. "Isn't this a really weird puzzle?" She showed Doll the box cover.

"M.C. Escher," Doll said. "Have you heard anything I've been saying on the phone all night?"

"Sorry. I wasn't paying attention." Gloria, forever bored to death by Doll's political stuff, had learned to tune out most everything that had anything to do with Doll's work. "What's M.C. Escher?"

"The puzzle you're doing."

"What?"

"The puzzle. It's a lithograph, I think, by Escher. He did drawings based on math or something."

"Math?" Gloria looked at the box cover. "Where?"

Doll straddled the chair behind Gloria, wrapped her arms

around Gloria's waist, and pressed her cheek against her back. "I'm going to have to cut off Judd Hansen's balls," she said out loud, though she was speaking to herself.

"I thought you liked him," Gloria answered. Then added, "I don't get the math thing. What's this got to do with math?"

Doll had no idea. "Beats me," she said, and she closed her eyes, snuggling up against Gloria as if she were a body pillow.

"Will you help me?" Gloria asked.

"With what?"

"The puzzle!"

Doll lifted her head to look again at the dizzying array of puzzle pieces in shades of black and white. After a moment, she said, "I guess Hansen's balls can wait until tomorrow." She pulled up a chair alongside Gloria and joined her in staring at the puzzle, looking for a place to begin.

Sharp claws, digging in

Kenny is nervous and fidgety. He hasn't been back to his house—now literally his house, used to be his mom's house—he hasn't been back since he found her. Linni is driving him there and he's all twitchy in the passenger's seat of a BMW i3, watching the centerpiece LCD screen like it's showing Emily Ratajkowski prancing around with Robin Thicke rather than the current mileage, the temperature outside and inside, and whatever. "So," he says, trying to distract himself, "this is like one of those all-electric models, huh?"

Linni and Claire have been looking after Kenny, attending to him, chauffeuring him wherever he needed, running interference when his friends, Bobby and Amayr, came by with a pocketful of pills, as if a little pharming might be just the thing. Kenny has spent the last couple of days in a mystifyingly incapacitated state. He knows, sure, his mother died and that's fucked up. He's got a right—but it feels like something weirder. Like there's a wall around him or something weighing him down and he can't see it and doesn't know what it is, except maybe he kind of does. He's not a good person. He's shallow and insincere. He's a liar. He'll lie whenever necessary to avoid having to deal with something or someone. He's all about himself and no one else, not really. What has he ever done but get high and screw around? What has he ever done for anyone but himself? The thing maybe he knows is that he's not the kind of person his mother wanted him to be. And she knew it, even if she ignored it. He's not the kind of person his mother taught him to be. And she knew it, even if she ignored it because she loved him. And what maybe he kind of knows is that he let her down. He let his mother down. That thought is like a weight. That thought is like a wall around him.

"Kenny," Linni says. "You're crying, Honey." She hands him a tissue.

Kenny wipes the tears from his face. Goes back to staring at the LCD screen.

"I wanted to get the Tessla S," Linni says, "but we would have had to wait and we could pick this one up right off the lot. Claire was more interested in getting something electric than in the particular model."

"Cool," Kenny says, and his voice cracks, something he can't remember happening since he was like twelve.

At the house, Linni follows Kenny into the den where he retrieves two photo albums from a bookcase and drops them on a cherry wood executive desk facing a window onto the back yard. The albums are old fashioned, leatherette, post bound—the kind with black pages.

The light in the den is eerie. It's late morning on a day that can't decide between spring and fall, fast moving clumps of dark clouds between which stretches of bright sunshine light up the back yard, the wide flat leaves of a tree neither Kenny nor Linni can identify spooning chunks of light across a lawn that needs cutting. Sunlight flashes through the window over the desk, lighting on the black pages of the photo album. Sunlight disappears and the room is gloomy. Before it reappears and all is bright again. Kenny's gaze is fixed on an 8x10 color image of his mother and father looking out at him, both of them dressed in white, his father in a white tuxedo with matching white shirt and tie, his mother in a white bridal gown. They're holding each other, her arm on his shoulder, his hand on her waist, about to begin a slow dance. Surrounded in a semicircle by family members. Standing on bright red carpeting.

His mother looks like a little girl, sixteen seventeen maybe, though he knows she was twenty when she married his father. She's a pretty girl, a bright smile, bright eyes, confident.

His father is a little chunky, with goofy long hair that looks like it's been styled. He's grinning, like he's getting away with something.

He has only another ten years to live.

His mother, another twenty-two.

And that's making Kenny think about his own life, given his genetics.

He has absolutely never before in his life given his death a moment's thought. Never. It's not that he thinks he's immortal. It's just that he never thought about it at all. Now it occurs to him that, like his father, it's possible he could have only another ten years to live—which would make him, in a way, already an old man. Or like his mother, another twenty or so years. So, he'd be middle-aged already. The possibility that he would lead a short life occurs to Kenny as a very real prospect as he gazes down at his dead parents' wedding picture.

"That would be a good choice," Linni says, coming around behind him, looking over his shoulder." They're choosing pictures for the funeral, where there will be a display of photographs of his mother throughout her life. Claire and Linni are making the arrangements. They thought Kenny, though, should pick out the photos.

"Okay," Kenny says before rubbing his eyes and forehead and then resting his head in his hands, his elbows on the desk. Linni massages a space between his shoulder blades. She thinks he's moved by the wedding picture, grief-stricken by a photograph of his dead parents in their youth, when instead Kenny is thinking about himself. The possibility that he could die young is descending on him like a creature with talons, sharp claws digging in and holding him fast.

"My parents," Linni says, "are a pair of old fools." She doesn't wait for and doesn't seem to expect a response from Kenny. "First they only disapproved of my career as a model. Then, when they got wind of stories about my, admittedly, reckless behavior—I was young once, like you, and there's lots of drugs and sex in modeling, at least there were when I was doing it. Anyway, after that, they would have nothing to do with me. Didn't invite me for holidays. Didn't answer my letters. They were, truly, ashamed of me. I haven't seen or spoken with them in a decade."

"I'm sorry," Kenny mumbles, through his fingers.

"No," Linni says, meaning she doesn't want him to be sorry. "What I'm saying is, your mother loved you. She loved you—what is it you always say here?—unconditionally. She loved you no matter." Linni is quiet a moment, then adds, "That is something very special that you had, Kenny. And that she had, too. A great gift, I think. For her, too. Is what I'm trying to say."

Kenny nods in his hands and then the tears come as his feelings shift from fear to sadness. It's exhausting, this grief stuff. This loss. Exhausting and demanding, the things it makes you think about, the feelings it makes you feel.

"I let her down," Kenny says. "I've been such a—"

"You're not hearing me," Linni interrupts. "Your mother loved you. She saw everything that's special about you. Sure, you've screwed up, and I'm sure she knew it, but life's long and she knew you had plenty of time to figure it out, and she believed you would. That's how it is when you love someone. Now," she ruffles Kenny's hair, "come on. Time to go." She leans over the chair to give Kenny a hug.

Kenny grips Linni's hands in his and holds tight for a second or two before letting her guide him to his feet, where she puts an arm around his shoulder and leads him out of the now bright den, a pair of old photo albums held securely under his arm.

What Angel Misses About Gardening

Sunlight. Dirt. Tending. Cultivating. Planning. Arranging.

Watching plants come up. Looking after them. Pruning.

Color. Arrays of color.

Cuttings. (What saint however dismembered ever rose again to such new life?) (That's Ted Roethke, Angel's favorite poet, paraphrased.)

Hours in the sun, sweat dripping into my eyes, my hands gritty with dirt, tending, caring.

When I'm gardening, I'm there. I'm out in the weather, peeling apart roots, digging into the earth with a trowel, testing the firmness of a bulb, placing it in the ground. I'm nowhere else.

I'm not in the basement apartment where I grew up choking in cigarette smoke, not in the dark in bed awake waiting through the hours till dawn, not strapped to a chair my father standing over me, not in bed with Dolores talking about whatever, sometimes politics, we both liked to talk politics, her ambitions my disdain. Once I felt something in me leave my body and travel in a short arc into her body. She laughed at that until I insisted it was real and then she watched me, tenderly, but also with a touch of worry, of concern.

Dolores' body in moonlight through bedroom windows. Stretched across the bed, her legs over my legs. My body is much darker, so much darker her skin flares where it crosses my skin. Together our bodies form a V, our legs meeting at the vertex. We lie on our backs. The palm of my hand touches the palm of her hand. It's summer. We're slicked with a sheen of perspiration. Through the open window, a breeze.

When he's gardening, Angel is absorbed by the labor, by dirt and light, planting and tending, by color. When he's gardening, he's nowhere other than where he is.

He misses that.

Now, without work, he's in his living room at night reading

Paradise, a book of poems picturing Bosch's *The Flight to Heaven* on the cover. The house lights are dim. He closes the book and considers the cover image of a naked body midway to heaven, a red-winged devil on one side of him, an angel on the other. He's in his favorite recliner, his legs tucked under him, slim volume of poetry in hand.

Cranston called earlier in the day and asked him to stop by his office. He was mysterious about why.

Angel has to quit obsessing on Neighbor. Today he saw him strutting around his fields with a gun strapped to his hip. Fucking idiot.

Angel is not dumb.

Angel knows what he's doing.

Angel does it with politics, he does it with Dolores, he does it with his father and his childhood and his family. Which is to say they are all lenses through which he diffuses his frustration with himself. It's easier to be angry with his father than it is to face his own failures.

Though his father was a nut case. Come on.

He was the angriest man alive, his father, and he took it out on his family.

Mean and humiliating and abusive.

Still.

Angel is way past all that.

When Angel tried to get out of the meeting, Cranston insisted. That was worrisome. It wasn't like him.

Is there a problem? Has one of the kids complained about reading Sylvia Plath? What, the holocaust imagery in "Daddy"?

Angel slaps the book of poetry closed. He can't concentrate.

He thinks maybe he'll try to work a little on his play, *The Man with an Ugly Heart*.

For that's the real problem. That's the root that needs tending. It's not about Neighbor or Dolores, or politics and the world. It's about, who is he? Who is Angel? Since his late teens, he's imagined himself as a writer. Specifically, as a playwright. Yet here he is at forty-one and he has yet to complete a satisfactory draft of the play he started in college.

Still.

The play has potential.

And forty-one is not old.

The central character in his play is a man who has terrible, vile thoughts about everything. Unspeakable, really. Humiliating. He thinks ugly things all the time. Violent things. Beating people to death with a pipe. Mutilating them. But the interesting point is that he's good. To counter all the ugliness in his heart, he becomes—by the end of the play—something like a saint, doing charitable work, giving away most of his possessions, keeping only enough to get by.

It's a great idea, and he thinks he has a great character to make the play really pulse with true life.

The problem is the plot. Every time Angel tries to make something happen, things go wrong.

Still.

He needs to apply himself. You can't write a great play, you can't win the Pulitzer and show everyone, including his dead father, if you go into your study once every six months, reread what you've already written, and add another line or two. If that. You've got to be diligent and persistent. You've got to be everything Angel has not been and can't seem to make himself be.

Angel tosses his book of poems onto the coffee table.

In his study, he sits at the computer and opens up the MS Word file, *The Man with an Ugly Heart*. He reads through the first act with growing excitement. It's good. It's seriously good. And he wrote this stuff. Him. Angel Maso. So, right, things bog down in the second act. In the first act, the guy, the central character is tempted. He's a banker and he has a chance to invest in a startup that makes facial recognition software. It's his best friend from college who was always a computer genius. First he thinks the software is going to be used to help prevent terrorist attacks. Once a terrorist's face is in the system, the software can pick him or her out of a crowd in the middle of Times Square on New Year's Eve. He—the central character, Andy—has some privacy concerns, which works as an early complication, but then he resolves that the good uses of the software outweigh those privacy concerns, and he invests everything he has in the startup because he doesn't want to be a banker, he wants to be an artist. If his friend is right and this software is as good as he says it is (and he has every reason in the world to believe him) then he's going to make a ton of money and he can quit his soul-sucking job.

This is all going on while, under the plot, he's wrestling with his corrupt heart, the anger and lust and pettiness he always has to fight to tamp down. This is the real theme of the play, this conflict within him. This desire not to be the person he seems to be right under the surface. If he can get out of the job that he hates, he hopes the ugliness that festers within will abate and he'll be able to be a better person, someone who isn't always thinking the kinds of ugly things he finds himself thinking.

So, at the end of the first act, the complications with his privacy concerns resolved, he goes ahead and makes the investment, which is substantial, which is just about every penny he has. Next thing, right away, there's a buyer for the software. Everyone is knocked out by how good the software is. The money offered is fantastic. Then in the final scene of the first act, when Andy and his friend are celebrating with champagne, the friend lets it come out that the buyer—who he has said he had to keep secret as part of the deal—is the U.S. Air Force. The software will indeed be used to prevent terrorist attacks. But it will also be used in drones to hunt down terrorists and blow them to pieces with Hellfire missiles. That's where the first act ends. With that revelation. Andy can't live with this; the audience understands that from his character develop-ment. He hates the use of drones and the unavoidable and inevitable loss of innocent lives. But Andy has invested all his money in the company. All his money and all his dreams of a different and better life as an artist, they're all in the balance. End of Act One.

Now, Act Two.

So far, the second act keeps going nowhere. Though the writing itself, the dialogue, is still damn good. That's something. Still, he's written so many versions of the second act it's wearying just to think about it.

Andy accepts that nothing in life is pure, and he takes the money and goes off to be an artist. He goes off to do charitable work, gives away the money, his possessions, etc. Problem with that, there was no Act III. How long can he go back and forth on whether to take the money before he just…takes the money. Not much of an ending, or at least Angel couldn't come up with much of an ending. Or even much of a middle.

Andy gives up the money. He loses everything he has and goes off to be an artist—and a better person. Again, not much drama after the first act.

Andy gives up the money and goes back to work as a banker. Depressing. He still has an ugly heart. Even uglier. Nothing's changed.

Andy kills himself.

Andy kills his friend.

Andy goes back to the bank and kills all his co-workers.

Andy breaks into the production facilities of General Atomics Aeronautical Systems Inc. in Sabra Springs, California, and straps himself to a MQ9 Reaper. The staging of that version was fun to think about, but then what, after he straps himself to the drone? 1) He blows himself up. Dramatic, but kind of way over the top. 2) He's arrested and goes to jail. Yawn. 3) He commits suicide strapped to the drone. Again, kind of way over the top.

Andy…what? What does Andy do in the second act that leads to complications and rising action and a climax that makes sense and is moving without being sentimental or absurd or preachy or obvious, and gets him around to being saint-like even though he still has an ugly heart? What?

Angel stares at the screen. He wishes he hadn't waited till so late in the day to get started. His thoughts keep switching back to Neighbor and the gun on his hip. Is it possible that the guy could really be dangerous? First the shotgun, now the pistol. Maybe he could ask Dolores to check him out for her, see if he's got a record or anything, if Angel should be worried. Dolores must have an in with the cops.

She could get someone to look into Neighbor on the QT. Angel has Neighbor's last name: Blakemore. (He found a piece of misplaced mail in his box addressed in a child's scrawl to Mr. Blakemore.) He has the address. Beyond that, nothing. No phone number listed. Nothing comes up in an online search. But it's not like Angel has put in a serious effort—any effort at all beyond looking in the phone book and a Google search—and surely with Dolores' connections…. She could just look at the property registry or something.

Angel resolves to call Dolores and ask her to check out Neighbor. It's a small thing. He has no doubt she'll do it for him.

He goes back to staring at the computer screen and Act II of *The Man with an Ugly Heart*.

Andy takes the money, becomes a sex addict. Why? What does that mean?

Andy takes the money and soon after initiates an affair with his friend's wife, the friend who's a computer genius (for now his name's Bob, the friend, but Angel isn't happy with the name and keeps changing it). But, Bob (in this draft). Bob didn't tell Andy his software would be used to blow up terrorists, as well as anyone who happened to be unlucky enough to be in the vicinity of the terrorists, like that wedding party that got bombed, or that hospital. So, the reason Andy is having an affair with his friend's wife is because he's a) angry with his friend, or b) has lost his moral compass, or c) he has finally given in to his inner ugliness, or d) all of the above. That's interesting. That's possible.

Angel writes that down: *Andy has an affair with Bob's wife.*

After he writes it down, he takes a little break and looks at Facebook.

He has six notifications!

Angel clicks on the little globe and a drop-down list of the notifications appears. Two of them are birthday notifications for people he has no idea who they are; one of them notifies him that he's been added to some group he has no clue what it's about; and the other two are from Tiffany.

Tiffany has invited him to Skype with her. Again.

Angel had resolved to quit doing this kind of thing, but Tiffany has included a picture of her at the beach. She's standing with her feet in the water, her head cocked just slightly, a come hither look in her eyes, one hand on her hip, as if waiting. She's wearing a one-piece red bathing suit that looks bright as a flare against the pale blue background of the sea. She's in her twenties, probably. She's pretty. Her body is still perfect. Under the picture, three words: *I'm lonely, Angel.*

Angel sighs. He looks at his play. He looks at Tiffany. He closes his eyes.

A long time goes by in silence, Angel seated at his desk, in front of his computer, his eyes closed, before finally he rises, grabs his credit card and his iPad, and heads for the bedroom.

Aye, Captain!

At six a.m. birds were chirping up a ruckus outside Ginny's condo, a flock of starlings screaming in the purple crown of a redbud that reached up to just below her back windows, a single black crow on her rooftop looking down at the sparrows as if wondering what the hell all the commotion is about. Cranston, behind the wheel in his Civic, cell phone in hand, deliberating in a small courtyard parking area, looked up at Ginny's back windows while he went back and forth between calling her and going up to have the talk he needed to have with her, or driving off, waiting for another time and giving himself more space to think through what he wanted to say and how he wanted to say it.

But he knew what he needed to say.

What had happened between them was wrong from every possible perspective. Part of him, a fairly big part of him, could still hardly believe that it had truly happened. He, Cranston Wade III, principal of Redvale High School, a happily married man with four wonderful daughters, in an adulterous relationship with a younger woman who was effectively in his employ. My God. It could only be more clichéd if she were his secretary.

From the late afternoon moment when he had left Ginny's apartment to this early morning moment in her courtyard parking lot, Cranston had suffered under a suffocating weight of guilt. He was a fool. What was he thinking? How could he risk his relationship with his wife and daughters, as well as his career should it ever become known that he was sleeping with one of his teachers. Though, of course, she wasn't really one of his teachers, even if she did occasionally teach a course in the high school. She was really an administrator for a program—oh, stop. She was effectively one of his teachers. He could lose his family and his job. What in hell were you thinking, Cranston? She put her arm around your legs and her head on your knee, and next thing you're both ripping off your clothes like you'd been waiting for that moment forever.

My God. No.

Cranston's finger hovered over the red call button on his phone.

He looked up again at the dark back windows of her condo. She was still sleeping. Though how she could sleep through the damn racket of those starlings was amazing.

He checked his reflection in the rearview mirror and considered the black pirate eye patch with skull and crossbones. The kids loved it. But did he really want to be wearing his pirate patch when he had this talk with Ginny? Was there something unconscious going on when he picked it out of the pile of eye patches he wore to school every day? Did it make him feel tougher? Amusingly wicked? Stop. He checked the glove compartment looking for a plain black patch and found only a single Sponge Bob: A yellow rectangle with, from bottom to top, blue pants, an upward curved line representing a smile, black eyeglasses, and three black pipe cleaner strands sticking out of the top, representing hair. Sure. Good thinking, Cranston. Show up at Ginny's place to have a serious conversation wearing either a) a ridiculous pirate patch, or b) an absurd Sponge Bob patch. Excellent.

Cranston hit the call button. (He went with the pirate eye patch.)

Ginny picked up on the fourth ring. "Cranston? What time is it?"

Cranston, ignoring the Caller ID that had already clearly identified him as the caller, said, "Hi, Ginny. It's Cranston. I was hoping I could talk to you this morning, before school. I'm in your parking lot. In my car."

When Ginny appeared at the back window, cell phone to her ear, Cranston experienced a quick rush of…what? Happiness? Happiness tinged with fear? Dread? Dread tinged with excitement?

"Sure," Ginny said. "Come on up. I'll buzz you in."

At her door, Ginny looked Cranston over, and grinned. "Aye, Matey," she said, "come on aboard."

Cranston shoved his hands into his pockets, as if to signal his intention to keep them to himself and sidled past Ginny into her apartment. He crossed the room and positioned himself with his back to her unmade bed, facing her.

Ginny closed the front door and leaned back against it. In the morning light, the green in her hair deepened to a dark sea blue. She crossed her arms, which only served to enhance the already substantial amount of skin exposed by a low cut, black chemise.

Cranston said, "We have to talk, Ginny."

Ginny raised her eyebrows, as if to say Well, go ahead. Talk.

"What happened between us," he said. "You know, of course. I'm married. And I have a family." Cranston had rehearsed a speech in which he explained that although he was obviously attracted to Ginny, that though there was something about her that seemed to awaken a long dormant, youthful excitement in him, and that though there was something about her that he responded to intensely, sexually—nonetheless, they couldn't, he couldn't, continue to have a romantic, sexual relationship with her. It wasn't fair to the wife and children he loved. And it wasn't fair to her since there could be no future in the relationship. Cranston had rehearsed the main points of what he wanted to say several times. He had started rehearsing it as soon as he left her apartment that afternoon. Hell, he had started rehearsing it even before he left her apartment. Now, however…. Now, there wasn't a word in his head beyond the few he had just spoken.

"Sweetie," Ginny said, and she rubbed a patch of red skin next to her eye as if it was itching her. She looked down at the floor, concentrating on scratching the itch. "I know you're married." When she looked up, she was smiling. She crossed the room, took Cranston by the hand, and led him back to her bed, where they both sat on the edge of the mattress. "I understand," she said as she crossed her legs and folded her hands over her knees. "You're married. You have a family. And you don't want to risk all that just to have a fling."

"Well, not exactly," Cranston said. "I wouldn't call it a *fling*."

"See," Ginny said. "There's your problem. Of course it's a fling." She pushed his hair back off his forehead. "It doesn't have to be a big deal," she said. "Or it doesn't have to be at all, if you don't want it." She laid her hand over his knee. "Me," she said, a playful smile blossoming, "I just think we could both use a little more spice in our lives."

Cranston looked down at his knee. What the hell was it all of a sudden with him and his knees? She lays her head on his knees, and next thing you know they're both naked. Now she puts her hand on his knee and his head turns to mush, his heart starts racing, and his vision tunnels till all he can see is the white of her thighs against the silky black fabric of the chemise.

"Just a fling," Cranston said, posed as neither a question nor an affirmation. The three words merely slipped over his tongue and out of his mouth, mindless.

"Aye, Captain." Ginny removed his glasses, folded back the stems, and placed them on her night table, before beginning to undo the knot of his tie.

Cranston thought, *Okay, just a fling*, as he lay back on Ginny's still sleep-warm bed, the sun high enough in the sky now to light up her white sheets with the bright colors of the prayer flag. *Just a fling* he repeated to himself as Ginny went about undressing him and he pushed the chemise's straps off her shoulders, his head emptied of everything but the light on her body and the expression on her face and the racing and rising of everything within and without. *Just a fling*, he repeated, as if the words were a magic talisman that might make it all okay.

Poor Baby

Angel, happy to be out of the house, dressed, shaved, spruced up, on a lovely spring day, white dogwoods and purple redbuds in bloom, a clear blue sky. The temperature mild enough for short sleeves, though Angel had put on his establishment outfit—khaki slacks, crisp white shirt and yellow tie, navy blue blazer—for this meeting with Cranston. There had been something in Cranston's voice when he asked for the meeting that worried Angel at first, something formal, serious. As if there was a problem. Later, though, the more Angel thought about it, the more he came around to a different opinion. He was well-liked by the other faculty and the students. In school, conducting classes, his best self came forward. He loved poetry, had loved poetry since discovering e.e. cummings as a sixteen-year-old in high school. When he was in front of the class, a room full of kids with their eyes on him, words came to him, a way of speaking came to him, and he was able make them feel the power of a poem to make language spark and jump and connect them to ideas and emotions that they understood, that they connected with, that were meaningful and powerful.

Angel was a good teacher.

He was a friendly colleague.

Truth was, he often hadn't spoken to anyone all week before showing up at school, and thus he genuinely enjoyed the company of both students and faculty.

He was sure he was well-liked. He was sure he was a good teacher. By the time he had put on his best blazer and driven off for the high school to meet Cranston, he was thinking that maybe he'd be offered a full-time position. That possibility, the more he thought about it, the more it appealed to him.

It would solve his financial problems.

It would get him out of the house and back into the world.

Of course, his real ambition was to be a writer not a teacher, but still. History was full of writers who had to work unlikely jobs to support their art. Wallace Stevens was vice president of Hartford Life Insurance. That always struck Angel as especially improbable. He imagined Stevens in a meeting with a bunch of big shots, thinking *Let be be finale of seem! The only emperor is the emperor of ice cream!*

Weird.

T.S. Eliot was a clerk for Lloyd's Bank of London. He worked in a basement office at a desk in a long line of desks with other clerks calculating foreign transactions. No wonder he wrote "The Waste Land." But, again, weird.

Angel parked beside a blue Toyota Corolla, its hatchback plastered with bumper stickers. One of the senior's cars, he guessed, and probably an athlete still here for practice, given it was after school hours and one of the stickers read *My Daughter Got Pregnant at North Vista High School.* North Vista was Redvale's big rival.

Angel straightened out his tie and looked himself over in the rearview. He placed his forefinger in the pronounced cleft in his chin, an old habit from childhood when kids teased him for being short and wide and having a chin that looked like it was split in half. Not to mention being named Angel. Though he didn't have it as bad as the lone Puerto Rican kid in his middle school, Jesus Gutierrez, who was scrawny and bookish and suffered mightily for being the teachers' favorite. Middle school bullies thought it was hilarious to grab Jesus by the hair and shove him into Angel, laughing like hyenas that they should hang out together.

On his way into the school, following a neat concrete path that curved around a well-kept lawn, Angel met Lucy Merola and stopped to chat. Lucy was one of the front desk secretaries, a dumpy, broad-faced, strikingly unattractive woman who smiled easily and genuinely. She stopped as she neared Angel. Her smile fired up and she put her hands on her hips. "Honey," she said, with her wide Southern accent, "aren't you handsome today!"

"Thank you," Angel answered, flashing a smile in return. "Cranston asked me to stop by for a meeting." He exaggerated a look of stunned surprise. "I have no idea what it's about!"

"Well," Lucy said, and she reached out to touch Angel on the arm, "you'll just have to go and find out, won't you?"

Angel agreed that he would, and they chatted a little more, briefly, about students and teachers and local news, before exchanging parting greetings as Lucy went on to her car and Angel proceeded to the principal's office, where he found Cranston seated behind his desk, looking out over a mess of manila folders, his expression as serious and dark as Lucy's had been friendly and bright.

Without rising, Cranston pointed to a chair. "Have a seat, Angel."

Angel managed a slight, amused laugh as he sat on the edge of the waiting chair and pointed to Cranston's pirate eye patch. "Sounds like you're ordering me to walk the plank. Something wrong?"

Cranston's gaze shifted from serious to angry. He got up, crossed the room, and closed the door.

"What?" Angel tended to sound angry when he was nervous or scared. This was a trait he suspected he had in common with his father, who was probably, God help him, nervous or scared most of his life. "Is it the Sylvia Plath poems?" he asked, following Cranston as he retraced his steps and retreated again behind the barrier of his desk.

"I can't tell you," Cranston said, "how disappointed I am in you."

"You're disappointed in me?" A bright flare of blood shot up to Angel's face. "What's the problem? If it's the Sylvia Plath—"

"It has nothing to do with Sylvia Plath," Cranston said, the pitch of his voice sharp and seriously pissed off.

"Then what?" Angel, knocked off balance by Cranston's deadly seriousness, fell back in his chair and waited.

Cranston hesitated long enough to let the silence build. "You are not X. J. Williamson," he said, and now the anger in his voice was tinged with weariness. "X. J. Williamson is a black woman from Denver. And you didn't graduate from the Iowa Writer's Workshop. They have no record of a graduate by your name."

Angel watched Cranston with a glint of amusement in his eyes, a dumb, entirely out of place, ludic smile on his face—as if there were an obvious and entertaining misunderstanding between them and he was about to explain away the confusion, after which they would both laugh at the mix up. Problem was…well, there was no mix up. Angel *wasn't* X.J. Williamson and he *hadn't* graduated from the Writers Workshop. Those lies were so old and he had shoved them so far back in his mind that he had pretty much forgotten about them.

"Well?" Cranston sat up straight and placed his folded hands on the desk. "Do you have anything to say for yourself?"

"Look," Angel said, and then his eyes were welling up and he blushed at the humiliation of being reduced to tears. He was a grown man, for God's sake. Cranston was treating him like a boy. He covered his face quickly, rubbed his eyes as if tired, and hoped that Cranston hadn't noticed—but of course he had. It would have been obvious. He took a deep breath. He gathered himself. "Look," he repeated, and now, thank God, he sounded in control. Serious, even-tempered, rational. "What does it matter that I'm not X.J. Williamson? She's a terrible poet anyway. I know poetry. I've been reading poetry all my life. I am, in truth, a playwright—with a love of poetry and language." Angel opened his arms, leading into his pitch. "So I told that character, Ginny with the crazy hair, that I published under a pseudonym because I knew all she'd care about is whether or not I had published anything—didn't matter if it was good, didn't matter if it was terrible. All that mattered was the publication. I wanted a chance to teach poetry to kids, so I hustled my way into the program. Ok, shoot me, I lied." He fixed his eyes on Cranston. He stared with what he hoped was a passionate and sincere gaze. "The point is, I'm a good teacher. I thoroughly know my subject. I'm good at conveying an enthusiasm for poetry to young kids. Isn't that what matters? Why does publishing terrible poems make someone more qualified to be a good teacher? You should hire teachers because they're good teachers, which I am." Angel paused, breathless from pleading his case, and then before Cranston could respond, he added, "And I never said I graduated from the Iowa Writer's Workshop. I said I graduated from the University of Iowa. Which I did. That Ginny character just assumed I meant the Writer's Workshop."

"And you didn't correct her?"

"No. I didn't." Angel pushed himself forward in his seat, leaned toward Cranston. "But, again, to the point. I'm a good teacher. You're not likely to find anyone who can do this job better than I can. Isn't that the heart of the matter? Isn't that the real point?"

"The point," Cranston said, "is that you're a fraud."

Angel, stung, dropped his hands. He looked at Cranston as if the man were transforming into a monster before his eyes.

"I can't have you around our students, Angel. After today, you'll be banned from school grounds." Having pronounced his verdict, Cranston softened a bit. "Listen," he said, "I'm sorry. You have been a good teacher. But you lied to me, you lied to Ginny, and you presented yourself as someone you're not. There's no way I can keep you on. I'm sorry."

Angel nodded. "It's a stupid system," he said. He lifted himself out of the chair, feeling his weight, wrestling the bulk of himself up onto his feet. At the door he turned back to Cranston. "Really?" he asked. "You're going to tell the secretaries, everyone, that I'm banned from the grounds? Can't we just agree that I won't come back?"

Cranston shook his head. "Sorry."

Angel thought, "Fuck you." He thought, "Fuck you, you sanctimonious, self-righteous pig." He said, "Okay, sure. I guess you have to do what you think is right." He nodded, a parting nod that said *Okay, fine. Whatever.*

Back at his car, he found Shelly waiting for him in the passenger seat. A teenager again, in leather boots, shredded jeans, and white mesh crop top over a slinky black bra, she crossed her arms over her bare stomach and glared at him, her eyes dark and furious. "What?" she said. "The fuck? Was that?"

"I screwed up." Angel backed out of his parking spot and headed onto the road.

"You?" Shelly, flabbergasted, jumped up onto her seat, folding her legs under her. "You're only the best fucking teacher they ever had in that second-rate bastion of mediocrity supposed to be such a great high school!"

Angel's heart beat steadily but loud, hard pulsing in his chest. Outside, the flaming dogwoods and redbuds flew past. He slowed down. He was driving too fast. Shelly seemed to be watching him carefully. She had her hair cut short and punky, a dark outline of mascara circling her eyes. Angel glanced at her quickly before turning back to the road. "This is new," he said. "Never seen you out of the house before."

"Because this really pisses me off," she said. "This whole thing." She slid closer to Angel, put an arm around his shoulder and kissed him on the neck. "Who is he to treat you that way? It's infuriating."

"I did screw up," Angel said. "He does have a point."

"Please, Angel, stop." Shelly snuggled closer to him, wrapping her arms around his chest, laying her head on his shoulder. "You had to hustle a bit to get yourself into the classroom. So what? Isn't that how things work in this country? Who doesn't pad their résumé? This is America, isn't it? Everybody hustles!"

"I'm tired," Angel said. "I feel like I haven't slept in years."

"You poor baby!" Shelly ran her hands through his hair and kissed him on the temple. "Listen to me, Angel Maso. You haven't done a single bad thing. Think about it. You were teaching those kids to love poetry! What could possibly be wrong with that?"

"I lied."

"Oh, please." Shelly ran a hand over his chest, massaging his heart as if trying to quiet the loud, rough beat of it against his skin. "You're fully qualified for the job. You're an excellent teacher. That's what matters. All the rest is bullshit." She kissed him on the neck. "Cranston's the fraud. If he were a competent principal, all he'd be concerned about is hiring the best teacher for the job."

"In the halls a few weeks ago," Angel said, his eyes on the road, his voice a whisper, "I overheard a student refer to me as Mr. Mumbles."

"Big deal." Shelly was busy kissing him softly on his neck and up behind his ear, one hand on his chest, the other on the back of his head. She was getting into it. "We talked about that. They're kids. They make fun of their teachers. That's what kids do."

"I do mumble to myself," Angel said. "I've been trying to get a handle on it."

"Angel, please." Shelly let him loose and shuffled around until she was in front of him, her back against the dashboard, looking him in the eyes. "You're a sweet guy," she said, firmly. "Everybody thinks you're a sweet guy."

"I hold grudges," Angel said. "I nurture wounds. I never give it up. I never let it go. I remember insults from when I was a child. They fester. They eat at me. This thing with Cranston, it'll never quit. I'll remember it on my death bed. The kids calling me Mr. Mumbles. I won't let it go. I'm incapable of letting things go."

"Look at me." Shelly maneuvered her head alongside the steering wheel. She was beautiful: her skin bright in sunlight through the side window, her eyes burning inside black ovals. "You're an artist," she said. "You're sensitive and you're surrounded by dull, stupid people, like those idiot kids and that jackass Cranston. You don't fit easily. You've never fit easily." She dropped down to her knees, slipped her head under the steering wheel, and kissed Angel's belly as she started to undo his pants. "You're an artist," she said, "and you're a sweet, decent man."

Angel pulled into the parking lot of a strip mall, found an alley that led around back, and parked behind a green dumpster. After looking around quickly to be sure the car was hidden, he released the seat and stretched out. In the back seat, he found his overcoat and tossed it over Shelly's head as it bobbed in his lap. Soon—that was better—his mind emptied—that's good—a glass of water spilling into the ocean, everything for the moment, thank God, absent except for Shelly's ministering, this girl who was as real now to Angel as sunlight streaming into the car.

God, he's sleepy. In a moment, when it's over, he'll close his eyes. He'll allow himself a little nap.

After all, it's not like he has anywhere to be.

Moody? Needy? An Emotional Wreck?

So, was Gloria a *femme*? What exactly was a femme, beyond the obvious of being a gay woman who was into looking sexy and dressing attractively? If even that was right. God, this was a beautiful late afternoon: golden light shimmering in treetops, mountains in the distance outlined in alpenglow. It wasn't that Claire had a problem with lesbians. She had grown well beyond that. At first, yes, when she was thirteen and out of nowhere her mother was living across town with Gloria, who looked like she could still be in high school—back then she had a problem. Perhaps because she was herself in a clinch with puberty and sex was on her mind, Claire couldn't help thinking about her mother and Gloria in bed together, making out, doing the things—mechanically at least—that she understood they must be doing, and it troubled her so profoundly that she quickly developed a massively effective ability to not think about sex at all. In a period of months, she went from being a socially engaged teenage girl with an appropriate interest in sex to being a sex-averse teen whose social life existed exclusively in the digital realm of social media.

Given how things worked out, perhaps she should thank her mom.

Claire grinned at the thought as she navigated the streets of Redvale, driving slowly through a development on the way to her mom's house.

Now that Claire was an adult who saw herself as politically progressive, she accepted her mother's relationship with Gloria. It was what it was. Her mother was gay, she fell in love with a young woman, and now they're living together happily ever after. Fine. Back to the original question: Was Gloria a femme? The walled-off ghetto in Claire's brain seemed to be developing cracks. The district in her mind where thoughts of sex, especially thoughts of lesbian sex, were banned, a place populated with blank synaptic connections, threw off a few sparks as she neared her mom's house. Claire thought that she really should know more about Dolores's life. She should try harder. She should be a better daughter.

If she could have seen herself in the rear view, she'd have been surprised at how deeply she was frowning as these thoughts crossed her mind. All those years of resentment, of weekends with her mother and Gloria in their various cute little apartments, with their cute little mutt Jingo who they walked through their neighborhood's streets like a couple of parents pushing a stroller, with their dumb pickup trucks like that somehow made them tough characters.... Those angry teen years still held power internally. Try as she may, they still ruled.

Claire resolved to be good as she pulled into Dolores's driveway, though her first thought was that if her place were any cuter, passers-by would fall over gagging in the street. The boxy, sea blue gingerbread house, with its elaborate sawn details, its outer porch balcony framed with white frills of carpenter's lace, with its peaked roof and peaked dormer windows, looked like it had been snatched out of an illustrated children's book, the house where the fairy godmother lived with her seven dwarves…or whatever.

Stop.

Be good.

Claire parked behind her mother's pickup and alongside a red Prius, which was occupying the spot where Gloria's chartreuse Dodge Neon should have been parked. She engaged the parking brake just as Judd Hansen stepped out onto the front porch, followed by Dolores, the two of them looking like they were just leaving the home of a terminally ill friend.

Dolores waved, Judd nodded. When Claire joined them on the porch, she shook hands with Judd, accepted a perfunctory embrace from her mom, and then said she hoped she wasn't interrupting anything important.

"Nah, we're all finished." Judd fixed a baseball cap over his bald head, tugging the brim in place. He said, "Good to see you again, Claire," so distracted he sounded computerized.

Dolores said, "We'll talk again in the morning, Judd," and then held the door open for Claire as Hansen walked off solemnly toward his car.

Inside, the front door closed behind them, Claire said, "What the hell was that about?"

"Trust me," Dolores said, "you don't want to know." She took a seat on one end of the couch in the living room and motioned for Claire to join her. "What are you doing here?" she asked, as if annoyed at the unannounced visit.

"I can leave," Claire said, still standing, "if this is a bad time."

"No, no, no, sit, please! I'm just—" Dolores threw up her hands. "Hansen's making me crazy!"

"What?" Claire took a seat on the opposite end of the couch and pulled her legs up under her.

If you had snapped a picture at this moment, you'd have been unable to miss the mother-daughter relationship. Doll sockless in Birkenstocks, blue jeans, and a plain white blouse; Claire sockless in low cut sneakers, blue jeans, and a simple, pale yellow blouse. Both with the same dark auburn hair: Doll's shoulder length and brushed neat, Claire's chin length and carefully unkempt. Both with the same round face, big eyes and thin upper lip. Claire in her youth, slim and athletically fit. Doll middle aged thick in the thighs, developing a belly, but still tight and firmly muscled through the arms and shoulders. Their dark eyes, identical neon signs announcing a degree of intelligence and depth.

"Honestly," Dolores said, "it's just Board of Supervisors business. Hansen's been going around telling people that I'm backing an open carry ban on semi-automatics."

"I thought you were," Claire said. "Linni told me—"

"I never told Hansen or anyone else," Doll said, raising her voice, emphasizing every word, "that I would support a ban, let alone a buyback program. Ever."

"So, the newspaper article—"

"Was totally wrong."

"You won't support a ban?" Claire asked, a quick flash of anger lighting her up. "Even after that maniac guy shot up the market?"

"Claire…," Doll closed her eyes and took a breath. "Claire," she repeated, evenly, her eyes meeting her daughter's eyes. "Of course I'd like to see a ban on the open carry of assault rifles. I'd in fact like to see assault rifles outlawed completely. But this is politics, and the art of politics is achieving what's possible." She paused again for emphasis and added, "A ban isn't possible right now in Redvale. Period. End of story."

"But Judd Hansen does? Think it's possible?"

"Judd Hansen's read *Profiles in Courage* too many times. He's a smart guy. I'm sure he knows, in his heart, no, it's not possible."

"Sorry," Claire, suddenly glacial. "I admire Hansen. I don't think there's anything wrong with being courageous and doing the right thing. Actually, I think it's generally a good idea."

Doll nodded, giving up. "Fine," she said, "but you're not pursuing a career in politics. I am. Meanwhile, since that idiot newspaper piece got picked up by the AP, I'm getting so many phone calls, locally and *nationally*, that I've had to unplug the land lines."

"You're getting phone calls nationally?"

"CNN, the networks, *The New York Times*, *The Washington Post*—"

"Really? I'm surprised there's that much interest."

"It's a big issue." Doll made the observation as if it depressed her immensely. "Especially in an election year. Especially after the downtown fiasco made national news. Plus, all you've got to do is say the words *gun control* and the pro-gun people go into convulsions. Honestly," she added, discouraged, "let's talk about something else. Is there a reason for this visit? Or did you…."

"Just come over to visit?" Claire asked, seeing that Doll was struggling to finish the sentence. "No, sorry. I came over to ask a favor."

"What is it?" Doll perked up, a spark of eagerness animating her. "You know if there's anything at all I can—"

"It's a little thing…well, maybe not. There's a local boy I represent, Kenny Walker—"

"Kenny from Kroger." Doll, pleased with herself for knowing

something about Claire's business.

"His mother died."

"Oh, I know, Linni told me." Doll grimaced.

"The thing is, I care about him, Kenny, and...I'm not really sure why, but, I'd like it if you and Dad came to the funeral."

"Together?" Doll slid back a little, as if trying to put some distance between herself and the idea of attending a funeral together with her ex.

"No," Claire said, as if don't be ridiculous. "Not together. Just, both of my parents there. I think, you know, it would be a way of expressing to Kenny that he's like family to me."

"Well, sure," Doll said. "Of course. When is it?"

"This Thursday. They're doing a mass in the morning, and then the viewing later, and burial the next day."

"So you'd like me to come Thursday afternoon?"

"That would be great."

Dolores hesitated, her eyes on Claire's, an unspoken question hovering.

"Of course you can bring Gloria," Claire said. "If she wants to come, she's welcome."

"I'll talk to her about it." Doll, obviously relieved. "I'm sure she'll want to. You know, she does love you, Claire, even if, I mean we both know, you have your issues with her." Doll made a face and laughed, "Well, and me too, of course. I mean, that you have your issues with me, not I have issues with—"

"I get it, Mom," Claire said. "Look, Gloria's welcome."

"The only thing that might be a problem," Doll said, "and I don't think it will, is that there might possibly be a Board of Supervisors meeting that day."

"Might possibly be? You don't know?"

"I don't," Doll said. "I don't think there will be, but...," Doll leaned back as if accepting something unpleasant but necessary. "Judd scheduled a meeting," she explained, "for Thursday to discuss his proposal, and, of course, as soon as word got out, the Redvale Gun Club went nuts, BeDouchian brought in the NRA, and now Elvis Blakemore and his band of wackos are promising to show up at the meeting armed to the teeth."

"Elvis who?"

"Blakemore, president of the Redvale Gun Club."

"Elvis?"

"That's only the half of it," Doll said, and her foot started tapping in an obvious displacement of nervous energy. She noticed quickly, put both feet firmly on the floor, and sat upright. "I do not want to be put in the position of confronting Blakemore while he's holding an assault rifle."

"Can they do that?" Claire's expression was stalled someplace between concern and amusement. "Can they bring assault rifles to a Board meeting?"

"Honey," Doll said, a lecture clearly about to be delivered, "we're among the most conservative localities in the nation when it comes to gun policy. We have legislators who believe the Second Amendment is the only permit anyone needs to carry a gun, open or concealed, anywhere. So, no, there's nothing at all to keep citizens from showing up at a Board meeting carrying assault rifles. Not here. Not in Redvale."

"That's pretty crazy," Claire said, amusement moving past concern as a little smile broke out.

Doll, following Claire's cue, laughed, and the laugh dissipated a knot of tension. "Judd's like, Let them show up! Let's have a debate! Let's get our pictures in the paper with a bunch of machos toting assault rifles, trying to intimidate elected officials!"

"And you don't agree?"

"No, I don't," Doll said. "First of all— Do you want a cup of tea?" When Claire shook her head, Doll stood, stretched, and then bent over to touch her toes. "I do," she said, and motioned for Claire to follow her into the kitchen. "First of all," she repeated, "I don't think I can support Hansen on the open carry ban." She stopped midway and turned to face Claire. "It has no chance! It's an exercise in futility! And the buy-back program," she added on her way into the kitchen again, past Gloria's M.C. Escher puzzle spread out on the living room table, "that's like asking a congregation of evangelical Christians to burn their bibles and sell you back their crucifixes. Not going to happen. You sure I can't make you a cup of tea?" Doll pulled a tea ball out of a drawer and went about packing it and boiling water.

Claire pulled up a stool and took a seat at an L-shaped kitchen island splashed in sunlight. She watched Doll take a ceramic mug down from a cupboard and place it alongside a mason jar of honey, the kitchen suddenly fragrant with the mint of crushed tea leaves.

"So, anyway," Doll, returning to the subject of the Board meeting. "I told Hansen to either reschedule until we could work out something with Blakemore, or else I'd have to seriously consider being a no-show."

Claire glanced behind her, into the living room. It took her only a moment to figure out that the barely begun jigsaw puzzle on the table was a famous M.C. Escher print. It would probably take Gloria god knows how many hours to piece the thing together, after which she would frame it and hang it in the basement with the rest of her completed puzzles. Jesus. At least Dolores insisted they stay in the basement. "Where's Gloria?"

"Getting her hair done. I think she said she's getting a streak of color added. I think she said blue, or maybe red."

"Huh, well, she's young enough to get away with it." Claire, a little jab, nothing terrible, but enough that her mother would notice.

"Anyway," Dolores, a quick subject change, "pretty sure we'll reschedule the meeting." She took the tea kettle off the stove just as it was beginning to whistle. "That gives me a little more time to think things over, and maybe someone can talk some sense into Blakemore, though that's not likely." Doll poured her tea, carried it to the island, and sat across from Claire.

Claire pulled the teacup to her and sniffed the rich mint aroma. "I find it hard to believe it's legal to show up at a government meeting carrying a semi-automatic." She slid the cup back across the island.

"Welcome to Redvale. At a Board of Supervisors meeting, nothing to stop them. As long as there aren't metal detectors at the entrances, they're legal to carry in a cannon." Doll picked up the mug with both hands and held it in front of her. "And Blakemore," she said, looking over her tea at Claire, "the guy seriously worries me. I truly believe he's dangerous. He's one of those men-in-black nuts."

"What?" Again, a smile slipped out.

"I don't know," Doll said, "something about men in black who are either aliens or government agents or whatever and they're supposed to be coming to take over the world."

Claire's smile blossomed into a little laugh. "How come I've never heard of this?"

"Because you're sane?" Doll, now also smiling. "Actually, it's not the men-in-black thing that scares me so much, though that's pretty damn out there. "It's—" she said, and suddenly lowered her voice. "I happen to know he's had restraining orders taken out against him by his ex-wife. Twice." She raised her eyebrows, secret sharing over. "I'm not especially interested in facing down this guy," she added, "with a machine gun hanging off his neck."

"What were the restraining orders about? Did he beat her up?"

"No, not that she reported anyway. She said he was threatening to kill her and she had no doubt, I'm told, that he was capable of carrying through."

"Well, that's not good," Claire said. "On the other hand, he didn't do it, obviously."

"Not yet." Doll punctuated the observation with a brief stare. "So. Anyway." She took another little sip of tea. "Pretty sure there won't be a Board meeting on Thursday. Judd's just going to have to reschedule. But, even if there is— One way or another, I should be able to attend the funeral. Have you talked to your father? Will he be there?"

Claire hesitated before answering. Tentatively, she risked, "I've been worried about Dad. I think I've been avoiding seeing him."

"Why's that? What's wrong?"

Because it's weird to find your father reading a Buzz Feed site about masturbating too much? Because his house has the atmosphere of a mausoleum? Because she fears he's becoming agoraphobic? Because he always puts on an I'm-happy, I'm-fine act when she sees him, when it's obvious he's neither happy nor fine? "I don't know," she said. "Little things. He doesn't seem himself lately."

"Your father's always been moody," Doll said, shrugging off Claire's concern. "Moody and needy and emotionally kind of a wreck. That's just Angel."

"You know," Claire said, a bolt of heat driving down from her forehead into her cheeks. "I actually know my father pretty well, Mom, given he raised me largely by himself from the time I was thirteen."

"Uh, oh." Doll's eyes went wide with exaggerated concern. "I didn't mean to push any buttons, Honey."

"You're not pushing any buttons." Claire, as evenly as she could manage. "Just, you know, once, I'd like to have a conversation with you where you didn't wind up criticizing Dad."

"I'm not criticizing him!"

"Really?" Claire laughed. "Moody? Needy? An emotional wreck? That's not criticism?"

"No, Hon," Doll said, getting her back up. "Those are just facts, Darling."

"Okay, fine." Claire, rising, throwing up her hands in surrender.

"Have you ever considered," Doll said, palms cupped around her teacup as if trying to mold it into a new shape, "that maybe I get tired of being cast as the bad guy? That maybe our breakup wasn't entirely my fault?"

"What breakup?" Claire took a step back from the island and Doll. "I don't remember any breakup. What I remember is you met

Gloria and you walked. And why not? I mean, she was young, she was hot. Why stick with middle aged moody old dad and your nerdy teenage daughter? Who couldn't understand that?"

"Oh, Claire, please." Doll dismissed Claire's tirade with an eye roll. She sipped her tea.

"You seem to forget that I was there," Claire said. "I don't remember any drama with dad. Why isn't it entirely your fault?"

Doll sighed in a way that announced she was willing to make some concessions. "All right," she said, "I'm certainly not faultless. I was trying to be somebody I wasn't with Angel, from the beginning; and, I admit, that was never fair to him; and I behaved badly at the end. But, Angel, Jesus, Honey…between his moods and his neediness, it was like living with a weight tied around my neck, plus his aimlessness, his delusions of grandeur about being some kind of a great writer and his utterly stunning inability to get anything done, ever, to take control of his life, which left me to do everything in that household, all those years, from the cleaning and bill paying to most of the bread winning, to—"

"All right, stop," Claire said, raising her voice. "You know, it's funny, because I don't remember it like that at all."

"You wouldn't, Honey. You weren't married to him."

"Fine." Claire, furious. "I don't have time for this." She forced a smile, shoved her hands deep into the pockets of her jeans, immediately pulled them out. "Some day," she said, her eyes welling up, "maybe we can talk about these things civilly. Right now…." She shook her head, threw up a hand in a quick wave goodbye, and walked off through the living room and out of the house.

In her car, in Doll's driveway, Claire glanced back to be sure Doll wasn't watching before she retrieved a pack of tissues from the glove compartment and dabbed away tears. She should have known better. Every time. Every damn time. Once, she'd like to have a simple, uncomplicated visit with her mother. Really, Claire, is that too much to ask? Did you have to essentially call her a coward on the open carry thing? Did you have to throw that little jab about Gloria's age? Did you have to get into it over Dad? Really, Claire? Every time? Can't you just once?

"Guess not," Claire said aloud, and backed out of the driveway and onto the road. She tried to shake off yet another disastrous visit with her mother. What made her think it would be any different?

It wasn't a disaster. Come on, Claire. You're not a drama queen. You're a businesswoman, and a very good one, a very successful one. Focus. You have a meeting coming up with ICM. You're in the middle of negotiating two international tours—once you get through this funeral.

It's dusk. A dreary, overcast day's last light fading. That's mom on the other side of a plate glass window. (Claire's thirteen, a few weeks after Dolores moved out.) It's almost dark and I'm in town alone, walking along Main Street. I'd acted up at dinner, told Dad that if I had to eat spaghetti and meatballs one more time I'd stab myself in the eye with a fork. Dad covered his face with his hands. He didn't make a sound. He didn't move. "Oh, please!" I left the house and walked and walked, all the way downtown, to the market—and then there's Mom, a glass of wine in her hand, amid a crowd of well-dressed women at an art gallery opening, eating hors d'oeuvres, drinking wine, laughing. I'm on the other side of the window. On the street. In the shadows.

Claire stopped at a light. For a second, she forgot where she was. She found her phone and while the light was still red sent a text to Linni.

Be home in a sec!

Before she could put the phone away, it chirped a return text.

Drive safe! Big hug!

Claire smiled. The light turned. She drove off, phone in hand, composing a return text, something bright and witty to dash off at the next light.

Drone Dreams

Angel is surrounded by ghosts.

It seems a bomb…a missile…something has crumpled buildings, twisted iron girders, left a field of blood and rubble. He steps barefoot over jagged hunks of concrete. Snaking tentacles of rebar reach out for him, inanimate furious arms. Smoke drifts over the devastation, morning fog scented with blood and tar.

And bodies. And parts of bodies. And ghosts picking through the rubble, searching, human forms Angel sees and sees through, which is how he knows they're ghosts.

He's in Syria. Or Afghanistan. Or Lebanon. Or Iraq.

A boy approaches. He's wearing a red T-shirt and black pants and black sneakers. He's all wet, his slicked back hair dripping water.

Angel asks him why he's all wet when everything and everyone else is dry and chalky, coated gray.

The boy shrugs. He doesn't know. He says, "Drone," and walks away.

Someone is knocking on a door—only there is no door, only rubble.

"Did you get them?" a woman asks. "Hurry," she says. The knocking grows more insistent. "Did you get the terrorists?"

It seems to Angel that somehow he's the terrorist. He doesn't know how this can be, but that's what he seems somehow to know.

"Hurry," the woman says. First she was dressed in a pants suit, then in a burka. He looks away and when he looks back she's older. "Hurry," she says again. "Tell me."

"It's me," Angel says. He's frightened. Someone is shouting at him. "It's me," he repeats.

"Are you okay? Are you okay? Hey! Buddy! You all right?"

It took Angel a moment to remember where he was. He pulled himself upright, raised the seat, lowered the window. "Yeah. Yeah," he said, and made a show of shaking off sleep.

Hunched over beside the car looking in: a skinny guy with a comb-over that looked like an animal's tail draped across his head.

"I must have really conked out." Angel rubbed his eyes with his fingertips. It was nearly dark. He looked around, at the dumpsters, at a slate sky tinted red on the horizon. "What time is it?"

"Well, you can't just pull up behind my store and go to sleep, you know!" The guy gripped the door frame with both hands. "Someone else might have called the cops on you."

"Sorry." Angel started the engine. "I needed a few minutes sleep. It wouldn't have been safe for me to keep driving, tired as I was."

"Well, you can't sleep here!"

For reasons Angel couldn't divine, the guy seemed seriously angry. "Okay," he said. "I'm on my way."

"I've got your license plate number, just so you know!" The guy gripped the door frame like he was thinking about picking up the car and tossing it in the dumpster.

"There's really no need to be upset." Angel, foot on the brake, put the car in reverse. "I stopped to catch a quick nap because I was too tired to keep driving." He shrugged. What's the big deal?

"Do you always unbuckle your pants when you take a nap?" The guy's face a caricature of disgust.

Angel's overcoat had fallen off his lap and his pants were open to the crotch, revealing wrinkled, rust red boxers. "I must have loosened them in my sleep," Angel said. "To make myself more comfortable."

"Yeah, well, be comfortable someplace else from now on! Understand?"

Angel thought about getting the tire iron out of his trunk and beating to death that dead animal on top of the guy's head. "Hey," he said, "I loosened up my pants to make myself more comfortable. Do you mind?"

"Yeah! I do mind!" The guy leaned closer. He was shouting in Angel's ear.

"Okay," Angel said. "Well. Fuck you." He hit the gas and the car lurched out from behind the dumpsters. The guy jumped back, his arms flailing, nearly losing his balance before he bent over, hands on his knees, mouth open in a mix of fear and shock as he watched Angel drive off.

"Asshole," Angel said, not really angry. More pissed off. More, slightly pissed off. And then—God, Angel, you're really losing it, aren't you?—he was crying. Great big sobs and copious tears as he navigated the darkening streets of Redvale.

No One Hears the Bullet That Kills Them

In Redvale, all the funeral parlors look like haunted houses: sprawling Victorian mansions with cupolas and parapets, widow walks and round towers and polished wood Gothic interiors, sweeping staircases. Claire, seated in an isolated room on a wooden bench with a red felt cushion, holding Kenny's hand, had the sense of being dropped back into an earlier century. The room had once been a library, well, technically was still a library, with its floor to ceiling built-in bookcases and rolling ladder and centrally positioned seminar table, though Claire doubted anyone had taken a book down to read in generations. Now the whole building—this library, the porches and viewing rooms and hallways where the bereaved gathered—had become a theatre set for solemnity, a place to stage a somber ritual, as if only the polished and elaborately crafted past had the power to soothe the blow of a loved one's death.

"I'm better now," Kenny said. He had broken down in sobs and tears at the sight of his mother's lifeless body stretched out along the velvety interior of a brass casket. "Damn. She looked like someone turned her into a spooky action figure." He pulled a white handkerchief from his pants pocket and dabbed his eyes.

Kenny laughed and Claire smiled along with him. She rubbed his back.

They both looked like different, and much more elegant, versions of themselves. Claire, who was partial to yoga pants and Ts, had chosen a simple, black, A-line dress for the funeral. Kenny, photographed most frequently in faded tight jeans and a form hugging thin cashmere sweater, wore a sleek black suit with narrow lapels that he had purchased and had tailored for him overnight.

"You ready to go back out there?" Claire, a little burst of tough brightness.

"Sure," Kenny said, and then added, "but wait." He rushed

his fingers through the bright locks of blond hair tumbling over his forehead. "Something I need to tell you," he said. He laughed again. "I don't suppose there could be a worse time, but...."

"What is it?" Claire, an alarm going off somewhere, one only she could hear. Something in Kenny's tone.

Kenny, scratching the back of his neck, looking away, then, resolved, sliding back a little on the bench, putting space between himself and Claire but turning to face her. "You know how I promised to...if I got with a girl, to be sure she signed that contract we agreed on?"

"The contracts...," Claire, a quick computer search of her hard drive. "Yes," she said, remembering. "And?"

"I didn't." Kenny looked off again, focusing on a wall of books, their somber, jacketless spines lined up like an army of little soldiers in formation. "I slept with this girl...girls, actually. Sisters—"

"Oh, Kenny. Sisters? Really? Here in Redvale?"

"I'd been partying with Amayr and Bobby at Willies," Kenny, his eyes fast to the bookshelves, as if he were reading the titles. "We all went out to the car. We got wrecked. Next thing I know...."

Claire, a long, slow exhale of breath, joined Kenny in studying the bookcases. The two of them, side by side, staring straight ahead.

"Honestly," Kenny said. "I was so wrecked, between the drinking and the coke, I don't even remember going home with them. I'm sorry about the contracts. I just...I didn't know what I was doing."

"The contracts," Claire said, as if amused. "The contracts are worthless, Kenny. They don't, they never meant a damn thing. They are, proverbially, not worth the paper they're printed on."

"Then how come—"

"Linni had this crazy idea," Claire, animated, throwing up her hands, "that some girls might actually be so insulted at having to sign a contract to sleep with you that it might slow things down, just a little bit at least."

Kenny shrugged. The contracts had not only not been a

problem, they had seemed instead to amp up the excitement.

"The contracts are not what you should be worried about. The contracts are not the problem. The problem is getting so wrecked that you don't know what you're doing."

"I'm quitting that," Kenny said to the books. "I've already got the address and meeting schedule for an AA group. I'm going to start there, give that a try, though…."

"Though what?"

Finally, turning to face Claire. "I don't think I'm an alcoholic or an addict, really. I think I just got…out of control."

Claire, a little gesture, slight shrug of shoulders and turn of head saying, yes, maybe he had a point.

Kenny put his hand on Claire's knee. "I'm going to pull myself together. I promise. I'm not like…the way I've been lately…." He wanted to tell her that he was ashamed of himself, but the words wouldn't come. He wanted to try to explain how the death of his mother was making him feel, the things it was making him think about—but that was hopeless. Instead, he said, "I'm sorry."

Claire, the business side of her revving up, asked, "Who are these girls? If this kind of thing gets out, I'm sorry, Kenny, but your brand would be crushed. Forget about all the things I've got in the works for you—including a very possible movie deal. That…that would all be over."

"It won't get out," Kenny said. "Willow, the girl, she was doing coke like—"

"Willow?" Connections firing, alarm flares lighting Claire's eyes. She had been surprised to see the Graham family among the early mourners gathered on the porch. She had meant to ask Kenny about it. "Willow Graham?"

Kenny, reading Claire's eyes. "I don't know her last name. Why?"

"Please," Claire said, "please don't tell me that the sister's name was Aspen."

Kenny blanched, the color almost comically draining from his face. "Yeah," he said. "You know them?"

"You slept with both of them? You had sex with Aspen?"

Kenny, corpse like in a house of corpses, didn't answer.

"The girl is still in middle school, Kenny! Do you understand that you could go to prison? Do you understand the position you've put me in by telling me?"

"I met her in a bar," Kenny, his voice scratchy, choked. "You have to be twenty-one to get in."

"Please. Give me a break." Claire got up, brushed off her dress, color rising in her cheeks, her eyes fiery. "There's no way that girl looks like she's within a mile of twenty-one. Were you so wrecked that you were blind too?"

"Yes," Kenny said. "Pretty much."

"Great. Excellent." Claire took a step back from Kenny. To say she was glaring at him wouldn't do justice to the combination of disgust and fury doing a cramped dance in her eyes. "I don't know what the hell to do with you," she said, and started for the door. With one hand on the knob, she turned to look back. "Alfred Graham, by the way, is president of Redvale College. He has enough power and influence to bury both of us," she said. "Just something to think about." She opened the door, took a step out, then stepped back in and closed it, hand still on the doorknob. "While you're at it, you might also think about what kind of a man sleeps with an underage girl, sister or no sister." She opened the door, stepped out, stepped back in, closed it again. "Jesus, but I'd like to strangle Willow Graham! And you!" She leaned toward Kenny as if she might actually do it, then, finally, left the room, snapping the door closed behind her.

Angel, in the back of the viewing room, fidgeted in his seat. He had come at Claire's request, and now Claire was nowhere to be found. Dolores and Gloria were out on the porch, along with what looked to Angel like a fashion show line up of young women, a couple of them wearing slinky black dresses better suited for a night club than a funeral parlor. Crossing the porch, on his way to the gloomy innards where the corpses were displayed, he had waved to Dolores, who, involved in conversation with Gloria and another woman, hadn't noticed. In the reddish, late-afternoon light, the figures gathered on the porch spoke softly among each other. A portly man in a shiny suit laughed at something a woman said, her hand on his arm. A stout, short woman sobbed and blew her nose into a man's white handkerchief. Angel thought about approaching Dolores and Gloria but chickened out. He wasn't sure why. They had both always treated him decently. Well, since the divorce anyway. Still, he crossed the sunlit porch and followed a somber hallway to the viewing room, where, after not locating Claire, he took a seat in the last row of gray folding chairs and joined others in looking at the waxy corpse of a dead woman center stage, in an ornate casket, surrounded by bright flower arrangements, posters with pinned photographs on easels, and, in a new twist, something Angel had never seen before, a wall mounted flat screen monitor flashing pictures of the deceased and, Angel assumed, her friends and family.

Angel's parents were buried in Calvary cemetery in New York, a jammed-up necropolis of marble headstones stretched over endless acres fitted between a maze of highways. The one time he'd visited, it had taken him an hour wandering among the dead to find the burial site. Angel, standing over the graves, reading his parents' names, buzz and growl of cars and trucks like white noise background static. A windy day, the breeze in his hair, no one else in sight, only endless fields of headstones. What can you recall, Angel, that was good between you and your father? Nothing. The mud of his anger buried all of us. You were fifteen when he died. Surely there were tender moments. If there were I don't recall them. The man didn't like me, let alone love me. I was a habitual disappointment. He called me Stupid. He called me Idiot. Think of the stepchild and the cruel stepmother of fairy tales: that was the nature of our relationship. I stood over his grave and tried to think of something good, something to mourn, and instead I remembered the acid fury of his gaze, the back of his hand, the rages, the tirades. What about your mother, then? She was a quiet, ineffectual woman. She protected me when she could. There, then that's something. Who said it wasn't? I stood over the grave site and did my best to pray for both of them. The man was not well. His life was a struggle. I can be big enough to see that and to forgive. I have it in me. I can be the better man. But he still turns up in your dreams? Frequently. Sometimes I wake up surprised that he's not still alive. Sometimes I wake up furious.

"Dad?" Claire, behind Angel, her hand on his shoulder. She spoke softly, leaned close. "Are you all right?"

"Sure. Why?" Angel, startled, jumped up. He looked around, got his bearings. Put his arm around Claire's shoulder and whispered in her ear. "Was I sleeping?"

Claire led Angel out of the viewing room, into the hallway. "You were muttering," she said, as if embarrassed to have to tell him.

"I'm sorry, Honey." Angel straightened out his tie, ran his hands through his hair. "I think I was dreaming. I haven't been sleeping well—"

"It's all right." Claire slipped her arm though Angel's and started for the porch. "You need to get that under control, though, Dad. The muttering. Really."

"It's just I was dreaming." Angel, softly, his eyes cast down. "I'm sorry about your friend—"

"My client."

"I'm sorry for his loss."

Claire nodded. A distracted nod, edged with anger.

On the porch, clusters of dark-clad mourners talking among themselves. The late afternoon sun splashed over railings, a hanging swing in which two young women holding hands listened as an older man spoke to them. Claire's entrance on Angel's arm caused a little stir. People looked their way, a few approached and expressed condolences as if it were Claire whose mother had died. Claire, polite and serious. She was an amazement to Angel, always. Somehow this beautiful, composed, extraordinary human person was his daughter. Angel Maso's daughter, already well off at twenty-two, already not only in control of her own life, but leading others, building a business, a mover and shaker. He had no idea where she'd gotten it from. Well, okay, her mother was always a formidable presence. He had to give her that. Really, if he was honest with himself…when he was honest with himself, he'd admit that everything had started to fall apart the day she left and had continued falling apart ever since. Oh, it's not that bad, Angel. It is. Admit it. You let her handle all the details of managing a life, from balancing the check book to keeping the house in order. You left it all up to her. Because she was good at it! Right, fine, but once she left you never could manage it all on your own. Admit it. You loved her but you also needed her, and now look at you.

Claire, who had been exchanging courtesies with a stranger, at least a stranger to Angel, turned to her father. "Did you say something, Dad?"

"Just…" Angel said. Had he said something? "There's your mother."

"Excuse us," Claire, to the stranger. Her arm still in Angel's arm, she crossed the porch and joined her mother and Gloria where they stood in a spike of sunlight, Dolores in a knee-length black skirt, a white blouse, and black jacket; Gloria in a short black skirt and boat neck, navy blue blouse. They both looked lovely, though Gloria seemed to be pissed off about something.

After a polite round of exchanged greetings, Dolores asked after Kenny. "I didn't realize his mother was so young," she said. "How's he doing?"

"Just about what you'd expect from Kenny," Claire said, and then seemed surprised when the others watched her, waiting for more.

"Is something wrong?" Dolores, reading Claire.

"No. Nothing." On the other side of the porch, the Graham family had spotted Claire and were approaching, all five of them: father Alfred mother Charlotte daughters Willow and Aspen, and son, Birch. The tree kids. (What in God's name were the parents thinking?)

More greetings exchanged as others on the porch watched surreptitiously. The Graham family knew Dolores, Gloria, and Claire. Angel had to be introduced around.

"Our daughters are friends of Kenny's," Alfred said. Three-piece suit, buttoned down from head to toe, an air of money and entitlement.

"He's such a sweet guy." Willow, dressed demurely as a saint, black dress high neckline.

"We love him." Aspen, in tight black dress and shimmering blue blouse, the top two buttons open, the prettier of the two with silvery blond hair, bright intelligent dark eyes.

Both of them with voices like squeaky toys.

Claire taking in the two girls recalculated her apportioning of guilt. One look and it wouldn't shock her if Aspen was the prime mover.

"What grade are you in?" Claire asked Aspen. Claire, a bright smile tattooed in place.

"Eighth." As if ashamed. "But I'm going to skip ninth, so next year I'll be a sophomore in high school."

"She's the genius of the family." Mrs. Graham, her arm around Birch's shoulder.

"I'm sure," Claire said, in a way that confused everyone.

"Well…," Alfred Graham, signaling their departure. More handshakes, parting greetings. "We've already expressed our condolences to Kenny, but do tell him that he'll be in our prayers."

"I'll do that." Claire did her best to smile graciously.

"Is everything all right?" Dolores asked Claire, once the Grahams were out of earshot.

"Fine. Why? I mean, other than Mrs. Walker in there." Claire, a bright, clearly artificial smile. When she tired of everyone watching her, she turned to Gloria, whose face had regained its stormy air as soon as the formalities with the Graham's were over. "What about you?" she asked. "Is everything okay?"

"Everything's fine," Dolores answered for Gloria.

"Actually it's not," Gloria said to Claire. "Good read. Your mother here's been getting death threats and refuses to do anything about it."

Dolores attempted to quiet Gloria with a look. She turned to Claire. "There's nothing to be done," she said. "The threats are vague—"

"*No one hears the bullet that kills them* is not a vague threat," Gloria said.

"And we don't know—"

"Elvis Blakemore."

Dolores, exasperated. "Gloria. Please."

"I'm sorry," Gloria said, and then lowered her voice to a near whisper, "but there's no way I'm going to let that low life snake son of a bitch threaten you like that and get away with it!"

"Elvis who?" Angel had been hanging back, relieved to be left out of the conversation, until he heard the name Blakemore.

"This is the guy," Claire said, ignoring Angel and addressing her mother, "who's president of the gun club?"

"One and the same," Gloria answered. "Redneck shit-for-brains recidivist."

At the word *recidivist* the conversation came to a jarring milli-second halt, as if everyone took a fraction of a second to think *What?* before moving on.

"Blakemore?" Angel stepped closer into the circle of women. "That's my neighbor's last name, the one who's been giving me so much trouble."

"There's about a hundred Blakemores in Redvale." Gloria, to Angel, wondering once again what in hell Doll could have ever seen in this short, stocky guy with a cleft in his chin that looked like some kind of deformity.

"This one's tall." Angel held a fist high on his forehead. "Wears his hair in a pompadour, like Johnny Cash, only ugly, with crooked teeth."

"That's him," Dolores said, "the inimitable Elvis Blakemore."

Gloria cut her eyes at Dolores, made a mental note to look up *inimitable.*

"If you know it's him," Angel said, "can't you do something about it? I wouldn't mind seeing that clown in jail. I just myself—" Angel froze. First, Dolores and Gloria were looking at him as if he had just beamed down from a spaceship and landed in their circle; second, an eruption of self-consciousness overcame him, and he feared saying something stupid or sounding dumb. "Um...," he continued, "I had a bit of a confrontation with him."

"Over what?" Dolores asked.

Oh, Angel didn't want to tell them about the trees. If he told them about the tree that fell on his car, that might lead to the other trees that crushed his fence, and Dolores might look at him pityingly, as if he didn't have the balls to sue Blakemore, to take him to court, to do whatever he should have done the very first time one of those trees damaged his property instead of being such a spineless wimp about it. You weren't a spineless wimp, Angel! You were trying to get along with your idiot neighbor! Do you want to be like your own maniac father? Always in to-the-death combat with neighbors? Do you?

"Dad?" Claire, with a little bit of annoyance, a little bit of anxiety. A quick look at her mother, as if they had both been talking about him and now Claire was saying See? "Dad? Mom just asked what the confrontation was about."

"I heard," Angel said, brushing off Claire's concern. "I was just thinking how to explain. You know, though? It doesn't matter." Angel, pleased with himself, finds his way out of the woods. "The point is that he's been marching around with a gun strapped to his hip. You know," he said to Dolores, "I think he might potentially be a dangerous character."

"He is dangerous!" Gloria, a bit too loud. "But you know who's more dangerous?" She aimed a meaningfully look at Dolores.

"Gloria, please stop." Dolores hooked her arm through Gloria's and pulled her close. To Angel and Claire, "We don't know for certain that it's Elvis making the threats, and, in any event, this isn't the right time to talk about it."

"But he is dangerous," Gloria said to Angel, calmer. "He's a nut and I happen to know he's armed to the teeth. If I were you, I'd be circumspect about getting into a confrontation with him."

"What happened with the Board meeting?" Claire asked Dolores.

"Cancelled till next Thursday. That at least gives me time to work out a position."

"What position?" Angel, curious.

"Gun control policy," Dolores, as if cursing.

Behind their circle, a small commotion broke out as Linni exited the funeral parlor with her arm around Kenny, who was quickly, if politely, mobbed by several young women in black offering condolences and hugs. Kenny, his face wrecked in comparison with its usual bright innocence, nonetheless managed a lower wattage version of his much-photographed, luminous smile.

Linni, leaving Kenny to his admirers, touched Angel's shoulder as she positioned herself next to Claire. Always the mediator, the reconciler, her touch was a warm gesture of good will, a greeting and a welcome.

Angel shrunk from it. He didn't know why. Had no idea in the world why. His body tightened. His heart seemed to clench. "I should be going now." He managed what he hoped was a shy smile. To Claire, "Please express my condolences to Kenny." He considered reaching through the circle to shake Dolores's hand, but then wouldn't he have to also shake Gloria's hand, and Linni's, and wouldn't that be too much? Yes, probably. So, no. "Okay, then," he said, and nodded in response to the quick barrage of brief parting greetings from all these women, all these women in his life: Claire and Linni and Dolores and Gloria. How did that come to be? All these women….

"You attract women." Shelly's voice, as if walking alongside him, on the way to his car. "Women are drawn to you. You're a good man, Angel Maso. You're decent and gentle, and women like that. You're a good man," she repeated. "Women like you."

"That," Angel answered, "is obviously not true." Still, it gave him pleasure to hear her say so. He hurried to the parking lot, anxious to get home, where he knew Shelly would be waiting.

With the Bright Birds, In the Near Dark

As the sun came up and the apartment's shadows dissolved, the living room sofa emerged first, a dark throw flung across its beige cushions. Then the coffee table with its scatter of papers and books. The black leather recliner across from the couch, still a shadow within a shadow. Ginny and Cranston were both awake, in bed, cuddled up, watching the night's dark fade away, listening to the cacophony of bird song on a spring morning. They were each of them in their own world, Ginny on her side, curled into Cranston, her head nestled comfortably on his shoulder, knee over his thigh, arm across his wide belly. Cranston on his back, one arm around Ginny's shoulder, the other elevating his head. He'd arrived an hour earlier. This coming Thursday was awards night. He'd explained to his wife that he needed to be at the school early to catch up on the extra work required by the evening ceremony. Theresa, his wife, didn't question. After twenty years of marriage, she'd never dream…. No, it wouldn't occur to her. Cranston, a big, sometimes goofy guy who loved his kids—which is what he called all the students in Redvale High, his kids—and his family, a man dedicated to his work, maybe a touch of a workaholic, but that was okay with Theresa. His job was important. He made a difference in the lives of his students. No, she slept soundly as Cranston crept out of the house in the still dark, and crossed town to Ginny's, where she had left the door open for him, as agreed.

Ginny wasn't thinking of anything at all. She was full of a delicious bodily satisfaction as she clung to the warmth of Cranston's big body and watched the morning light come into her apartment. In a moment, she knew, the sun would come rushing through her windows and the Tibetan prayer flag, and the rooms of her little home would be full of color and light. The bright red throw across her couch would light up like a flare. The prayer flags, caught in a current of air from the slightly open windows, rippled and swayed. When the sunlight hit them, little ghosts of color would dance across the room. Her head on Cranston's shoulder, her lips near his breast, she watched and waited.

Cranston wished that somehow these moments could last forever. It made no sense, he understood that. He didn't really want to stay in this one place forever, in this one position, Ginny close to him with her crazy spumoni colored hair, with the bright birds that circled her breast, in the near dark, the commotion of sparrows and crows and robins outside, the quiet inside, quiet and warmth, a moment in between everything, just him and Ginny. And the birds. And the sun rising.

It made no sense and he didn't really want it and still, yes, he did, he wished the moment might go on forever.

Come and Take It

Gloria pulled up to the open gates of Elvis Blakemore's place to find him straddling the shingled ridge of his house's gable roof, where a shiny metal flagpole some ten or twelve feet high appeared to rise out of the attic below. As she watched, he raised a large white flag picturing a photograph of an assault rifle under a black star and above the words "Come and Take It." Lord a'mercy, does he know what a doofus he looks like? He's seen her. He saw her pull up and stop at the head of his driveway, if you can call this strip of mud and gravel a driveway. Went about raising his asshat flag with the red sun at his back before turning to stand there, glaring down at her. Gloria knew she shouldn't be there, that Doll would throw a fit, but shit. Twenty minutes earlier she had come home from shopping at the mall to find still another death threat among the voice mail messages and now here she was looking up at dumb ass Elvis Blakemore standing on his roof under a shithead gun flag with his arms on his hips looking at her with hate spitting out of his eyes. Right next door to Angel's rundown boxy little in-need-of-a-paint-job clapboard house. They should call this road Doofus Drive.

Gloria hit the gas, a rooster tail of dirt and gravel following her until she skidded to a halt beside Asshat's 250. Elvis scurried halfway down an aluminum extension ladder before turning, leaping to the ground, and stomping heavy footed toward Gloria's yellow Dodge Neon, which looked like a Matchbook car alongside his 250.

Gloria, out of the car, chest stuck out, a cocky five-foot-four sprite with her newly dyed bright blond with red streaks Miley Cyrus boy-short spiky hair sticking straight up off her head like static electric shock, perfect angry little live wire look.

Elvis hulking over her, leaning in, fists clenched. "What the hell you want, Tiller?"

Gloria turned her head and spit. The sound of her family name a time machine whisking her back to the double-wide where she grew up playing outside in the woods with a half dozen cousins, every one of them a Tiller, which is what most of her life Gloria knew herself to be, a Tiller, as if it were a race like blacks or whites. Tillers. Well, yeah, she supposed she was still underneath it all a Tiller. No change of lifestyle, tattoo or nose ring or spiky haircut ever likely to change that. "Elvis," she said calmly, even though she could hear her blood pumping, feel it in her ears, "cut it the hell out with the threatening phone calls, or you're the one will wind up getting hurt."

Elvis took a step back in mock fear. "Are you threatening me?"

"Of course I'm threating you. Are you a fucking idiot? Or are you deaf?"

"Get off my property." Elvis, smirking. "Before I shove a shotgun up your dyke cunt."

Gloria had to look up to make eye contact with Elvis. She pulled a stick of gum out of the pocket of her jeans, bit down on it, her eyes never leaving Elvis's eyes. "You grew up here," she said finally. "Which of our families harbor the greater number of dangerous lowlifes?" She gave Elvis only a second before she answered her own question. "I win that prize, as you well know. Not even close. How many uncles I got in jail currently?" She scratched her chin, thinking.

"I'm surprised you got any left on the outside." Elvis, watching Gloria carefully.

Gloria scoffed. "Please, Elvis, they don't have enough jail space to lock up all the Tiller men in these parts. You know that."

Then it was Elvis's turn to look away and spit.

"Plus," Gloria went on, "I hear Uncle Ronnie just got out a few weeks ago. Uncle Ronnie's the one killed that guy from Ellensburg."

Elvis nodded. They both knew it was Travis Tiller who'd killed the Ellensburg man in a knife fight following a poker game. He'd just been released after serving ten years in Greensville. Ronnie Tiller shot a state trooper in the balls and was like to be spending the rest of his life in the Red Onion.

"Oh, it's Uncle Travis just got out." Gloria threw up her hands. "I get all the hateful lowlifes in my family confused."

"What do you want?" Elvis looked past Gloria, across a muddy field where two of his donkeys stood side by side, their heads hanging, looking abjectly bored. Beyond the donkeys, his patched up wire fence and his sicko neighbor's house.

"What I just said." Gloria raised her voice a little, as if talking to an idiot. "Cut it the hell out with the threatening phone calls."

Elvis nodded again. "Is it true what I hear," he asked, "that this jerkoff lives next door to me used to be married to Supervisor Maso?"

Gloria cast a quick look over to Angel's house, as if to confirm what she already knew. "So what? What's he got to do with anything?"

"Shouldn't be surprised." Elvis, a sneer of contempt.

"What shouldn't you be surprised about?" Gloria, annoyed but also curious, put her hands on her hips, waited for an answer.

Elvis nodded toward Angel's house. "Sicko came running after me the other day with a boner."

"What?"

"A boner," Elvis repeated. "You remember what a boner is, don't you?"

Gloria turned to look again at Angel Maso's house, as if she might have suddenly been transported into a parallel universe. "Angel Maso came running after you with a boner? What? Was he trying to rape you?"

Elvis's expression shifted from contempt to disgust. He looked at Gloria as if some ungodly form of contagion had risen up out of the dirt.

"You know what?" Gloria aimed her index finger at Elvis's face. "I don't give a shit whatever the hell you're talking about. You heard what I said. We get another phone call from you, you'll be looking at the kind of trouble you know you don't want no fucking part of."

Elvis nodded. He heard her. But he didn't like it. "I hear your family don't have a thing to do with you anymore."

"That's right." Gloria leaned against the front fender of her car.

"But I'm still blood, and you know how that works. Plus, the Tillers don't need much of an excuse to go after a Blakemore. Trust me," she said, "it wouldn't be a salubrious move on your part to mess with me or Doll."

Elvis, momentarily perplexed, squinting. "I'll be at that Board meeting on Thursday, and I'll be carrying—and so will lots of other folks."

"Did I ask you not to show up at the Board meeting?" Gloria, like she had no idea what he was talking about. "Show up dragging a damn cannon with you, for all I care. Just quit threatening Doll. And," she said, her expression going suddenly so dark and malevolent that Elvis despite himself took a step back, "God help you should anything happen to her." Gloria turned her head, spit, took another quick glance at Angel's place, and then got in her car and drove off, leaving Elvis fixed where he stood, looking after her.

Long after the little Dodge Neon's taillights disappeared around the bend, Elvis continued staring out at the empty road, his thoughts a thick sludge of contempt. Sick fuckin' bitches. Both of them. Shit, all of them. Had his way, he'd put an end to all such sick shit. Supervisor Dyke and all the rest. Still, he wasn't dumb. He saw how things were. Thing was, to draw a line.

For Elvis, guns were the line. Let them get married. Let them run the damn country. They'd turn it all to shit soon enough—already had, far as Elvis was concerned—but sooner or later everything might fall apart. Then. Then. Them with guns, the ones armed, the ones could provide for themselves and their families. Then it would be their turn.

Elvis glanced up at the Come and Take It flag, the black star and the huge black assault rifle on a field of white, fluttering in a breeze as he returned to his house. He found Annie at the door waiting and his kids in the kitchen, the girls, Barb and Sue Ellen, at the stove, his boy, Elvis Jr., at the table talking back and forth with the girls. He and Annie had their kids close together, planned it that way. Barb, twelve; Sue Ellen, fourteen; Junior, 16. Between the three of them, they hadn't given him a bit a trouble.

"What was that all about?" Annie, hands crossed over her chest.

A tall woman, only a couple of inches shorter than Elvis. She'd run track in high school and played center on the girl's basketball team. The years had been kind to her, and she still sometimes, to Elvis at least, looked young and pretty as some of the college girls he was always seeing all over town.

"Nothing much." Elvis paused in the doorway, leaned against the door frame. "Fool got it in her head I been threatening Supervisor Maso."

Annie watched her husband a moment. "Honey," she said, lowering her voice so the kids wouldn't hear, "is this whole thing about to get out of hand?"

"What whole thing?"

"All of you all carrying your guns to that meeting on Thursday. I've been hearing talk, and some of what I'm hearing is worrisome."

"Like what?"

"Like wild talk about some of the supervisors needing a bullet in their ass."

Elvis dismissed her concern with a quick shake of his head. "I'll send everybody an email and tell them to tone it down." He kissed her on the forehead. "There's nothing to worry about. We're just making a point." He looked to the kitchen. "How long before dinner's ready?"

"'Bout a half hour." Annie closed the front door and started back for the kitchen as Elvis headed for the basement, where he'd made a little office for himself. He took a seat at a metal desk pushed up against a wood paneled wall—and then got up immediately and opened the gun cabinet beside the desk to look over his arsenal, the AR 15s hanging beside several handguns, each in their cases; the tactical jackets and assault vests; the holsters; the boxes of shotgun shells, the various extra clips and magazines for the handguns and rifles. He ran a finger along the barrel of his favorite AR-15's front sight assembly. A weapon of lethal beauty, it won out in his deliberations over which gun to carry to the Board meeting. He removed it from the cabinet, attached one end of a sling to the rifle, tossed the length of it over his neck, attached the other end, and tested the tautness of the hold and the rifle's ease of handling before retaking his seat.

Many were the evenings Elvis sat quietly at his basement desk dreaming of changing the world, of bringing it back to a time more firmly grounded in the kind of morality that anybody with an ounce of sense knew to be the way things were supposed to be. He meant obvious things, like men were meant to marry women. That's what marriage was. Anything else was a perversion. Like, we couldn't just let any damn fool who could walk across a border come to live in America and take away jobs from hard working citizens. That's just following the law. What's complicated about that? Like, we just don't give away money to any lazy fool and his dozen kids out of wedlock. Make the son of a bitch work to take care of his own damn kids, see how fast he learns to keep it in his pants. Really, not complicated stuff. Stuff he could handle. He was pretty damn confident he'd make a good mayor for Redvale. Maybe even this next election, if he got the kind of attention that made people notice, that gave him a chance to express his views. Not impossible. Not impossible at all. He was doing a damn good job running the gun club, wasn't he? Yes, he was.

At the moment, though, it was the Tillers he was worried about. That was a pack of fools he didn't want to mess with if he didn't have to.

He pulled the phone to him and dialed Buddy.

Buddy was the oldest of the brothers. After him came Elvis and Rick, then Vince, the youngest of the Blakemore boys, engaged to be married in a few months.

He'd call them all. Best just to let them know what was going on.

Act I, Scene 6 *The Man with An Ugly Heart*

SETTING: ANDY'S study. A desk against
             the wall, 27" computer
             monitor, ledgers, various
             papers on the desk. A single
             window that looks out to the
             street.

AT RISE: ANDY at the window, his back
             turned to ROBERT. Silence, an
             air of tension between the
             two men. Both men holding
             Champaign glasses.

                    ANDY
          (Turns to face ROBERT. He looks stunned,
          struggling to find the right words.)
Drones? Hellfire missiles? You told me this software would
be used to spot terrorists in a crowd! You told me it would
be used to prevent violence!

                    ROBERT
          (Nonplussed. Completely taken aback by
          ANDY'S reaction.)
I did. And it will. But it can also be used in drones to
target terrorists. And, truly, I don't see your problem.
The software will be used to spot bad guys, so the good
guys can be sure they have the right target.

                    ANDY
You don't see my problem? A drone spots a terrorist in a
crowd and then what? Blow up everybody? Including women and
children.

ROBERT
(Getting angry)
First, we have no control over that. Second, this is the
U.S. Government. We're not going to blow up innocent people
if it can be avoided.

ANDY
(Frustration growing)
Really? We must be reading different newspapers. What about
that wedding party in Yemen that our drones turned into a
funeral?

ROBERT
(Upset to have to concede the point)
Yes. That was horrible. I admit. But still. We have to go
after the terrorists!

ANDY
(Despairing, pleading)
We're surrounded by violence! We live and breathe bloodshed
and mayhem. And now you're asking me to be a part of it! I
want to be an artist! Not a killer! That's what this
investment was supposed to be all about. Doing something
good. And now this?

ROBERT
(Has had enough.)
Hey. Grow up. This is the world we live in.
(Exits)

(ANDY, alone. He knows his own true
heart is a dark hole of violence and

I Love You, Dad. You Know That.

Angel looked like he hadn't slept in days.

Claire at the stove boiling water for tea. Angel at the kitchen table in his ratty terry cloth robe, the same robe he wore all the mornings of her adolescence as he stumbled through the kitchen making her pancakes or scrambled eggs, always timed so that she'd have to gulp them down if she wanted to catch the bus.

Her back turned to Angel, Claire watched an enamel blue tea pot atop the glowing red coils of the stove's front burner. Around her the house was silent, only the low growl of a dehumidifier humming away in the basement, occasional bird squawks from beyond the kitchen window. Claire had learned from Linni who had learned from Doll who had learned from Gloria who had learned from Elvis Blakemore that Angel supposedly chased Elvis while he was sporting a boner. While Angel was sporting a boner. Her father. How exactly does one bring up such a subject with one's father? This was not going through Claire's mind as she stared at the blue enamel of the tea pot, more like it was percolating under the surface of her thoughts, which were, at that moment, about Frankie, the groundhog who had made a home for himself under their porch right around the time Dolores left for parts Gloria.

What's a groundhog's lifespan? That would have been more than nine years ago. Yet, a half hour earlier, when Claire pulled into the driveway, Frankie popped up from his burrow under the porch and came all the way out to the top step to watch as she got out of the car. Stood up straight, the way groundhogs do, and watched her approach until she was halfway up the drive before darting back under the porch. Frankie, the groundhog, greeting her return, like an alert but skittish puppy. Was that possible? Could a groundhog come to know their human neighbors? She used to collect piles of dandelions and dead insects and leave a trail of them leading from his burrow out to the driveway, hoping he'd follow the trail right up to her waiting hand. Angel encouraged this, insisting that groundhogs could be trained. He claimed to have fed Frankie out of his hand on numerous occasions, though Claire had only once or twice managed to tempt him out of his burrow and on those occasions he had merely snatched up the nearest dandelions, watched her from a distance, and hurried back underground.

For that matter, Claire thought, why did we assume he was a Frankie and not a Francine?

"Hey, Dad." Claire lifted the tea pot from the burner just as it threatened to start screaming. "Did you ever really feed Frankie out of your hand?" She threw a quick glance back to Angel at the kitchen table. It was two in the afternoon and he was still in his pajamas and robe, a clump of hair toward the back of his head sticking straight up like a horn, dark circles under his eyes. A broad panel of light from the window over the sink held him bright in its frame.

Angel nodded, smiled. "Haven't done it in a long time," his voice scratchy and tired, "but, yeah, I used to pretty regularly for a while there."

Claire found the familiar yellow and red box of Lipton tea bags, same spot in the cupboard as always. Dust and sugar crumbs and mouse dropping behind the boxes and cans. She considered insisting on having a house cleaning service come in once a week. Again. But that was an old argument. "Then how come I could never get him to eat out of my hand?" she asked. "I used to try all the time when I was a kid."

Claire seemed to be succeeding at lifting Angel's spirits. He'd been zombie-like morose when she'd first arrived. Now at least he was smiling.

"You didn't know the secret." Angel propped his chin up on his hand, watched Claire pour hot water into a pair of black cups.

"Really? There was a secret? What was it?" Looking through the cupboards, searching for a snack to go with the tea. When all Claire found was a box of Ding Dongs, she said, "Oh, for God's sake." She couldn't help herself. She glared a second at the split open chocolate cakes pictured on the box cover, their centers filled with some kind of gooey white mix of sugar and chemicals, before giving up and pulling two of the plastic wrapped probably petroleum-based products from the box and tossing them onto the table. "I can't believe you still eat this crap." She delivered Angel his tea and took a seat across from him, teacup in hand.

Claire at one end of the table, scrubbed clean, hair pulled back into a pony tail that stuck out the back of a cute red baseball cap. White sneakers, sea-blue yoga pants, a white Spiritual Gangster T. Her eyes on her father, a doctor doing a visual diagnosis of her patient.

Angel, on the other end, a depressed mess. Hair all over the place, sleep deprivation bags under his eyes, cheeks puffy, his skin sallow. He watched the Ding Dong as if it might leap up and bite him.

Claire considered getting to the subject of this visit. *So, Dad, Linni told me something about somebody having an erection, or something like that? So, Dad, what's this crazy story I hear about you running after your neighbor and, like, you have an erection?* "So, Dad," she said, and choked. "What was the secret?" she continued. "How'd you get Frankie to eat out of your hand?"

"Honey Nut Cheerios. He loves them." Angel, grinning. "I still dump a bunch of them under the porch now and then."

Claire, amused, smiled as she pensively dunked her tea bag up and down in her cup and watched the water darken. "Could it possibly still be the same groundhog?" she asked. "After all these years? They don't live that long, do they?"

"It's still Frankie." Angel, tentatively, pulled the plastic wrapped Ding Dong closer. "He's got a triangle of white spots over his nose."

"Huh." Claire poked at the chocolate cake with her index finger. The plastic wrap crinkled. "So, Dad," she said. "I heard there was some sort of incident between you and your neighbor?"

"Oh," Angel, the lights going on. "That's what you're doing here. What did you hear?"

"Just that there was some sort of…confrontation. You were running after him or something?"

Angel's face reddened. He clasped his hands together and rested them on the table. As if restraining himself. As if trying to keep from exploding.

"Dad," Claire asked. "Are you all right?"

"I'm fine." Angel doesn't want to tell her about the trees and his car and the fence and how Elvis Blakemore (who used to just be Neighbor but now has a name and that somehow makes it worse), how Elvis Blakemore didn't even have the decency to apologize for *his* trees, the trees on *his* property, falling over and doing damage to Angel's property, on *multiple* occasions, and how it wasn't even the trees and damage that was getting deeper and deeper under Angel's skin, but the lack of respect it showed, as if Angel could be dismissed, as if Angel were a nobody who he could walk all over, and how Angel had thought he was being a decent guy, just trying to get along with the neighbors, but now he wonders if he's the nonentity his father always told him he was, if he doesn't have the balls to confront Elvis Blakemore, that asshole—that is, until he did confront him, so, yes, that's what that was all about, my shouting at him, calling him a redneck asshole, and you know what? It felt good. I'm glad I did it. Fuck him and his fucking trees. Not answering me? Not even giving me the courtesy of a response? After his trees have fallen on my property and done damage to my property *multiple* times? Son of a bitch is lucky I didn't take a baseball bat to his stupid head!

"Dad. Dad." Claire behind Angel, massaging his shoulders. "Calm down, Dad. Please."

Whoa. There were tears in Angel's eyes. Apparently, he had raised his voice. Apparently, he had been shouting. This surprised and confused Angel. Some parts of his life—he had to admit this now—some parts of his life were in free fall, out of his control. He needed to get a grip. Apparently, he didn't know when he was talking out loud and when he was talking in his head. That wasn't good. That was a problem. Claire, though, Claire with her hands on his shoulders, and now a hand on his cheek. Claire, his daughter, touching him lovingly. That was good. How long had it been since anyone at all had touched Angel? A long time. A very long time. He'd have to think about that. "I'm sorry," he said. He put a hand on top of Claire's hand on his shoulder. The two of them framed in the sunny rectangle of light from the kitchen window. Claire in her bright colors, looking young and healthy. Angel in his tattered robe, looking sickly and old. "I'm going to start seeing a counselor," he said.

Would he? Would he do that? The words had just issued forth. "I haven't been able to sleep the past couple of nights. That's why my emotions—" he made a fluttering gesture with his hands, "—are all over the place."

Claire grasped Angel's hand as she took a seat close to him. "I'm worried about you," she said, and gave his hand a squeeze. "Is there something else going on in your life? I mean, you're not sick or anything, are you? Please tell me you're not keeping something from me?"

"No. It's just—" Angel's eyes fixed on the tabletop, as if looking through it into the swirl of his own thoughts. "Lack of sleep…. Stuff…."

"What stuff?" Claire's mind pulled toward the Buzzfeed excessive masturbation page, and the weird erection thing. Part of her wanting to know, to help; another part of her thinking, *What the hell is he going to tell me?*"

Angel took a deep breath and exhaled slowly. Claire's touch fixed something. He could feel himself reconfiguring, pulling together. He wiped the residual wetness from his eyes, took Claire's hands in his and turned to face her. "I'm sorry, Claire. I apologize for being so emotional."

"Don't apologize, Dad. Just tell me what's going on." Claire, relieved to see the shift in Angel. His dad voice back. His dad demeanor.

Angel ran his fingers through his hair, pushing it down, smoothing it in place. "I haven't been taking care of myself," he said. "I haven't been eating right. I haven't been exercising. I've let my work fall off. I guess, if I'm honest about it, I've let myself fall into at least a little bit of a depression."

"There's medications for that," Claire said. "And seeing a counselor, that's an excellent idea."

"You're right." Angel, a touch of brightness in his voice. He offered Claire the gift of a smile, which she accepted by smoothing down a clump of stray hair on the side of his head.

"Love you, Dad," she said. "You know that."

Angel answered by squeezing her hand in the affirmative.

Neither Angel nor Claire was the emotionally effusive type, and thus both immediately felt awkward.

"So," Claire said, "would you like me to make an appointment for you with a counselor? I can have Linni do the research. You know she'll find the best person available."

"No, no. Can we keep this between us, please? I don't want Linni, or anybody else…."

"Okay," Claire said. "Certainly. But you will do it, right? You'll make an appointment?"

"I promise."

Claire, just being who she is. "When?"

"Tomorrow. I've already started looking around, so…. It's just a matter of finding somebody."

"Excellent." Claire, with a grin, "I'll be checking up on you."

Angel, enough of the counselor talk. "What about you? What's going on in your life?" He dunked half a Ding Dong in his tea and took a bite.

For a moment, Claire considered telling Angel about Kenny. But only for a moment. Gee Dad, this guy Kenny, who I kind of like and who's my client, he just slept with an underage girl and her sister. Right. At the same time. What do you think I should do?

"I'm good," she said. "I'm a little worried about Mom. Your crazy neighbor and his gun club, and half the rest of the city from what I hear, plan on showing up at the next Board meeting with assault rifles."

"When is that?" Whoa. Ding Dongs! The sugar rush perked him up wonderfully.

"Thursday evening, seven o'clock."

"Ah, too bad." Angel, looking off, as if mentally reviewing his busy calendar. "That's Awards Night at the high school. Same time." Then, where did this come from? "I'm getting a teaching award. Best poetry teacher, or something along those lines." Really? Really, Angel? What the hell?

"That's wonderful, Dad. But I promised Mom that I'd be at the Board meeting for support."

Angel, relieved. A cosmic gift. "That's fine, Claire. It's not a big deal. I'm just saying, otherwise I'd be at the Board meeting, too."

Claire, out of her chair, as she carried her cup to the sink and rinsed it out. "But I would have loved to be there," she said. "It's nice that they're recognizing you that way."

And, all right, still more! "The kids love me," he said. "It's rewarding work. Of course, it doesn't pay much, but still."

"I think it's great." Claire, the cup washed and placed in the drain, stretched, ended up with her hands on her hips. "I've got to go," she said, "but you'll let me know when you've got the counseling appointment set up, right?"

Angel laughed, playing a father with nothing to worry about, indulging his over-protective daughter. "Promise." Up from the table, he kissed her on the forehead, followed her out the door, and waved as she drove off.

Back in the house, Angel wandered through the kitchen, paced its length, wound up in the living room where he fell back into his favorite overstuffed chair, the one that faced the fireplace.

He's scared.

He feels the fear in chill bumps up and down his arms. He might be shaking a bit.

What, Angel, really now, what is going on? You're talking when you don't know you're talking. You're lying. Big, silly, obvious lies, that Claire will inevitably at some point discover.

Take a deep breath, Angel. Gather yourself together.

Admit that you're in trouble. Go, seriously, go look for a therapist.

Angle covered his eyes with both hands and sobbed.

Angel in his living room, in his favorite stuffed chair, sobbing.

The Hour Come Round At Last

Snow.

Well, the suggestion of snow.

A tentative white patina of frosting thinly coats green lawns, flowering dogwoods, the purple blossoms of redbuds.

Cranston is at the window in Ginny's apartment, under the fluttering colors of the prayer flag. He's dressed and ready for work. He's allowing himself a quiet moment before leaving. First the school day and then Awards Night. There won't be time to go home for dinner. Theresa will meet him at school with the kids.

Beyond the window, winding lines of brick, two-story houses, each with a small lawn, many with a redbud or dogwood tree, here and there a red maple. Concrete sidewalks follow the contours of the road, though no one walks anywhere in Redvale, except to walk the dog or to exercise. Otherwise we drive. We drive everywhere.

This morning, on the way to Ginny's, the snow was still falling. Snowfall so light, you could count the flakes as they drifted through the fading dark of early morning.

Behind Cranston, Ginny is in bed, sleeping on her side, facing him, her chin tucked into her chest, her clasped hands extended toward the edge of the mattress—as if she's diving, the moment before a diver hits the water.

Cranston can see her reflections in the windowpanes. In front of him, rare April snow, morning quiet, his home and the city and the people he loves. Behind him, Ginny. How is it possible he feels the swell of emotions, the desire to embrace, to pull close to him, to pull into him, this girl he has on any number of occasions described to others as kooky, a bit of a nut?

He has no idea. He can't answer the question. Yet, here he is. Again. Another early morning in Ginny's apartment.

And again

And yet again

Wishing he didn't have to leave.

Gloria and Doll are sleeping, Gloria's petite body curled into the bulk of Doll's belly and chest, Doll's arm wrapped around Gloria, holding her close, the top of Gloria's head nestled securely against Doll's neck and under her chin. They're fitted together neat as puzzle pieces.

On the night table behind Doll, her iPhone is minutes away from breaking into a hokie electronic rendition of "By the Sea," which Doll detests waking to but can't figure out how to change.

Outside, the light dusting of snow that fell overnight has already melted away. When Doll eventually makes it out of bed and shuffles to the kitchen where she'll put up a pot of coffee, slice and toast a bagel and slather it with cream cheese for breakfast, she'll see no trace of the snow out the window over the sink, only the green, neatly mown grass of her back yard, contained by an actual, honest-to-goodness, white picket fence.

Doll's eyes will linger a long moment on the elaborate doghouse in the far back corner of the yard. She and Gloria built it for Jingo, a rescued terrier-poodle mix that looked like a little ball of fur when they took her home from the kennel. By the time she was a year old, she looked like a cute doggy version of Yoda, with a coat that was mostly shaggy tufts of brown and white fur. When she died in the middle of the winter last year, during a day of wind and rain, they both fell into an embarrassingly long period of somberness and mourning. Who would have ever guessed you could grow so close to a pet? It surprised both of them. For months, the tenor of their lives together was tinged with something that had be called grief. And still, every morning, ever since, Doll's eyes lingered a long moment on the abandoned doghouse before she could pull herself away and get back to preparing breakfast.

This particular spring morning, however, after the alarm eventually goes off and the tinny notes of "By the Sea" wake Doll, it will take a considerably longer time before she's up and out of bed and in the kitchen. This particular morning, which Doll will remember always, Gloria rolls over onto her back, wakes with a devilish smile, and says, "I was dreaming about us."

Doll doesn't have to ask. She knows by the impish smile and the mischievousness in her eyes exactly the nature of Gloria's dream.

God, she's beautiful.

Especially in the morning, in the sun that flows through the skylight.

Doll silences her phone and places the flat of her hand low on Gloria's belly. The three red stars between Doll's thumb and forefinger absorb sunlight. Gloria slides up and toward Doll. Doll's hand slides down.

Slowly, luxuriously, the day begins.

Claire is in bed with Kenny. Hell if she knows what she's doing, but there he is in her bed, that famous mop of blond hair bright against a jade pillowcase, her new cerulean lightweight down comforter, the one that arrived only days ago via post, pulled up to his neck.

It's kind of amazing.

After the funeral, she came home seriously thinking about going to the police. Okay, sure, Aspen probably knew exactly what she was doing. Certainly Kenny was not her first. You don't do a threesome with your own sister if you're some innocent flower. More likely the spider underneath. But still. Still. Even if she planned arranged organized motivated and scripted the whole debauched encounter. Still. She was in eighth grade. Eighth grade! Kenny on the other hand was of fully legal age. An adult. A grown man. Even if he still looked like a teenage boy. By the time Kenny returned from the funeral in that ridiculous red sexmobile of his, Claire was leaning heavily toward reporting him to the police.

Then he came into the house with eyes red and puffy from crying.

Claire, steeled against him, went up to her bedroom and locked the door. Where she remained for an hour or so, until Linni returned, and Claire heard her talking with Kenny, their soft voices unintelligible, a murmur from someplace far away in the silent house.

Then, Linni at the bedroom door.

Linni explaining Kenny's remorse, his humiliation.

She knew, yes. He told her.

And didn't Linni think it was a crime? Didn't Linni think that Claire, and now her, now Linni also, didn't she think they had a responsibility to report this crime?

No. Linni did not. Linni, the fashion model. Linni, in Paris. Linni, in Milan. Linni, in Manhattan. Linni Sorland, with a view of sexual morality far more fluid than Georgia born and raised Claire Maso. Please. Three willing bodies. Not just consensual but in Kenny's version, the girls were trophy hunting. There's probably not a teenager in Redvale they haven't told every detail.

Oh. Great. Wonderful, on several counts.

Let him talk to you. He's like you, you know. He's guilty. He's sorry. Linni, a look like she didn't know what all the fuss was about. He wants to talk to you. Linni, ever the negotiator. Ever the facilitator.

Then, Linni left the house.

Then, Kenny climbed the stairs. Knocked on Claire's bedroom door.

Tears in his eyes. Choked voice.

For a long time, they talked. Kenny on one end of the bed, Claire on the other.

She'd go to the police if she ever heard of anything like the Aspen thing again.

It was never going to happen again. That's not who he was. He's done with it. The promiscuity. The drugs. Everything. He doesn't want to be a model anymore. He doesn't want to make movies. He wants to get into Redvale College. He wants to get a degree, the way his mother had always hoped. And then, crying, at the mention of his mother and what she had hoped for him.

And then, Claire holding him.

He's done with it all. He wants a different life.

Claire reassuring him. Claire stroking his hair.

Kenny embracing her.

The two of them falling back onto the bed as gears switch and they become all hands and mouths, drifting out of one world and into another, disappearing together, sliding into each other.

That was two days ago and they hadn't gotten out of bed a whole lot since.

Linni made herself scarce.

Claire adapted. She could let the past, it turned out, be the past. She felt light-headed a lot. They talked about the future, about possibilities, for both of them.

And now, here she is, sitting on the edge of the bed, the *Redvale Times* in hand, a serving tray with a pot of freshly brewed coffee and two cups on the night table. She's been up for an hour already. She's letting Kenny sleep.

Tonight is the Board meeting. She's reading about it on the front page of the paper, under a picture of Elvis Blakemore and, according to the caption, three of his brothers. All three with AR 15s strapped to their chests.

Claire hopes they all know what they're doing. The story says the guns are a peaceful gesture of protest against any proposal that limits the open carry of AR 15s in Redvale. At least two of the Supervisors, Williamson and BeDouchian, both opposed to any restrictions whatsoever on the right to carry, plan on bringing their own sidearms to the meeting.

Great.

Claire drops the paper to the floor, climbs up on the bed, and begins gently massaging Kenny's back and shoulders.

She's looking forward to his waking.

Angel Dials The Right Number

Angel at one end of the kitchen table, Shelly across from him, Uncle Augie in the living room.

A regular circus this morning while outside the day turns springlike sunny after a night when it snowed. In April.

Angel's hands are encrusted with mud. As are his khaki slacks at the cuffs. Probably ruined. Clumps of mud caught in the cuffs. Both knees black with dirt, streaks of mud up and down. The black hoodie he's wearing also mud streaked though it doesn't show. Angel looks at his hands, the black curves of his fingernails, the prominent veins. He's getting old. His hands look old.

Shelly watches him. She's New York professional sleek in a black pencil skirt, a black blouse cut to show off the tanned skin of her neck and chest and just a touch of cleavage under a salmon blazer. If it weren't for the blazer, she'd look like a judge in all that black. She should be in a corner office high rise with a view of the New York skyline. Of course she's young and gorgeous. Her makeup perfect. Her hair lustrous. Her hands folded in front of her on the table. Eyes fixed on Angel.

Uncle Augie is out of sight, but he's there, in the living room, in the stuffed chair facing the fireplace, his feet folded up under him.

The house is quiet. It feels like waiting. Like a moment in-between.

Angel hasn't slept in days. Or, really, it's fairer to say that he hasn't fully slept in days because there have been periods here and there when he's probably been sleeping though not been aware of it. But certainly not restful sleep, not refreshing sleep. That feels like forever. Since he's had a refreshing night's sleep.

The night before this morning with Shelly watching him at the kitchen table and Uncle Augie out of sight in the living room, last night a single gunshot interrupted his pacing of the house. He couldn't sleep, he couldn't sleep, he couldn't sleep: then the gunshot and he was animal-sharp awake.

Neighbor was always out there shooting—but not at night. That was unusual. But it wasn't that late. Just barely dark. Still. Unusual.

Angel threw on khaki slacks and sneakers—he'd been in pajamas and slippers—and a black hoodie, went out in the yard to look around.

He couldn't see much, the gardens all shadows, everything a deep shade of gray under a full moon peeking out through a break in smudgy thick clouds. At the fence, he looked over toward the lights in Neighbor's house. In the fields between him and the house, a couple of shaggy donkeys side by side.

Angel was cold out in the yard. He went back inside and resumed his pacing.

Later that night, much later, he noticed rust red stains on the toes of his sneakers. On closer inspection, the stains appeared to be blood. Or maybe it was blood. What else could it be?

He went back out into the yard and this time it was snowing. A scattering of flakes visible in intermittent moonlight as clouds rushed past.

He retraced his steps and there, in one of the flower beds, a small puppy-size creature with most of its head blown off.

It took him awhile. It didn't occur to him.

Back in the house, hunting up a flashlight, back out to the yard. Two in the morning. Silent out in the dark, only wind through trees, leaves and branches rustling. The dead creature in the flashlight beam is a ground hog. Still it didn't register. Not until he saw the triangle of white spots in what remained of the snout. Then he understood and he waited out in the cold and wind, trembling, under a freakish drifting down of snowflakes, in the on-and-off light of a full moon behind a rush of dark clouds.

He waited out in the dark forever, until Uncle Augie emerged from the house carrying a shovel.

Uncle Augie again dressed in a white three-piece suit, a Southern gentleman out of the civil war era, immaculately groomed, a gold watch chain looped from pocket to pocket across the belly of his vest.

"Do the right thing." Uncle Augie handed Angel the shovel. He raised a finger. "Don't listen to her," he said. "Do you hear me, Angel?"

Angel nodded. Uncle Augie looked up at the moon and the drift of falling snow. "It's cold," he said, and returned to the house.

Angel dug a deep hole between the garden bed and the fence. The bullet, he realized, could not have come from Neighbor's property. First, Frankie's body was too close to the fence. The bullet would have had to come through one of the wire rectangles of the cyclone fencing. Which was not likely. And, anyway, Frankie's body had been blown back toward the fence. So the bullet came from the other side of the yard.

He lay Frankie in the ground, filled in the dirt, patted it down.

So Neighbor—Elvis, Elvis Blakemore—had been in Angel's yard. He must have been there a long time, waiting, armed.

He'd had the balls to take the shot while Angel was right there, in the house. What would have happened had Angel rushed out and caught Neighbor before he could cross the yard, climb the fence, cross his own fields, and disappear into his house?

Whatever, Neighbor obviously wasn't worried about it. He took the shot, ambled across Angel's yard, probably thinking Angel was cowering inside, probably assuming Angel didn't have the balls to confront an armed man.

"Probably," Angel said to Shelly, back in the house, that night.

"Probably?" Shelly, outraged. Dressed like a businesswoman, only with spikey high heels. "What do you mean probably?"

They were in the hallway between the bedroom and living room. The lights were all on now. The house lit up bright.

"Probably," Angel repeated. "We don't know for sure that it was him."

"Oh, please!" Shelly put her hands on Angel's chest, hesitated a second, and then shoved him.

Angel fell back against the wall. Slid down onto his butt.

Shelly, hovering over him. "Your father cowed you," she said. "He turned you into a weakling. You've got no balls."

Angel, "You can't talk to me like that. Can you?" What was it he felt? Something like shock. Or extreme surprise. Shelly had physically shoved him against the wall. He was looking up at her from the ground. "I'm a decent man," he said. "I'm a reasonable man."

Shelly knelt beside him. "You're a coward. You're afraid of them all."

And what was Angel thinking in that moment?

That, oh God, she was so beautiful. Her eyes were crystalline blue. Her mouth, her lips….

He grasped her arm. "Let's get under the covers." Pulled himself to his feet. "Please. Let's go to bed."

Shelly's face soured into a sneer. She yanked her arm free. "Not interested," she said and walked off into the bedroom, slammed the door behind her.

"Wait," Angel called after her. "You can refuse me?"

From behind the bedroom door. "Apparently."

Angel knocked at the door. "Hey," he said, "that's my bedroom."

"You're such a disappointment." Shelly, climbing into bed. The rustle of the quilt being thrown back.

Angel, banging on the door.

Shelly, "Just quit it, will you, Angel?"

"What do you mean, *quit it?* What's going on, Shell? You can't do this. You can't tell me to *quit it.*"

"Well, apparently I can." Shelly, fluffing up the pillow. "Quit it. Go away. Go bury another pet or something."

Angel, bewildered, waited in the hallway. Paced the length of it once or twice. What did she want? What did she expect?

Was he supposed to march over to Neighbor's, drag his ass out of bed, beat him with a baseball bat till he was a bloody mess?

And so the night passed with Angel barred from his bedroom, pacing through the house.

The night passed. The snow stopped. The sun rose. The snow melted away. Angel at some point collapsed at the kitchen table.

Now it's morning and he's looking at his hands. They're mud smeared, dirt thick under the fingernails.

He looks up to see Shelly sitting across from him, watching him. He hadn't heard her leave the bedroom, but there she is. Looking solemn as a judge.

It confuses Angel, that solemn look on her gorgeous face. Again he thinks, What does she want from me? What does she expect me to do?

He opens his mouth to ask her, but she seems to know the question in advance. She makes a face that says she's disappointed in him. It reminds him of the way his father used to look at him. She gets up, shows him her back—which is stunning in that pencil skirt! Good God!—and returns to the bedroom, clicking the door solidly shut behind her.

Angel holds his head in his hands and sobs. He's been doing a whole lot of sobbing the last few days. Really, he's had enough of it. He's disgusted with himself. He needs to pull himself together. Come on, Angel! Really, you're turning into a pathetic figure! Get it together! Figure it out!

But still, there he is, sobbing. Angel at the kitchen table, a panel of sunlight creeping over the sink, making its way to him.

When next he looks up, Uncle Augie has taken Shelly's place at the table. He's still dressed like a rich Southern plantation owner out of a Tennessee Williams play.

"What are you doing here?" Angel asks, calmly at first, but then he's angry. "And what the hell are you doing dressed like that! You were a slob when you were alive! And you lived in Brooklyn!"

Uncle Augie looks down at himself, hooks his thumbs in the pockets of his vest. "This? This is what I always looked like. You just never saw it." He smiles a little, thinking, then adds, "Your Aunt Mary saw it."

One more stupefying piece of information Angel has no idea what to do with. Again, "What do you want Uncle Augie? What are you doing here?"

Uncle Augie pulls Angel's cell phone out of his pocket and slides it across the table. "Make the calls, Angel. I'm proud of you. You're doing good. You're staying out of the bedroom." He pushed the phone closer to Angel. "Now it's time to make the calls. You know you need to."

Angel hesitates. Then nods.

Uncle Augie produces the local phone directory, opens it to the necessary pages, slides it to Angel.

Angel dials the right number.

A woman answers. She tells him the name of the hospital and the unit. As if he hadn't just looked it up. As if he didn't know where he was calling.

"Look," he says. "I need help."

And Who Knew What Political Office Might Beckon?

By Thursday afternoon the weather was gloriously springlike, and the men—and they were all men—of the Redvale Gun Club were gathered on the patio behind Elvis' house. Elvis had fired up the grill and was busy flipping hamburgers and chatting with his brothers, Buddy, Rick, and Vince. Of the four of them, Vince was the only one harboring any reservations about the upcoming Board meeting—and his concern had nothing at all to do with the issue of open carrying guns to a local government meeting. His concern was with the Tillers. He didn't like the idea, didn't like at it all, of a bunch of Blakemore men and Tiller men all in the same place carrying loaded assault rifles.

"It's just a little crazy," Vince said. "Isn't it?" Vince, the youngest of the Blakemore boys, was still in his twenties. After a relatively few wild years of teenagerhood in which he had dropped out of high school, been arrested several times on drug offenses, and been sentenced the last time in drug court to a year-long stint in a court-appointed drug rehabilitation program, he had found religion, been reborn, attained his GED, and currently was in night school at Redvale Community College while working full time at the nearby Adamsville Army Ammunition Plant, better known locally as the Adamsville Arsenal.

"There won't be any trouble," Elvis said.

Buddy said, "Peaceful show of political opposition." The oldest of the brothers, Buddy was dressed in chocolate chip camo pants and shirt jacket. He was understandably proud of 1) being a combat vet, and 2) still fitting into his old Army gear. He wore his short gray hair in an old-fashioned crew cut, waxed to stick up straight off his forehead.

Rick, the Blakemore brother nearest in age to Elvis, was the most athletic of the boys. He'd played baseball in high school the year Redvale High won the state championship and consequently he was locally famous. Also, the best-looking boy in the family. By far. With the manly, handsome, angular face of a Rudolph-Valentino-era movie star. Trim and fit, he had a reputation for travelling to New York to buy his clothes, which included expensive Italian shoes and silk shirts. He worked behind the desk at the Holiday Inn, and had to be the best dressed desk clerk in the entire world wide chain of Holiday Inns. You hardly ever saw him when he wasn't wearing a suit. Also, he was still single. And he traveled a lot to New York. So, there were rumors. This afternoon, standing beside the grill, hands in pockets, pensively watching Elvis arranging rows of sizzling burgers, he was dressed casually in crisp blue jeans, a black knit shirt, and a tan blazer. He didn't talk much to his brothers, or anyone else really. But he was there. He was a Blakemore boy.

"We don't stop them, they'll be coming to confiscate our guns." Elvis pointed his spatula to the Come and Take It flag flying over his house. "And then they'd better bring a shitload of body bags."

Buddy grunted in affirmation but Vince said, "Yeah, yeah," uninterested in the rhetoric. "I'm talking about if Spider's there. Then what?"

At the mention of Spider Tiller, Buddy and Vince were instantly quieted, and Rick, surprising all of them, turned his head and spit in the grass behind the grill.

Fifteen or so years earlier, when Buddy was in Afghanistan, Spider Tiller raped his daughter, Ellen Blakemore. Or so the Blakemore family believed, since Ellen, who was fourteen years old at the time, swore to it in video testimony used in Spider's trial, testimony that included excruciatingly ugly details that every Blakemore man in the courthouse listened to in a state of barely controlled rage.

Spider at the time was a man in his mid-forties, and he swore it never happened. The whole thing, he claimed, was a malicious attack on his family, a fabricated rape that grew out of a fight between his daughter, Jesse Tiller, and Ellen, who used to be her best friend.

The case was byzantine in its complications and filled the front page of the Redvale Times for weeks. Jesse had stolen Ellen's boyfriend. That was pretty much a fact, or at least Ellen was dating the boy first and Jesse wound up with him. Ellen spread rumors about Jesse giving her own brothers blow jobs. There was a rumor that they both did it, gave Jesse Tiller's older brothers blow jobs, both the girls, at the same time, with both the brothers. The brothers, fifteen and seventeen, well liked at school, were outraged at the accusation. Jesse denied it. Ellen denied that she was involved but swore that Jesse told her it happened all the time.

The events and rumored events whispered around town or stipulated to in trial testimony were said to have happened in the basement of Spider Tiller's home, in the hours immediately after school let out.

Spider was home from work on the afternoon of the alleged attack. That too was a fact. He claimed, however, that he never stepped foot in the basement, that he'd seen Ellen running across his front yard wiping tears from her eyes, asked Jesse what had happened, and had been told they'd had a fight about a boy. And that was the extent of his involvement in the events of that afternoon.

Redvale itself was divided in its opinions once the Not Guilty verdict was delivered.

The Tillers were as furious about the rumors of their family's sexual misbehavior as they were about the false accusation leveled against Spider.

Spider had packed up his family, moved down to Florida, and hadn't returned until a dozen years later, at which point Ellen Blakemore was married—to a Tiller!—and had three children of her own.

So, it was all a big mess. Nothing had been forgiven and nothing forgotten. Spider, a man in his mid-fifties now, kept himself largely out of sight. Ellen's mother, Merri Blakemore, swore on everything holy that there was no force on earth would keep her from putting a knife through that son-of-bitch Spider's heart should she ever cross his path.

"He won't be there," Elvis said, finally. "He's not that stupid."

"Might be," Vince said. "Never was the brightest bulb, what I've heard."

Buddy said, "Shut up, Vince," and the way he said it put an end to the discussion.

So, yeah, the Blakemores and the Tillers. They're not bad people, really. There's even a societal success here and there—a couple of doctors, a novelist of some fame—though most of them, descendants of tenant farmers, have been and always were dirt poor, with all the attendant limitations and burdens of poverty. Some of them are outlaws and mean as snakes, yes, but far more of them, almost all of them overall, are solid members of the community, church goers and civic volunteers.

And here's Elvis, the Blakemore in question, President of the Redvale Gun Club, a man with political ambitions. Yes, he believes there's something called a New World Order, run by Jews, that's trying to control the U.S. population through the media and with the use of chemicals, that those contrails you see all the time in blue skies are really chemtrails, clouds of mind-altering chemicals sprayed down on us by the Illuminati; yes, he believes that Obama is just waiting for the right moment, the trigger crisis, to institute martial law and establish a police state metropolitan government that will round up patriots and send them to FEMA concentration camps; that it's likely the metropolitan government will allow Red Chinese troops to occupy America because the extra bodies will be needed to man their police state; that door-to-door gun confiscation is coming and that the Redvale Board of Supervisors is part of the plan, along with those dykes, Dolores Maso and Gloria Tiller; that fluoridation of the U.S. water supply is part of the New World Order's population control program; that the High-frequency Active Auroral Research Program, better known as HAARP, is a government agency tasked with creating directed-energy weapons designed for weather- and mind-control; that the Federal Reserve was created to spread Jewish banker domination over every aspect of American life; that the Men in Black are aliens aligned with the New World Order who will most likely be granted territories of their own once the metropolitan government is in place. And, yes, he does have a violent streak, which his ex-wife will affirm. And he did shoot Frankie. He doesn't like groundhogs. And he doesn't like his perv neighbor.

But he's really not such a bad guy.

The stuff with his ex happened years ago and he regrets it. The political stuff, well, sure, he believes it all, kind of. But it doesn't have much influence on his day-to-day life, which is mostly about his work and his family and keeping up his fields and taking care of his animals. Or maybe it's more accurate to say he's not such a bad guy where his family and friends are concerned. He just doesn't do very well with others, which includes anyone outside his family and his friends, which includes anyone who doesn't look like him or is from some other country.

Anyway.

There he was in his backyard, on his patio, grilling hamburgers with his brothers on a bright spring day, a dozen gun club members ambling through his fields or standing around nearby talking politics and guns, some of them with their assault rifles already strapped in place. They'd just had a meeting and by unanimous vote elected him to be their official spokesperson at that evening's upcoming Board of Supervisors meeting. He'd already written up a statement that proclaimed their Second Amendment right to keep and bear arms, and that any law to the contrary was a violation of the constitution, and therefore illegal and the Redvale Gun Club would stand up for their inalienable rights. He was looking forward to delivering the statement—and if that fucking prick Spider Tiller was stupid enough to show up, well, whatever happened, that was on him.

Seeing the burgers were ready, he yelled "Who wants them a hamburger?" and then glanced over at his neighbor's yard, where he had already noticed the freshly turned earth at the spot where he'd shot that damn groundhog.

He smiled and greeted everyone by name as they held out a paper plate and he placed a patty on a fluffy white Sunshine hamburger roll.

He was a shoo-in to be reelected as President of the gun club.

And who knew? Who knew what he might do next? Who knew what political office might beckon?

Transcendent Gardening

Angel waited until the last of the cars and trucks were gone before he went out into his yard to do some gardening.

No one could help him right away. Best he could do was get an appointment for next week.

But, fine, he could do it next week. He could hold on. It wasn't like it was some kind of dire emergency.

Having made the appointment, he already felt better.

Shelly, however, wouldn't let up. All day she'd been sulking around the house, coming out of the bedroom to harangue and insult him, returning to the bedroom, slamming the door behind her.

Angel didn't know how it could have come to this. As if he were under siege. Nor did he know what she wanted from him, though he had asked her repeatedly.

She was disappointed in him.

It was time for him to act.

What? What do you expect me to do, Shell?

Be a man! He came into your yard with a loaded weapon! He shot your pet!

He shot a ground hog. There's a difference.

Shelly, disgusted, stomping back to the bedroom. You make me sick!

And so on.

All day.

Out in the yard, under the late afternoon sun, Angel strapped on knee pads and knelt in a garden of flowering yellow and purple tulips. As he dug up weeds with a trowel and a hand fork, he tossed them and the dirt clumped to their roots into the bright red belly of a wheelbarrow he had rolled up behind him. Jesus, the sun felt good on his back. As did digging in the dirt. Such a simple thing and yet a kind of peace radiated through him, up out of the dirt and into his body.

Angel on his knees in the dirt. A short, bulky man, gardening in mud-streaked khaki slacks and a black hoodie. A red wheelbarrow at his back. From a distance he might look like a man who, after work, has decided to go out into his garden to do a little weeding. Up close, a different picture. His skin is sallow. There are dark circles under his eyes. His profusion of dark hair, usually combed neatly in standard conservative male fashion—a tight part on the left, swept back off his face—is a mess. Clumps of hair stick up here and there, morning head, just out of bed head. Something rattled and jerky in his every motion. The cleft in his chin red and irritated.

Angel, busily weeding, made the mistake of taking a break to look around him at his yard. Everything needed upkeep. The gardens were all going to weed. Tree branches and various wintry debris were scattered everywhere. And then, finally, his eyes lighted on the fresh patch of dirt where he had buried Frankie, and, beyond that, Neighbor's patio, the black grill, the cheap lawn furniture. All of it under the fluttering Come and Take It flag.

"What are you going to do about it, Angel?" This is Shelly, behind him. She's lost the salmon blazer and the black of her skirt pops beside the enamel red of the wheelbarrow.

"I'm weeding," Angel says. "It feels good out here in the sun." He twists around to look up at Shelly, at the curves beneath the black boat neck cut of a sleek long sleeve seamless top. "You look great all in black," he says, a little breathy. Is he exhausted from this little bit of gardening?

"Please, Angel," Shelly says. She's pleading now. She looks down at him with big eyes, hopeful.

"I'm a good man," Angel says. "I'm a man of peace."

"Oh, Angel…." Shelly, sorry for him. "Wake up, Honey. Look at the world you live in. That *good man* shit, that *man of peace* shit, it's an excuse for not acting. You don't have to be a coward, Angel. You don't have to let everyone walk all over you."

Angel goes back to weeding. "What do you want from me?" he says into the dirt. "What do you expect me to do?"

"It's time for some real gardening," Shelly says. "It's time for some genuinely transcendent gardening."

Angel pretends he doesn't know what she means. He digs up a clump of bittercress and tosses it into the wheelbarrow.

Shelly won't allow it, this playing dumb. "Time to get rid of those Blakemore weeds," she says. "What are they, the whole bunch of them? All of them. They're the weeds and you're the gardener."

"Stop it," Angel says, dismissing her.

"All those redneck weeds," Shelly says. "All those idiot creepers and stupid vines choking the life out of things."

"Stop it," Angel says again. He tosses his tools aside and digs his hands into the dirt and then Shelly's gone and he's alone again in his garden, among yellow and purple tulips, on his knees.

Angel dug into the dirt with his hands. It felt good. The more he dug the more the peace of the earth flowed up into him, so he dug deeper and deeper, up to his elbows, until he forgot that he was weeding. In the back of his head, Shelly's words repeated over and over, an ear worm, the chorus of a song stuck in mind.

Time for some genuinely transcendent gardening.

Try Real Hard Not To Shoot Yourself In the Ass

Forty-five minutes before the scheduled start, when the parking lot of the County Administrative Center was already overflowing with cars and pickup trucks, the Board of Supervisors meeting was moved down to the first-floor auditorium, a space usually reserved for large public events. The Board's meeting room had space for fifty. The auditorium held two hundred and fifty. By seven o'clock, the meeting's scheduled start time, the auditorium was filled to near capacity with a tense, well-behaved crowd of Redvale citizens, the majority of whom were there to speak out against any regulations or policies that might limit the right to keep and bear and openly carry semi-automatic weapons in the city of Redvale. A substantial percentage of the audience, however, was there to support Judd Hansen's proposed policy banning the open carry of assault rifles within Redvale city limits. Judd had spent a busy week leading up to the meeting urging many of the town's most influential citizens to show up and speak in favor of such a ban. Among them, however, was not a single politician, not the mayor or vice-mayor, or any other elected city official, and not a congressman, state or federal. The political class had apparently decided to stay away for the time being. For the most part, this was a good thing by Judd Hansen's calculations, since all of them without exception would have been inclined to oppose the ban. However, given the recent shooting up of the Main Street Market, they were keeping their distance, waiting to see how things fell out.

You might think a crowd like this, in this situation, would be boisterous. Nope. Not this crowd—and that no doubt had something to do with the dozens of men in attendance, and several of the women, who were openly carrying weapons ranging from assault rifles to handguns. They carried semi-automatics dangling over their chests, strapped to their backs, or hanging from their waists. The preferred method of carry for handguns was a holster snug to the hip, though one cowboy, black cowboy hat and all, wore a Dodge-city style gun belt, with a holster low down on the thigh and tied in place above the knee, all set for a quick-draw contest. The number of deadly weapons on display seemed

to make everyone at least a little nervous. The crowd for the most part
was arranged in clumps of people familiar to each other talking quietly
among themselves. Which is not to say the auditorium was quiet. No.
Two hundred and fifty or so people talking is not quiet. Just, it wasn't
raucous. You might call it festive, in the way a big gathering after a funeral
is festive. Here and there someone laughed. Most everyone was talking
to someone. But overall the mood was...earnest. A large number of
people gathered to speak out in support of their beliefs, knowing there
would be strongly opposing opinions. That kind of tension. And, again,
the guns.

The auditorium itself was raked, with three rows of gray-blue
seating separated by wide aisles, leading down to a stepped stage—a
low semicircular stage one mounted by climbing four steps to the top
platform—where a lectern had been set up in front of a row of folding
chairs. A modern facility with oak laminate floors, the space had the
feel of a contemporary megachurch—though without an altar and not
very mega. A pair of black speakers was wall mounted on either side
of the stage, and two microphone stands were positioned one in each
aisle for commentary, questions, and statements from the crowd. The
possibility of a large gathering was something everyone had foreseen,
and so the auditorium had been decided upon as the overflow alter-
native long in advance, and all the appropriate preparations had been
made. There were volunteers to help usher people to their seats; there
was an assigned attendant for each aisle microphone; and there were
a half dozen uniformed police officers arranged around the front and
rear of the room. There were reporters, too, print and broadcast. The
TV news reporters, local celebrities to the crowd, were accompanied by
unfamiliar cameramen hauling television gear on their shoulders, trailing
black wires. Overall, it was a well-organized event. The atmosphere was
serious though not somber. There was a sense that an issue of great
import to the citizenry of Redvale was about to be debated, and the
people were here—in attire ranging from three-piece suits to casual dress
to chocolate chip camo and blaze orange—to have their impassioned say.

Claire Maso was seated second row center, Kenny on one side
of her, Linni on the other. Kenny's friends Bobby and Amayr were

behind them. In front of Claire, in the first row, only a few feet from the stage, Dolores was hunched over in intense, whispered conversation with Judd Hansen. The other three supervisors had already taken the stage, Williamson and BeDouchian face to face, BeDouchian's hand on Williamson's shoulder, LeDoux with his arms crossed over his chest, looking out glassy eyed at the audience. The meeting, one sensed, was not yet quite ready to come to order. Every few minutes, Gloria got up from her seat next to Dolores and pretended to stretch. She was wearing a polka dot red skirt and a navy-blue blouse, casual neat attire that seemed jarringly out of place with her short, spikey hair. Not that she wasn't gorgeous. The girl couldn't do anything but be gorgeous. Just, kind of, she looked like she was wearing her mother's clothes. Each time she got up to stretch, her eyes scanned the entire auditorium, but always lighted in the end on the clump of Tiller men seated toward the back of the room. There looked to be twenty or thirty Tillers all told, including her uncle Travis, fresh out of the penitentiary for manslaughter.

Gloria glanced behind her to Claire, who struck her as looking even more intense than usual. Well, at least more intense than she usually looked whenever Gloria was around. This had been going on forever and Gloria had long ago gotten used to it. She liked Claire a great deal. Maybe even loved her. Certainly admired her. It didn't take a genius to figure out why Claire might not feel the same way about her—even though they had spent so much time together as Claire was growing up, and even if, though Claire would never admit it, Gloria had always been good to her, and they'd had good times together. Gloria still held out hope that one day Claire's attitude toward her might change.

She was tempted in the moment to ask Claire what was up with the Graham girls. She'd noticed the way Claire had snatched Kenny away from them as if they were contagious. They'd been descending the aisle toward the stage when they passed the Graham family. The girls had called out to Kenny and waved, and Claire had yanked him away by the arm so forcefully they both tripped on the next step. She was also tempted to ask Claire if something was up with Kenny. The way she seemed with him, it appeared to Gloria something was going on more than a business relationship.

"Excuse me, Linni?" Gloria had already exchanged polite greetings with Claire and Linni, and been introduced to Kenny. "Would you mind guarding my seat for a minute? I'll be right back."

Linni said "Of course," and draped her white scarf over the back of Gloria's seat. She had the typical Linni royal beauty thing going on with a wine-red blouse and the white scarf.

Dolores popped out of her conversation with Hansen and looked up to Gloria. "Where are you going?"

Gloria bent to whisper in her ear. "To have a word with some of my darlin' kinfolk."

"Why? The meeting's about to start."

Gloria was about to explain that she didn't like the way her folks kept looking over to the Blakemores on the other side of the auditorium, and she wanted to put in a strong word against them making fools of the whole family by starting something that was going to make them all look trashy. She didn't get out a word, though, before she saw her Uncle Spider enter the auditorium with his wife on his arm and an assault rifle dangling at his side. "Oh, for Christ's sake," she said, and buried her face in her hands.

Dolores spun around in her seat and looked toward where Gloria had just been looking. "Is that who I think it is?"

Gloria didn't answer. She picked herself up and climbed the aisle toward her family. The other Tillers had shifted seats to make room, and Gloria reached Spider just as he was about to take the aisle seat, his wife alongside him.

"Uncle Spider," she said calmly, her hands folded at the waist, through a friendly if clearly forced smile, "what in hell are you doing here?"

Spider's wife, Terri, jumped up not only before Spider could utter a word, but before he could even think to say a word. "Because he's tired of hiding his face," she said in a loud, hushed whisper. She propped her hands on her hips. "That's why, Miss Gloria. Why shouldn't he be here? He's got a right."

Spider Tiller was a tall, angular man, bony all over, as if his skeleton were trying to pop out through his skin. He had the look of a man who saw the world through a two-second delay. Terri, too, was a quiet woman—until she got mad, which was not infrequently. Her head only came up to Spider's chest, and whatever skeleton she had was buried under pounds and pounds of jiggly flesh.

"Uncle Spider," Gloria said, angling her body away from her aunt, "you're likely to start a riot being in the same place with the Blakemores."

Terri yanked Spider down into his seat. "We're not going anywhere," she said, and flopped down into her seat beside him. "Why don't you go back and sit with your girlfriend where you belong?"

Gloria ignored her aunt and knelt in the aisle beside Spider. "All I'm saying," she whispered, "is maybe this isn't the best time for a coming out party. You know what I mean?" She glanced across the auditorium to the Blakemores, several of whom were looking back at her. When she spotted the person she was looking for, she turned back to her uncle. "Merri Blakemore's here," she said. "You know she'll make trouble. No two ways about that."

Spider looked straight ahead, toward the stage, where Dolores had joined the other supervisors and Judd Hansen was at the podium, tapping on the mic to be sure it was working. "Well that's on them now, ain't it, little girl?" He paused a second before adding, "I got a right."

"Sure," Gloria said. "And I bet you feel a lot better about it with that cannon hanging off your hip."

"I do," Spider answered, still looking straight ahead, no expression in his eyes beyond blankness.

Gloria stood and looked over her family. Within her she felt a familiar tearing. They were looking back at her, some of them fiercely, more of them with bewilderment. It wasn't that she loved the whole lot of them, it was more that she was bound to them on a kind of cellular level that she both resented and couldn't resist and didn't want to resist. The whole stupid, evil, scofflaw idiot bunch of them. But then she looked at her own mother and father who immediately looked away, as if she were nothing more to them than an unpleasant memory—and that allowed her to fall back into her own comfortable, familiar anger.

"Well then," she said to her uncle, "try real hard not to shoot yourself in the ass." She patted him on the shoulder and returned to her seat just as Hansen, at the lectern, began to speak.

"So glad to see you all here," he said. "You see? This is how democracy works!"

Hansen went on while Gloria, anxious for the evening to be over, tuned him out and allowed herself to drift off into thoughts of her morning in bed with Doll.

Once Hansen launched into his introductory remarks, Gloria might have been the only person in the auditorium smiling.

Powerized!

Angel, on the concrete floor in his basement storage room, back against the wall, chin resting on his knees, hands wrapped around his legs. In the dark. Well, not dark entirely: a misty haze of early evening light sweats through a single narrow dirt-encrusted window near the ceiling, provides enough illumination to see stacks of cardboard storage boxes, a clutter of brightly colored garden tools, a coil of bright orange extension cord hanging from a hook beside a spastically unraveled plumber's snake. Shovels, rakes, a pickaxe, a pitch fork, long-handled tools lined up along a windowless concrete wall. Alongside Angel, a tall green bag of potting soil, open at the top. The rich, loamy smell of dirt mixed with the mildew and dank odor of a damp basement. Outside, a lovely early spring evening. Angel in the near dark, hiding from Shelly.

He's having trouble keeping it together. As if the ground might fly out from under him, as if something within him might detonate, his heart beating fast and hard, his thoughts a loop and a swirl: he thinks this thing or that over and over before the loop snaps and swirls off in a fast litany of words images memories, too fast to contain, to think over, until something sticks and loops, etc. He feels like he might come apart, thus he has taken a seat on the ground in the dark basement storage room, pulled his knees to his chest and wrapped his arms around his legs, holding himself tight. The smell of dirt and mildew. The beat of his heart. Somewhere outside a lawnmower or leaf blower. Upstairs, through the ceiling, Shelly's footsteps pacing the hall between his bedroom and study. Uncle Augie is gone. Just him and Shelly now: Shelly pacing upstairs, Angel in the basement.

He's so damn tired. Something has to be settled. Something has to be rectified. Before he can sleep.

That's the loop he's on now: something has to be settled, something has to be rectified, before I can sleep. Over and over.

What? What, Angel?

I don't know. How long have I been down here? Jesus.

Angel pulled himself to his feet. He felt as though he were waking from a dream, but he hadn't been sleeping or dreaming, only sitting on the floor in the basement, avoiding Shelly. He located the pull string to a bare light bulb fixed to a ceiling rafter, hesitated, like waking in the morning and not being quite ready to open your eyes, then snapped the string and there he was, near the door to the storage room with its boxes and clutter and array of tools. He turned to the door and froze. Jesus Lord, he was afraid to go back upstairs.

Okay. Stop. Pull yourself together.

Angel puttered through the storage room, flipping open the tops of cardboard boxes, rummaging inside. His hands were black with dirt. He could feel the grit of soil all the way up to his shoulders. He needed a shower. Put that on the list. Inside the boxes, junk mostly. Old stuff that should have been thrown away. In one box, a stack of Claire's childhood school lunch boxes, bright plastic contraptions decorated with Disney characters. He pulled out a shocking pink one, unlatched it, and found that it contained piles of 4X6 photographs from all the way back in another lifetime, when Claire was a toddler, when Claire was in pre-school, family pictures with him and Dolores and Claire, though most of them were Dolores and Claire because he was the one snapping the pictures, all the way back to the days of cameras and film, when he carried those little bright yellow canisters to a drug store and waited a week to pick up the prints. Another lifetime. Another house. Different people. Different world. And what was Angel thinking as he browsed through these pictures of young mother Dolores and baby Claire, pictures of a birthday party with a living room full of friends? Nothing good. Nothing sweet and nostalgic. Instead, a dense fog settled over. A darkness. Was there really a time when he had a house full of friends and neighbors, a house full of rowdy shouting kids, a house full of adults milling and chatting?

Yes. Of course there was.

And what he was thinking was, You wrecked my life. Dolores. You told me you lost your wedding ring and of course that was a fucking lie. How long had you been cheating on me? How many nights were you in bed with that girl, young enough to be your daughter? How many nights, Dolores?

I'm a man to be stepped all over. My father. My wife. My employer. My neighbor.

Angel, you're tired.

He tossed the lunch box to the floor, where the pictures scattered. Maybe if he called Dr. Wilkinson he'd prescribe him a sleeping pill right away, if he explained. Something that could knock him out. That was a thought.

He was so damn tired.

Angel puttered. Opened another cardboard box. Inside, bright new Transcendent Gardening sweatshirts and caps. The sweatshirts were dark blue with a left-of-center picture of a blossoming yellow rose, the word *Transcendent* curling down above it, and *Gardening* curling up below it, also in bright yellow. Yellow rose over the heart.

Dr. Wilkinson was his family doctor, though he hadn't seen him in years. Still, he was his family doctor. Even if he didn't have a family anymore. Still. If he explained, maybe. He felt sure with a night's sleep, a real night's sleep, he could hold on till his appointment. He might come apart. His heart was beating crazy hard.

The caps were bright blue, with a yellow rose above the brim. He took off his black hoody and his undershirt came off with it. His skin pale and doughy. He laughed at the sight of himself under the harsh light of a bare bulb. His hands and wrists were black, his arms up to the shoulders dirt-streaked. Somehow his chest too was streaked with dirt.

First he'd call Dr. Wilkinson, then he'd take a shower.

He pulled on the Transcendent Gardening sweatshirt, fit the cap on his head, and started for the door.

Jesus, is that what you think it is?

Had you asked him earlier, Angel would not have been able to tell you that his father's old baseball bat was downstairs propped up in a corner of the basement storage room, but that's exactly where it was. Angel pulled up at the sight of it, the worn white ash at the batting end, the handle wrapped in black tape. He picked it up and the solid, weighted heft of the thing demanded he swing it, and he did. It felt good. It felt solid. His father's name burned black into the wood, still quite clear, and alongside it, the coinage *Powerized!* under a lightning bolt.

He took another swing and the power of the bat extended up into his arms and shoulders and chest. He could do some damage with this. Is that what his father thought that night, all those years ago? He'd bet it was. He swung again.

Yes, it was. Angel was certain.

The bat silently spoke to him. It said *powerized!* He felt it in his arms and shoulders: *powerized!*

Shelly said, "There you go, Baby! Now you've got the idea!" She massaged his shoulders, kissed him on the back of the neck. "Who's the man?" she whispered. "Who's the man now?" She wrapped her arms around him.

"I should, shouldn't I?" Angel said. Such sweet relief, Shelly's arms around him, her embrace.

Angel turned to face her. First he smiled, then laughed, then covered his mouth with his hands and bent over laughing.

Shelly's smile said she was in on the joke. A busty twenty-something with frosted blond and feathered shoulder-length hair in a camouflage strapless corset and thong. A garter belt held up thigh-high fishnet stockings with dollar bills folded over the elastic top. Knee-high black leather boots with spiked heels finished off the outfit. "It's your reward," she said, and spun around to show off a perfect ass framed by the corset ties and stockings. "You like it?"

"You're crazy," he said into the palms of his hands. "You're out of your mind." He wiped away tears. Yes, he was crying. Either from laughter or despair. He couldn't tell. "I take it," he said, "you think this is a good idea?"

"Shit yeah!" Shelly leaned in and planted a wet kiss on his lips.

"About time!"

"Okay then." Angel swung the bat up onto his shoulder and threw open the storage room door. When he stepped outside into the early evening spring sunlight, he had to pause and throw a forearm over his eyes to protect against a screaming blue sky and green everywhere like flares in the trees and grass. He waited till his eyes adjusted to the light, in blood-stained sneakers and muddy khaki slacks, in a crisp, clean, navy-blue Transcendent Gardening sweat shirt and bright blue cap.

How long could a heart keep beating this fast before it burst?

He swung the bat and it felt good in his hands and arms and chest.

Powerized!

"Go ahead!" Shelly behind him in the open doorway, in the shadows of the house.

How must Angel have looked marching across his neighbor's fields with a baseball bat slung over his shoulder? Though we know now that no one saw him, he must have been a sight: mud-black hands, dirt-streaked face, hair wild sticking out the sides of a baseball cap.

On Neighbor's patio, he changes plan. Fuck that, running around the outside of the house smashing windows. Leave that shit to his father. He wanted Elvis Blakemore—either to cow him or crush him, either would do. Just to watch him back down, throw up his hands, to see fear, to see him fear for himself for his family. Maybe to hear him plead. Maybe he'd do that, make him plead. Or else just smash his fucking head in.

All of which meant getting to him before he could get to his guns, thus the change in plan.

Piece of luck, the back door had a glass pane above the knob. He smashed it in, quick opened the door, charged into the house shouting Neighbor's name. Elvis! You son-of-a-bitch! You here! Charging from room to room. Sweating up a storm. Elvis! You miserable redneck prick! Come here! I want to talk!

Down the stairs to the basement, two at a time. Angel is flying.

He's running around like a kid. His heart a revved-up engine.

Basement empty, up the stairs again. In the living room. Oh, look, a wall-mounted flat screen TV. Smash!

An antique brass lamp! Smash.

X-Box. Smash! Smash!

Angel, muddy sweat dripping into his eyes. Breathing like a freight train. Did he know no one would be home?

Of course, they were out at the Board meeting.

Did he know that before he broke into the house? Maybe. Maybe not. But now he knows and so he sits on a brown leather couch in the living room and looks around. The house to his surprise is tastefully decorated. Well, except for a mirrored wall, though it did make the living room appear larger. Still.

He looks at himself looking at himself in the mirror. Wow, he's a mess. Dirt-smeared sweat-streaked face, muddy pants, knees caked in mud. Baseball bat resting in his lap. The cleft in his chin is somehow clean so it looks like someone has drawn a white line from the bottom of his lip down under his chin. Is he getting fat? A little. Maybe.

What now? A terrible fatigue is nearby, threatening. Angel lifts himself to his feet, hefts the baseball bat to his shoulder. The bat is in communication with a mysterious source of energy located somewhere inside Angel. When he grips the bat it's like plugging in.

He goes back down to the basement, finds a small room with a desk and a tall cabinet. Opens the cabinet.

Jesus Lord. Guns. All manner of guns. Military style assault rifles, shotguns, hunting rifles, handguns....

Drawers stuffed with shotgun shells and gun clips and magazines. Boxes of ammunition.

A small wardrobe of camo hunting jackets with big cargo pockets. A tactical vest? Is that what it's called?

One of those green camo armored vests the soldiers wear in Iraq, slips over the shoulders with a million pockets for who the hell knows what.

Angel tries it on. It's heavy! But the straps are wide and padded and it carries easy on his shoulders.

He grips the barrel of an assault rifle, the metal cool and slick in the palm of his hand. He starts to lift it out of the cabinet, but already his eyes are on this strange looking sawed-off kind of shotgun-looking thing.

He lifts it from the cabinet.

It is a shotgun.

But strange. A single wide barrel, but a pair of closed off barrels beneath it, making a small triangle.

Angel fits the rubber butt against his shoulder, aims the gun out the office door at an armoire in the adjoining room, a nice piece of furniture, cherry it looks like, or cherry finish, two long doors and a wide drawer beneath.

He tries to pull the trigger and gets nothing.

He looks the weapon over, figures out that it's pump action. He pumps and pulls the trigger and Jesus Lord! If the butt hadn't been snug against the padded strap of the armored vest, the recoil might have broken his shoulder. And the noise! Like a cherry bomb going off next to your ear.

Holy shit! Look at the armoire! It has a hole in it the size of a football!

Angel snatches a pair of earplugs out of one of the open drawers of the cabinet, from between a scatter of shotgun shells. He fits the earplugs in place as he looks over the weapon. He can figure out this thing. It's not complicated.

He carries it upstairs, stands back from the mirrored wall and there he is: a short, stocky guy in an armored vest and a Transcendent Gardening cap, with a yellow rose above the brim. He steps back from his reflection as far as he can get, aims, and holy shit, the mirror explodes, shards of glass in a quick silvery explosion. A glittery scatter of mirror and plaster.

Shit this feels good! Powerized? Yes, seriously.

He blows up the dishwasher, the refrigerator, the kitchen cabinets. In the living room again, he blows up the leather couch. The house stinks of cordite. His ears, even with the plugs, are wounded by the sound. He doesn't care. In the master bedroom, he tries to blow up the headboard, but nothing. He looks the weapon over, finds a lever near the trigger. He's already figured out that the shells are loaded into the two bottom barrels and feed the firing barrel. He pushes the lever. Bang! The headboard is dust! Bang! He blows a hole right through the wall out to daylight.

This feeling…. Give him something else to blow up! Give him something else to explode!

What tiredness? What fatigue?

Elvis, you son-of-a-bitch. Dolores, you wouldn't recognize me now, would you? Shelly, where are you? It's me. It's Angel Maso. That's fucking right. That's fucking right!

Just how does Angel feel in the midst of his neighbor's blown to shit house? Dressed in armor, toting a shotgun?

Well…. Transformed.

A Fling, Ginny. Remember That.

Ginny arrived late for Awards Night. The high school auditorium gorgeously designed with two looming side walls constructed of massive glass panes that looked over the faint pink blossoms in an orchard of flowering cherry trees to the evening purple of the North Georgia mountains. Packed with parents and families there to applaud the year-end accomplishments of students and teachers. Alone in a long corridor that led to three triptychs of closed auditorium doors, Ginny braced herself for seeing Cranston and his wife and family as soon as she opened a door and stepped into the crowded room, where she could already hear the laughter and loud chatter and occasional girly screams of a pre-start, festive gathering. Of course the chances of her opening the door and running into Cranston and family were about zero, which is why she had arrived late, to be fairly confident Cranston would be backstage, his family seated somewhere in the audience, and she wouldn't run the risk of having to be introduced.

But enough, Ginny. This is a fling with a married man, a little thing, of no consequence as long as you are both discrete, which of course you will be or else you would have never embarked on the affair. Even though the man is impossibly cute, a big teddy bear of earnest beliefs and righteous commitment to his work. A sweet man, as transparent as a breeze. The first time they met, in his office, there was nothing special going on between them. He looked her over. This was a little more than a year earlier. She'd been wearing bright yellow skin-tight stretch pants and a loose sky-blue band T that fell to mid-thigh. When she took a seat, his eyes fell to her legs and thighs and lingered there long enough for him to blush before he looked up and met her eyes and began the interview. Which went well. They liked each other right off, Ginny with her passionate advocacy of poetry, Cranston amused, somewhat befuddled, but impressed by her energy and arguments for all the advantages of the Poets in the Schools program.

She never had any intention of seducing him, and then one day she did. Well, hardly a seduction. An affection, a connection growing between them for a long time had …what? Risen up and demanded completion. And the odd thing, the interesting thing to Ginny's thinking—she couldn't quite articulate it yet, but…. Even though she was the one who made the first move, who asked him to her apartment, who went and sat at his feet and wrapped an arm around his legs, laid her head on his knees, even though that was all her…it was about him. It was about Cranston and what she knew he wanted and would never ask for and so she had to offer. Like giving in to the desire he couldn't or wouldn't express, but still she felt the pressure of it, of how much he wanted it, and it was hers to give and so she gave it, willingly. A gift. For both of them.

And a fling, Ginny. Remember that. A fling and no one has to be hurt. In time, a memory for both of you, a sweet memory, as long as you remain reasonable and keep in mind the parameters of the relationship, the understood constraints.

Plus the crazy differences between you! You're a Yankee born and bred: raised in Boston, undergrad in New York at NYU, MFA at Syracuse, then back to Brooklyn and work for an arts advocacy program that eventually brings you here to the South and Redvale, Georgia, where, weirdly, you've come to love the place, especially the mountains. The gorgeous forever sweep of mountains. But no one will ever confuse you with a Southerner. You're an artsy Brooklyn girl—and Cranston? Born and bred in Redvale, Georgia. A fraternity boy in Athens. A math teacher. An older, married man with four daughters! So. Remember. There's nothing long-term here. That's not the plan and never was.

Ginny opened the doors to the auditorium and stepped into the crowded room just as Cranston was stepping out onto the stage and approaching a centered lectern to loud applause. The big goof was wearing his yellow Sponge Bob eye patch to the delight of the crowd. Ginny joined the applause, scanned the audience for his family, the wife and four daughters, found them lined up in the front row, or figured at least that it had to be them, five girls in a row, descending in height and age, their hands raised in applause.

Cute.

She found a seat on the aisle and settled in.

Watching Cranston as he straightened his tie while delivering opening remarks, she felt a crazy sweet swell of warmth that she knew it was unwise to be feeling—and she told herself to stop it. She told herself, calmly, reasonably, not to be a fool. Not to fall in love.

Though she feared it might already be too late.

As If Asking a Question of God

Several explosions in rapid succession interrupted Jimmy Whitmore, a downtown market businessman who owned a men's clothing shop shot up in the recent Redvale semi-auto rampage. He was in the midst of delivering a response to Elvis Blakemore's impassioned call for protecting citizens' Second Amendment rights, and Redvale Gun Club member Justin Bailish's unhinged tirade against the government and the Federal Reserve Board, which he tied to the necessity of an armed citizenry. Whitmore, a thin middle-aged man dressed stylishly in a blue, pin-striped suit, had been delivering an equanimous, carefully reasoned argument in support of Judd Hansen's proposed semi-auto ban when the explosions made him cringe and clutch the microphone stand before falling to the ground. Later, when the events of the evening had been dissected moment by moment, over and over again, video clips from television cameras and cell phones replayed endlessly twenty-four seven on cable and network news, it would be established that this was the instant Angel Maso, soon to be known worldwide as The Angel of Death, entered the community auditorium of the Redvale County Administrative Center and opened fire with a 12 Gauge shotgun on Redvale Police officers Caleb Barrett, Peter Levy, and Leslie Kolbert, all three of whom died from their wounds.

On the video, we see Whitmore standing in the aisle, holding the narrow microphone stand in one hand and gesturing with the other, situated midway between the stage and the entry doors on the left side of the auditorium, a column of seats to his left, a wider center column to his right, and, separated by another aisle, a third column of seats to the far right. You hear him say, "I would like to ask my friends—" before six shotgun blasts interrupt his speech. We know now that they were shotgun blasts, but in that moment, in the video, what you see on the faces in the crowd is confusion and shock. Everyone simultaneously hunkers down. A wave of fear crashes into them as some cover their heads, others shout, a few scream, but all of them are pushed closer to the ground. We get only those few seconds of clarity before the television cameras are jostled or dropped. After that the video record comes mostly from cell phones, and most of those videos are recorded after the carnage is over. The videos of the aftermath are extensive and gruesome. But of the event itself, we have only those first few seconds at the beginning, what one television camera manages to record while lying on the ground, and a complete audio recording which captures mostly screams and gunfire and here and there a decipherable shout, one of which, famously, is seventy-six-year-old Christine Wiley shouting "Terrorists! Terrorists!" Sometime later, on one of the morning shows, she'll swear she saw two swarthy, bearded men in black, wearing ISIS black flag T-shirts, shouting "Allahu Akbar!" Others will confirm this, though no such men were captured on video, no such shouts recorded on audio, and every official investigation will debunk the claims.

And of course there were no ISIS terrorists. There was only Angel, his cheeks and forehead blackened with camo face paint, his torso covered with a green camo tactical vest with body armor, its myriad pockets crammed with shotgun shells and ammo clips, an AR-15 slung over his back, and a Glock 19 tucked into a hip holster. On his head, a blue Transcendent Gardening baseball cap, bright yellow rose above the brim. In his eyes, which no video captures, a fierce fixed million-mile stare that nonetheless scans the auditorium as he moves toward a panicked crowd that flees at his approach, hurling themselves toward two stage-level exit doors on either side of the auditorium, where bodies immediately begin to pile up, where survivors will talk as their voices crack of climbing over the dead as they scrambled toward the last of the evening light coming in through the open doors, above the blockade of bodies. The stories of the survivors are terrible. They're horrifying—and repeated in print and television coverage in their every appalling detail, reporters digging for the deep human story, the visceral response, the heartbreak and tragedy.

Angel was hunting. He wanted Elvis and his family, all the miserable Blakemore clan, every one of them. He wanted Delores and Gloria. Both. Let's see how they feel now. Let's see what they think now. He had something to tell them, something he needed them to hear. Meanwhile, people were shooting at him. Bullets pockmarked the walls behind him, the ground at his feet. He was aware of this, but invulnerable in his tactical gear. Still, he ducked behind a blue green row of seats as the air filled with smoke. Switched to the rifle and fired blindly in the direction of the stage. Hunkered lower and reloaded the shotgun, fed it twelve shells, six in each barrel. There were other figures with guns shooting from behind the barrier of auditorium seats. Some of them seemed to be shooting at him, but others didn't. They appeared to be shooting at each other. Where the hell did all that smoke come from? (Smoke grenades, Angel. No one knows who detonated them. Most will speculate it was you.) Angel waited, butt on the ground, back against a seat back. Place sounded like a firing range, the gunfire pretty much constant. The air fuliginous, acrid. Who the hell were they shooting at? (Each other, Angel. The Blakemores believe the gunfire is coming from the Tillers and vice versa. Most of those two long-warring families, those who survive, won't know anything about you until it's all over.) Angel's head empty of conscious thought, though apparently he knew exactly what he was doing. He raised himself up, shotgun in hand, and fired on anyone with a weapon, which was everyone who was not fully prone on the ground or trying to get out the exit doors. One row he came upon didn't even see him until they'd never see anything again. They were shooting across the room, and he came up behind them, fired six blasts from the shotgun, switched barrels, moved down a row, same thing, emptied the other barrel before switching to the rifle and emptying a clip into the figures fighting to get out the door. And so on, making his way toward the front of the room, wreathed in smoke, hunting.

Does Angel see children in the line of fire? Yes. Does that stop him? No. He's weeding. He has a job to do.

Claire, on the stage, struggling to get loose of her mother.

"We can't, we can't," Dolores, as she drags Claire toward the backstage exit. She means we can't help them, though only the first two words come out.

Judd Hansen is dead. BeDouchian is dead. Both with head wounds they couldn't possibly survive.

Delores knew from the start.

Gloria is most likely dead. Linni Sorland is most certainly dead.

She saw Angel enter with the shotgun. She knew it was Angel, short and squat, the peaked cap with a yellow rose.

Kenny Walker is probably dead. LeDoux is probably dead.

While everyone else ran for the exits, Dolores leapt down the stage stairs and ran to Gloria and Claire. How long could that possibly have taken? How many seconds?

And yet. While still on the stage, a bullet strikes Judd Hansen in the eye. A chunk of BeDouchian's skull lands at her feet.

Before she reaches the first step, Kenny Walker's arms fly up in the air as if he's at a revival meeting and he's just been saved. He flops over the seat in front of him as Claire reaches for his folded-over body.

On the first step, Gloria grabs Claire by the arm, as if to pull her over the row of seats toward the stage, and then is thrown back as gouts of blood spurt from her neck. Linni Sorland shields Claire from behind, opening her own body like a wide sail, extending her arms, positioning herself behind Claire. Before her beautiful face largely disappears, transformed into something ugly, red, raw.

Off the stage, before she reaches Claire, who is blood-covered now, blood on her face and in her hair, LeDoux, walking calmly toward a side exit, red-eyed and dazed, is knocked to the ground, as if someone hit him in the back with a club, his suit jacket blossoming a red stain.

Claire, when Dolores at last reaches her, is silent. With one hand, she holds Linni by the wrist, the other hand is on Kenny's shoulder, and her eyes are on Gloria, sprawled on the ground, her arms flung wide. Claire, as if she's trying to keep Kenny and Linni from falling apart, as if trying to hold them together.

Smoke and gunfire. Bright flashes erupting out of the smoky dark. And screams. Screams and yelling. As the auditorium rapidly empties.

This all happens in seconds. Everything, so fast, the percussive clatter of gunfire from start to finish only a few minutes, the screams, the wafting smoke. And Angel, like the moon peeking out from behind fast-moving clouds. Angel appearing and disappearing behind smoke, behind chairs, between fleeing bodies. He has a handgun now and he's making his way toward the front of the room, firing down into bodies along the way.

When at last she reaches Claire, Dolores heaves her up and over the first row of chairs. Angel is moving down the left aisle. He doesn't appear to have seen them yet, but he will, soon. He pauses over a body and fires three times, picks up a weapon from the ground and slings it over his shoulder, pulls another clip from his vest, reloads.

All the gunfire—other than the pop pop pop of Angel's handgun—has ceased. The auditorium is almost empty of moving bodies, though not entirely. Still there are figures that jump up from a hiding place and charge out the side or rear doors.

Dolores has to drag Claire up the stage steps. She means to explain that Angel is the shooter, that he is approaching them, that they must get away, that there's a door back stage, but the only word that comes out is her daughter's name. "Claire! Claire! Claire!"

Claire struggles against Delores, but is off balance and can't get to her feet. In her mother's arms, being dragged away from Kenny, from Linni, from Gloria. A substantial part of her mind, of her thoughts, of her consciousness, stuck on Gloria. Gloria grabbing her by the arm, Gloria's neck seeming to explode, a spray of blood splashing back into Claire's face, Gloria falling over, falling sprawled out on the gleaming blood-marked oak of the auditorium floor.

"Claire." Dolores drops her voice almost to a whisper. They're in the center of the stage. The smoke is thinning, rising to the ceiling. And they freeze there, on stage, looking out into the auditorium.

Did Angel see Claire in Dolores' arms?

Kind of. Maybe.

Whatever is going on in Angel's head, it's not conscious thought. It's not reasoning.

Maybe he saw Claire. Maybe he heard her say something once and then repeat it a second time, as if asking a question of God. He had just put three bullets into the head of Elvis Blakemore. And then there was Gloria at his feet, another one of the hunted. And was that Dolores on stage now, with Claire in her arms?

Maybe.

Maybe Dolores' eyes met his and in that second he was frightened.

That might be what happened.

The Glock heavy in his hand, Angel tucked it away in its holster.

He turned his back on the stage and climbed the empty aisle toward the entry doors, eyes staring out at him here and there from between and under the rows of seats.

Outside, the howl of sirens approaching, cars and trucks tearing over grass and concrete, a chaos of moving vehicles, traffic laws suspended in panic. The night crisp. The familiar smell of honeysuckle in the air.

Angel finds his car where he left it, on the concrete entryway, between flag poles. He gets in behind the wheel.

Did he follow mass-shooter protocol? Did he put the gun in his mouth? Did he pull the trigger?

No. He didn't.

Shelly, bright-eyed, radiant, put her hand on his wrist and held it tenderly. "Stop," she said. "Not yet."

"We're Done Now"

They'd been told, Cranston thought, trying to maintain focus on the introduction he was delivering for Stella Dunnett, the darling sixty-nine-year-old history teacher who was retiring. She could have retired years ago and been off living in sunny Los Angeles, nearby her successful cardiologist daughter—but she loved teaching and hadn't finally decided to retire until arthritis and problems with her knees started making it hard for her to get around. Now, before giving her a lifetime achievement award, as Cranston was trying to extoll her virtues, to sum up a magnificent career dedicated to her students, cell phones throughout the audience beeped and chimed, and Cranston was getting angry. They'd been told to turn off their damn phones, he thought—and then there was a gasp from the back of the room, and someone else in another corner of the auditorium shouted *Oh my God!* and the room was suddenly full of loud chatter as a few got up and hurriedly left.

Cranston was about to ask what was going on when a man in military gear kicked open a door and entered the auditorium wielding what looked like a sawed-off shotgun, with another military-looking rifle slung over his chest. He scanned the room as some fled through the side exits but most twisted around or stood up in their seats to get a look at whatever was happening. The room a loud buzz of anxious chatter. The last of the evening light faded, the windows of both walls black lakes. Cranston tapped the microphone, again about to ask what was going on, when the figure seemed to find who he was looking for in a back row and strode purposefully in that direction.

Angel saw Ginny Diaz looking at him, no recognition at all in her eyes. Why should she have recognized him? His face was grimy with blood and black paint. The yellow rose on his cap streaked with blood. His khaki slacks black in places with gore. Arms and hands muddy, grimy with a grease of blood and dirt.

But Ginny was hard to miss, the blue hair, the yellow and green streaks. Angel's body jerked into gear. He raised the shotgun to his shoulder, and with that move there were screams and a panicked rush as everyone bolted all at once for the exits, shouting, yelling.

Except not everyone ran away. Not this time. This time a trio of boys rushed Angel. They tackled him, big kids, one of them it turned out a football player, the team's quarterback, DeShaun James. The other two, DeShaun's best friends, Scott Marshall and Nack Pacetti, pitcher and first baseman on the varsity baseball team.

DeShaun hit Angel first, but too late.

Ginny, at the last moment, recognized Angel. He could see it in her eyes, which were frightened, which were terrified. She raised her arms and crossed her hands, as if that might protect her.

It didn't.

The shotgun erupted.

Ginny lifted off her feet by the blast tumbled into the next row. DeShaun in that same second hit Angel in the back, and the shotgun flew out of his hands.

Angel's knees on the ground, his cheek on the arm of the aisle seat. DeShaun tries to get his arms around the tactical vest, another boy grabs a fistful of Angel's hair.

But Angel is built like a duck pin and he doesn't ever fully go down. He pulls a long sawback bowie knife from its sheath in the tactical vest, and slashes blindly. A moment later the weight drops from his back and Angel jumps to his feet, furious. He's outraged at the boys, the little bastards. Two of them on the ground, one holding his neck, blood spurting out from between his fingers; the other, his eyes blank, holding a bloody hand over his heart as if saying the pledge of allegiance. Mr. Mumbles!, Angel shouts. Or he thinks he does. Mr. Mumbles! Really, he doesn't know what he's saying. But he does know that he's furious, and he's at least thinking Mr. Mumbles as the one remaining boy, Nack Pacetti, backs away from him. He too with his arms raised and crossed as if it might help somehow against the rifle which Angel levels at him and fires twice into his chest.

Must be some kind of automatic reaction, the arms raised and hands crossed.

It doesn't help.

The force of the bullets tosses Nack backward, his body jerking with the impact, as if the bullets hold him up a second or two before he falls into the row of seats behind him.

And then it's still not over, the attack on Angel Maso.

First it's Matt Ramano, who appears to be trying to hug him as he shouts his name, *Mr. Maso! Mr. Maso!*

Angel clubs him with the butt of the gun, knocks him to the ground, puts a single bullet in his head.

And then it's Cranston, and Angel thinks *Thank you*. He may even say it in a whisper, *thank you*.

The hunt is over. Cranston is running toward him up the aisle while everyone else is fleeing in the opposite direction.

Angel doesn't wait for Cranston to reach him. He squeezes off several shots in rapid succession. One of them at least hits. Angel can't tell. Maybe more than one, but he's not much of a shot. What does he know about these weapons beyond aim and pull the trigger? And aiming is hard in these moments, so much blood pumping in his ears, so much shaking in his limbs.

But the weapon, which is determined later to be Elvis Blakemore's AR-15, is a lethal machine, and at least one bullet stops Cranston as dramatically as hitting a glass wall. One second he's running up the aisle, the next he's stopped. And drops to his knees. And falls forward on his face.

Angel empties the rest of the clip into the remaining crowd, which has thinned in seconds to almost nothing, a bunch jammed up at the side exits, a bunch jammed up at the back doors.

He tosses the rifle to the ground.

He removes the tactical vest and drops it on top of the rifle.

He's bleeding. In the bright light of the auditorium, inside black glass walls, he's bleeding. His Transcendent Gardening sweatshirt is relatively blood free but for a spreading circle of blood at his side.

He lifts the shirt to find a deep slash wound. Which he must have inflicted on himself.

He touches the wound and, crazily, worries about the possibility of infection. Which amuses him.

From its holster he removes the Glock with its fresh clip. He's tired again.

Outside, behind him, an orchestra of sirens getting louder.

He wanders down the auditorium aisle, toward the side doors, shooting the fallen along the way. But he's exhausted now and hardly looks at what he's doing.

Outside, in the dark, he makes his way toward the tree line.

Shadows dash out of the night. There's wailing and screaming behind him, in the lighted auditorium, behind the soaring glass walls.

Angel sits at the foot of a cherry tree, and now Shelly is beside him. She's an older woman, older than Angel, but beautiful still. She's barefoot in white capri slacks that show off the sleek turn of her ankles. In a loose black blouse with a cowl pulled over her head, out of which sea-blue eyes watch him. Or see through him. Or into him.

She kneels and kisses his forehead. "We're done here," she says, and kisses him on the lips. She says, "we're finished, Darlin'," and she rises to her feet, and walks off into the woods as Angel watches.

When the police arrive behind their black shields, emerging out of the yellow light of the auditorium, does Angel this time put the barrel of the Glock in his mouth and pull the trigger?

Yes. Yes, of course he does.

Bright Birds Flying Into the Light

Cranston drifts in and out of awareness of the world. He's in a hospital room, his oldest daughter, Marcy, at his side. She's an attractive woman, a young version of Theresa. The way other men looked at his wife in those years when they first started dating, Cranston is thinking of that, or that thought rips through his addled mind. They come and go quickly, one thought then another then nothing and he opens his eyes as if he's terribly sleepy but waking now and then to look out and see what he sees, though he can't put much together. He's in a hospital room. Marcy is holding his hand over the rails of a hospital bed. The light in the room is impossibly bright. There's a bustle of activity around him. A machine beeps incessantly somewhere close. There are loud voices, men and women. They're not shouting but they're speaking loudly, forcefully, giving directions. He can't tell what they're saying.

It seems only a moment earlier that he was holding Ginny in his arms, but that can't be right. That was there, in the high school auditorium, and now he's in a hospital room. In the auditorium a lunatic, someone…someone shot Ginny. That much he remembers, and yet there was no gunshot wound. He held her in his arms in a circle of white light and silence, as if they were alone on a stage, just the two of them under a spotlight. He held her in his arms and knew she was alive and knew the life was slipping out of her. He kissed her on the lips. He rested her head in his lap. He spoke her name and when she died the bright birds around her breast flapped their wings and flew up and away into the light. In that moment, as the birds twittered and flew away, he felt a great peace descend over him. A peacefulness like the peacefulness he feels in this moment as he slips off into the quiet, Marcy's hand over his hand the only thing connecting him to the world of light and movement and sound.

That night, the night of the shootings, Cranston believed his family to be safe. He had jumped down from the stage at the roar of the shotgun, after Ginny had been blown off her feet, and DeShaun and some boys tackled the shooter. He had gathered Theresa and the girls and pushed them out the door before he turned back and ran up the aisle to help subdue the attacker. Later, he will tell others, many times, that he remembers nothing clearly after that. Only sporadic, incoherent bursts of memory from the hospital room before he was taken into surgery, at the county hospital where the corridors were lined with the wounded on gurneys, where every doctor in the county and surrounding counties had rushed to aid the victims. What he didn't know that night, what he didn't know until he was out of surgery and out of danger, was that Ellen, his fourteen-year-old, had run back into the auditorium looking for Jack Neely, her boyfriend; and that Theresa had followed her; and that they had both been shot and killed trying to drag Jack Neely's lifeless body to safety. That story, the story of the high school principal who was shot trying to reach the shooter, and his wife and daughter who were killed when they ran back into the auditorium to save the life of the daughter's fatally wounded boyfriend—that story will be retold myriad times in the hours and days immediately after the massacre, repeated endlessly on news shows and written about again and again in newspaper and magazine articles.

There will be many similar stories. Stories of men and women shielding children with their bodies, of husbands dying protecting their wives, of lovers and colleagues and friends and the brave things they did and the terrible losses they suffered. The nation will gather in front of its television screens and the President will address the people and the world will weep with us, and it will go on like that for several days before the news and the world moves on, and then for them, as for the fifty-five dead that night, it will all finally be over—but for Cranston, and all the survivors, for so many in Redvale, Georgia that evening, it's only the beginning. They're entering into an altered world.

In the hospital room next to Cranston and Marcy on the night of the shootings, Buddy Blakemore looked down at his youngest brother, Vince, who was unconscious on a gurney, prepped and in line to be taken by helicopter to another hospital. Buddy wasn't able to keep the details straight. Merri was dead. Elvis was dead. Rick was dead. And Vince was hanging on. Only Buddy escaped unscathed. In the back of Buddy Blakemore's mind the facts of his wife and brothers' deaths replayed in an echo of bald assertions: Merri was dead, Elvis was dead, Rick was dead. And underneath those assertions was the fact of his own cowardice. Once the shooting started, he froze. He, Buddy Blakemore, who had lied so often to himself and others about being a combat vet in Afghanistan that he had come to believe it, believe that he had seen combat in Kandahar, when in fact he had never gotten any closer to the fighting then hearing gunfire in the distance—he, Buddy Blakemore, the oldest of the brothers, had found himself unable to move once the shooting started. His arms locked up, his heart seized, and then he was outside in the night and he didn't go back into the building until he had seen the shooter drive away, pulling out from in front of the main entrance and driving off over grass and onto the road. Then he went back in, and found Merri, and Elvis, and Rick, and Vince—Vince the only one still breathing. Amid the lingering smoke. Amid slick streaks of blood. Amid moaning and screaming and panicked yells. Amid the coppery smell of blood mixed with the acrid odor of cordite. When he carried Vince out of the auditorium, someone took his picture. That picture in the next few days would travel over the world, printed on the front pages of a thousand newspapers, shining out from television screens everywhere. Buddy Blakemore, his face blood-smeared, his eyes pleading, carrying his only surviving brother out of the carnage.

Vince would survive the shootings. He'd be married in the summer, though the marriage would soon be abandoned to a future of drinking and endless trouble.

Buddy wouldn't survive. Two springs later, on the anniversary of the massacre, the bullet he ran away from that night would finally find him, in an empty garage with an idling truck, his family away visiting family.

Another body to add to the death toll.

All Those Poor People

In Claire's den, on a red leather couch, with an amber bottle of Kentucky straight bourbon on a slate coffee table in front of them, Dolores and Claire sat side by side, their hands folded in their laps like a pair of somber, daydreaming schoolgirls. It was late and they were done speaking. They had spoken to the authorities. They each had told everything they knew. The talking it seemed had gone on interminably before finally they were released and escorted home, where Claire found her driveway full of cars. Then there had been more talking before finally they showered and got out of their bloody clothes and made their way down to the den in matching white terrycloth robes, where they watched cable news for a while before turning off the sound.

How strange. How otherworldly.

All around Claire and Dolores, throughout the various rooms of Claire's house, a contingent of friends was busy answering the phone and guarding the doors against an ever growing rush of reporters seeking interviews. Now and then Claire sipped her whiskey, as did Dolores, but neither of them spoke, each of them wearing silence like a heavy coat. Side by side, in parallel worlds.

What was there to say? What was there, even, to think?

The news stations had quickly assembled and reported the essential facts. Angel Maso was the shooter. At the Board of Supervisors meeting, where hundreds had gathered, many carrying semi-automatics and other weapons to protest a proposed open carry ban in the city of Redvale, Georgia, a pandemonium of gunfire had broken out in the chaos that followed the initial shootings by Maso, many of the gun-wielding protestors believing they were under attack by terrorists. Others thought they were under attack by the U.S. government. By the time the police arrived in force, thirty-five were dead in the auditorium of the County Administrative Center, and an equal number were wounded. Angel Maso by that time was already across town, at the high school, where an awards ceremony was in progress. There, with a shotgun, a semi-automatic, a handgun, and a knife, he murdered another twenty citizens of Redvale before taking his own life.

Already, seemingly within minutes of the shootings, Angel Maso was known worldwide as the Angel of Death.

Already, Angel was identified by commentator after commentator as the face of evil. *Today the people of Redvale, Georgia came face to face with evil.* With Angel Maso, the Angel of Death, the incarnation of evil.

Already, the multitude of stories surrounding the shooting were beginning to accumulate.

How Angel had sought and been unable to find psychiatric help.

How he was a quiet man, who kept to himself, who lived alone.

How he had been recently fired from a job at the high school.

How his ex-wife was on the Board of Supervisors.

How Ginny Diaz, his first victim at the high school, ran the Poets in the Schools Program from which Maso had been fired.

How the Tiller and Blakemore families, who accounted for twenty of the fifty-five dead, were enemies of long standing.

How some claimed to have seen Elvis Blakemore shooting at members of the Board of Supervisors.

How some swore to have seen terrorists waving ISIS's black flag at the Board meeting and the high school.

How some swore there were multiple men in black among the shooters at the high school.

Scores of stories even then, in the immediate wake of the shooting. Stories that would blossom, expand, and spread throughout the nation and the world.

What was there to say? What was there, even, to think?

Later, much later, in the months and years to follow, Claire and Doll, discussing these moments, this night, as they sat together stunned on the red leather couch in her den, will discover they at least had one thought in common, one refrain buzzing through both their dazed bodies in a counterpoint to their own particular grief, their own particular losses, a thought for the dead and for the survivors, for the labyrinthine network of the bereaved:

All those people. All those poor people.

The Redvale Times Lists the Dead

1.   Amayr Ahmed (DOB 10/2/1993)
2.   Justin Bailish (12/12/1972)
3.   Caleb Barrett (6/17/1983)
4.   Barb Blakemore (2/7/2004)
5.   Sue Ellen Blakemore(5/1/2002)
6.   Annie Blakemore (8/20/1981)
7.   Elvis Blakemore (3/6/1972)
8.   Elvis Blakemore, Jr. (1/17/2000)
9.   Rick Blakemore (11/22/1975)
10.   Charlene Blakemore (9/4/1987)
11.   Bowie Blakemore (10/10/1984)
12.   Jeff Blakemore (2/7/2006)
13.   Amy Blakemore (6/28/1961)
14.   Diana Blakemore (3/30/1975)
15.   Betty Sue Blakemore (5/7/1993)
16.   Robert Corcoran (8/15/1995)
17.   Peter DeBouchian (1/28/1954)
18.   Ginny Diaz (12/24/1986)
19.   Stella Dunnett (10/27/1947)
20.   Willow Graham (3/24/2003)
21.   Charlotte Graham (12/2/1977)
22.   Birch Graham (8/20/2007)
23.   Judd Hansen (11/26/1979)
24.   DeShaun James (4/13/1999)
25.   Elizabeth Jennings (7/30/1964)
26.   Leslie Kolbert (2/18/1990)
27.   Henry LeDoux (8/26/1951)
28.   Peter Levy (5/15/1988)
29.   Scott Marshall (10/19/2000)
30.   Lucy Merola (11/1/1965)
31.   Jack Neely (6/11/2002)
32.   Nack Pacetti (4/17/2000)

33. Mary Perez (12/15/1994)
34. Joseph Perez (7/27/1993)
35. Anthony Perrini (2/12/1980)
36. Esther Price (12/28/2001)
37. Joseph Riggins (8/29/1963)
38. Matt Romano (9/16/2001)
39. Vincent Sardinia (3/29/1968)
40. Linni Sorland (12/18/1973)
41. Gloria Tiller (4/14/1986)
42. Ronnie Tiller (1/11/1975)
43. Travis Tiller (9/12/1970)
44. Sperry Tiller (4/26/1965)
45. Terri Tiller (4/28/1965)
46. Jesse Tiller (10/13/1987)
47. Merri Tiller (8/3/1966)
48. Angela Tiller (6/17/1982)
49. Ellen Wade (7/9/2002)
50. Theresa Wade (3/15/1976)
51. Kenneth Walker (2/10/1995)
52. Harold Wilkinson (11/8/1954)
53. John Williamson (7/14/1983)
54. James Whitmore (5/27/1964)
55. Mikala Wolfe (10/22/1993)

When Night Eventually Comes

Some shake so hard their teeth chatter.

Some repeat mantras: I will be okay, I will be okay, I will be okay. Or God help me please God help me please God help me.

Some stare at the ceiling too exhausted to think or move.

Some try to imagine a course through the future.

Some remember the loved ones they've lost, as if they might hold off death another moment.

Some replay events, asking what if.

Some reach for the hope that they might yet wake from this dream.

Some get up and look at the newly empty beds in their quiet homes.

Some stare into silent rooms.

Some collapse where they are and curl up in a ball.

Some are sedated.

Some cry yet again.

Some can't stop crying.

Some moan softly.

Some moan so loudly they wake their remaining family.

Some drink.

Some take pills.

Some are alone.

Some are surrounded by friends.

Some pray.

Some have angry words with God.

Until the dark, atramentous, overtakes them.

In Descending Dark

It was winter before Claire and Doll visited Angel's grave. He had been buried by his brother, with no ceremony, his body secreted out of Redvale and delivered to the winding avenues of the dead in Queens, New York, Calvary Cemetery, to a plot among strangers, removed from the family plot for fear of vandalism, the majestic skyline of Manhattan on the horizon, the Empire State building, the Freedom Towers—and Angel in death as in life, isolated, one in a line of paltry headstones.

Doll had come along with Claire reluctantly. She hadn't complained or resisted, but she was only there because she wouldn't let Claire go alone, and Claire had made up her mind to visit the grave site. Angel, no matter what he had done, was still her father. No matter how much pain and grief and anguish he had caused, he was still her father. She wouldn't abandon him. She *couldn't* abandon him. Not for Linni, not for Kenny, not for Gloria, not for everyone. Night after night, he visited her in dreams—and some of the dreams were terrible. Angel blood-covered, a ghoul mauling a body that could be Kenny or Linni, or, in the worst of the nightmares, her, Claire. In some of the dreams, Angel was lost and Claire was panicked, searching for him. In cities. In mazes. Through the endless corridors of unfamiliar buildings. In one dream, a dream that had recurred a dozen times and was half a dream and half a between-sleep-and-waking memory, she was on stage the evening of the shootings in the auditorium of the County Administrative Center, struggling against Dolores who was trying to pull her away from Kenny and Linni and Gloria, in the moment when she saw the shooter and recognized him as Angel and said *Daddy*, twice, as if the word were a question with an impossible answer. In the dream as in that moment, he only turned and walked away.

When Dolores had asked, her face barely masking something between anger and contempt, why she would want to visit Angel's grave, Claire hadn't answered. Instead, she had said that she was going and Dolores was welcome to join her, an offer that they both understood as a plea. Claire didn't want to go alone, but she would if she had to. She'd had a dream the night before, before announcing her intentions to Dolores, in which Angel had faced her from behind a wall of smoke. Maybe they were in the auditorium. Maybe it was the smoke that had filled that room. Angel almost there, almost seen, behind drifting smoke. She had awakened grief-stricken and sobbing. She had gotten up that night, like so many nights before, and wandered through her house, going from room to room looking for something that might occupy her attention. Finally, out on the deck, looking toward the mountains, she'd resolved to visit her father's grave, and only then was she able to go back to sleep.

Now it's winter and snow is falling lightly over this seemingly endless necropolis where a headstone smaller than any that surrounds it marks Angel's grave. Dolores and Claire side by side, Claire gazing down at the grave, Dolores looking off toward a fluttering streetlight against a gray sky. All around them a circuitry of roadways hums with heavy traffic. In the distance, the hazy lights of the New York skyline. Doll covers her head with the fur-lined hood of a down parka. She's thinking about the obscenity of it all. Everybody's life, their life's story, Gloria's, Linni's, everyone's life, their stories, severed, ripped away, aborted in a second. The cruelty of that evening. The monstrousness of it. And here, at her feet, lies the body of the perpetrator. She asks herself what she's doing in this place and for a moment she's furious, her face already rosy from the cold grows redder—and then she looks to her daughter and sees that she's silently crying, her face wet with tears, and her anger dissipates and turns to sorrow as she puts her arms around Claire and holds her close.

In descending dark, in failing winter light, surrounded by the dead.

But That's Not The Ending

Another year goes by and there are more mass shootings. In high schools. In grade schools. In colleges. In factories. In malls. In bars. Sometimes it seems like there's one every day, but now only the most spectacular make the news. The nation continues its tiresome debate between those who believe more guns in more places will lead to less violence and those who think that's insane. Claire and Doll avoid the news. They hide out in their respective homes. They avoid the controversies, the lawsuits, the conspiracy theories, the denial nut jobs, the legions with causes they want Claire or Doll to support, the reporters, the endless, invasive inquiries. Claire sells off her businesses and her properties. Doll gets out of politics and lives off her savings. They see the same therapists and take the same meds. Then, one summer, when Doll has dragged herself out of her house to stroll through Redvale's annual downtown festival, she passes a booth manned by gun-rights advocates. There, in Redvale, Georgia, the site of the nation's most deadly shooting rampage, they are auctioning off a Glock 19, the gun that turned out to be the single most lethal weapon in the arsenal of weapons that took fifty-five lives. Or, at least, it had been assigned that status. Though many of the dead had been wounded by more than one weapon, it was Angel's final shots to the head with the Glock that were inarguably fatal.

For several minutes that felt to Doll like a few seconds, she waited with her hands on her hips and watched a sixty-something jovial-looking big man in a loud Hawaiian shirt and a straw hat as he talked and laughed with a trio of smiling young women. The booth was standard for a street fair, a flimsy construction of plywood and crepe paper with a waist-high desk that held pamphlets, stickers—and a Glock pistol attached by a thin chain to an eye bolt. The street fair was crowded with people in shorts and bright blouses and sandals and sunglasses and summer hats. They flowed around Doll as around a motionless stone in a slow-moving stream. For a long time, she seemed stuck in place, her eyes moving from the handgun to the man in the Hawaiian shirt to the NRA bumper stickers and an assortment of buttons and a round orange sticker that read Pro-Gun Voter, the words curled around a picture of a handgun. The three laughing young women each looked to be in their late twenties or early thirties, and they each wore one of the orange stickers affixed high on their blouses, just under the shoulder.

Doll had very little memory of what happened next, but between what she did remember and what was reported, she was able to put together a coherent story. Apparently, she approached the three women and explained that she once had a girlfriend around their age, and that she had loved her immensely. More love than she had ever known before in her life and would ever know again, because her girlfriend was murdered by a man with a gun just like the one this man in a festive straw hat is auctioning off here in Redvale, Georgia, the site of the massacre where her girlfriend—Gloria, her name was Gloria—was murdered. The three women looked at her in silent bewilderment as she gently peeled the stickers off their blouses, crumpled them up, and tossed them in the direction of the Hawaiian shirt. And then that man, the clown in the straw hat, after saying he was sorry for her loss, began to explain why the Second Amendment to the constitution protected the right to keep and bear arms and how the government wanted to use tragedies like her own to deprive citizens of their constitutional rights, which would turn them into a nation of sheep who could be—Doll, apparently, didn't hear him out before she began to scatter his buttons and tear up his bumper stickers while screaming that he was a bloody idiot and that men and women and children were dying every day because of morons like him.

By the time the police got to her, Doll had torn down the booth and was smashing a couple of cardboard boxes full of gun-rights literature with a length of two by four while a crowd of people gathered to watch her, some of them applauding and cheering her on, some looking stunned, a few cursing her. No one, though, tried to stop her before the police led her away to the station house, where she was held and finally released after the gun-rights guy declined to press charges.

So. That was the beginning. The incident made national news. The day after the street fair, she was giving interviews to newspapers and magazines all over the country. The day after that, she started appearing on the morning shows. After years of having refused television appearances and news and radio interviews, after years of avoiding the press, Doll found herself suddenly saying yes to everyone, appearing on every cable and network news show, becoming one of those talking heads who appear in one of a triptych of screens and answer questions posed by Don Lemon or Rachel Maddow or Chris Wallace, etc. She had a knack for keeping things simple, and the news shows loved her for it. No matter what the question, she was usually able to wind her way back to a few basic, winning arguments. You couldn't keep men from going crazy, you couldn't keep them from being violent, but you could make it harder for them to get their hands on deadly weapons. Nothing, she argued, was ever going to put an end to the violence in men's hearts, but you could at least limit their access to the weapons that encouraged it. The fact that her positions were not radical—she wasn't calling for confiscation or even buy-back programs—also made her popular. She called only for a slate of reasonable regulations, ranging from safety features on guns to banning military-grade weapons, to tight regulations on who could carry guns and where they could carry them. The fact that she was the ex-wife of a shooter and partner of a victim gave her a degree of authority that others found difficult to attack. And while, yes, it was hard to talk about Angel, and even harder to talk about Gloria, she steeled herself to do what was necessary.

Doll, after years in hiding, came back into the world as a woman with a cause.

Now, she and Claire are on the balcony of a second-floor condo, overlooking the ocean. They're on Jekyll Island, on the coast of Georgia, gearing up for a gubernatorial campaign. Yes, Doll is going to run for governor as an Independent. No, she doesn't have a chance. It's the middle of the night, still another hour or two till daybreak, and they're sitting side by side in a gliding loveseat, watching as distant lightning strikes light up the horizon. The salt smell of ocean is in the air. A steady breeze off the water. Claire isn't thinking about anything much at all. Mostly she's watching the ocean, waiting for the next branching network of lightning to momentarily scatter darkness. It's Claire who is largely financing this gubernatorial campaign—though it wasn't, originally, her idea. No, that honor goes to Cranston Wade III, former principal of Redvale High

School, current member of the reconstituted Redvale Board of Supervisors. Cranston approached Doll, who at first dismissed the notion. He was persistent, though. He had contacts all over the state. He believed in Doll. Eventually, he convinced her to run, and then he and Doll managed to coax Claire out of her house and into the planning—and now, here they are, Claire and Doll on Jekyll Island, waiting to meet in the morning with a series of potential donors and backers, while Cranston is off in Atlanta, doing the same.

Neither one of them slept through the night much anymore. Claire usually awakened around 4:00 a.m., sometimes from a dream, sometime just opening her eyes and finding herself fully awake. This particular night, she had awakened thinking about Angel, which was nothing unusual. She lay in bed for a while remembering his eyes. She took comfort in this, remembering her father's eyes while he made breakfast for her when she was still a child. There was a light in his eyes then, a liveliness. When her thoughts turned to Kenny and Linni, she made herself remember Angel's eyes. They were not the eyes of that man in the auditorium, the man who murdered so many. Those were someone else's eyes, a stranger who had possessed the body of her father. Believing that, *knowing* that, was necessary for Claire. It was the only way she could think about that night—and she couldn't avoid thinking about that night. It wasn't him. That wasn't Angel Maso. That was not her father.

Claire would love to see Doll defeat Governor Guns-Everywhere. In her mind, he's the one responsible for the massacre, his guns-everywhere policies that encourage easy access to all manner of weapons and the right to carry them everywhere. To Claire, Angel Maso may have pulled the trigger, but the Governor is responsible for that night. She would have loved to defeat him, and sometimes she even let Cranston's enthusiasm make her believe it was possible.

But it wasn't. They'd be lucky to get 5% of the vote. Doll's support for mental health reforms and drug rehabilitation programs, her support for increased spending on education and job creation, and the way she made links between these issues and gun violence—none of it showed any sign of connecting with voters. Add to that Doll being a gay woman, and, well, the proverbial snowball in hell had better chances.

Claire, thinking these things, laughs out loud. "You know," she says, "that this is all futile."

Doll understands that she's talking about the run for Governor. "Sure," she says, and grants Claire a smile. "This time," she adds, and sidles closer to Claire. "This time," she repeats as she puts her arm around her.

Claire leans into Doll, rests her head on her mother's shoulder.

Together, they watch lightning over the ocean and wait for morning.

Notes

Because my neighbor's tree did once fall on my car, and because my property and his property are pretty much as described in this novel, I feel compelled to point out that in no other way is the neighbor in this novel related to my actual neighbor, who seems to me to be a perfectly nice guy. The same is true for all the other characters in the novel: they're all invented.

I'd like to thank Judy Bauer, Stephen Gibson, Cloe Veltri Gibson, Weston Cutter, and Jeremy Griffin for being early readers. Thanks to my immediate family: Judy, Eli, and Susan; and to my larger family, including friends, fellow writers, editors, publishers, and former students. It is my great good luck that there are too many names in this community to list here.

And to everyone who was in Blacksburg, Virginia on April 16, 2007, especially those students who spent that day together, a very special note of…what? Love, I guess. I can't think of any other way to put it.

C&R PRESS TITLES

NONFICTION

This is Infertility by Kirsten McLennan
Many Paths by Bruce McEver
By the Bridge or By the River by Amy Roma
Women in the Literary Landscape by Doris Weatherford, et al
Credo: An Anthology of Manifestos & Sourcebook for Creative Writing by Rita Banerjee and Diana Norma Szokolyai

FICTION

Transcendent Gardening by Ed Falco
Juniper Street by Joan Frank
All I Should Not Tell by Brian Leung
Last Tower to Heaven by Jacob Paul
History of the Cat in Nine Chapters or Less by Anis Shivani
No Good, Very Bad Asian by Lelund Cheuk
Surrendering Appomattox by Jacob M. Appel
Made by Mary by Laura Catherine Brown
Ivy vs. Dogg by Brian Leung
While You Were Gone by Sybil Baker
Cloud Diary by Steve Mitchell
Spectrum by Martin Ott
That Man in Our Lives by Xu Xi

SHORT FICTION

A Mother's Tale & Other Stories by Khanh Ha
Fathers of Cambodian Time-Travel Science by Bradley Bazzle
Two Californias by Robert Glick
Notes From the Mother Tongue by An Tran
The Protester Has Been Released by Janet Sarbanes

ESSAY AND CREATIVE NONFICTION

Selling the Farm by Debra Di Blasi
the internet is for real by Chris Campanioni
Immigration Essays by Sybil Baker
Death of Art by Chris Campanioni

POETRY

Curare by Lucian Mattison
Leaving the Skin on the Bear by Kelli Allen
How to Kill Yourself Instead of Your Children by Qunicy S. Jones
Lottery of Intimacies by Jonathan Katz
What Feels Like Love by Tom C. Hunley
The Rented Altar by Lauren Berry
Between the Earth and Sky by Eleanor Kedney
What Need Have We for Such as We by Amanda Auerbach
A Family Is a House by Dustin Pearson
The Miracles by Amy Lemmon
Banjo's Inside Coyote by Kelli Allen
Objects in Motion by Jonathan Katz
My Stunt Double by Travis Denton
Lessons in Camoflauge by Martin Ott
Millennial Roost by Dustin Pearson
All My Heroes are Broke by Ariel Francisco
Holdfast by Christian Anton Gerard
Ex Domestica by E.G. Cunningham
Like Lesser Gods by Bruce McEver
Notes from the Negro Side of the Moon by Earl Braggs
Imagine Not Drowning by Kelli Allen
Notes to the Beloved by Michelle Bitting
Free Boat: Collected Lies and Love Poems by John Reed
Les Fauves by Barbara Crooker
Tall as You are Tall Between Them by Annie Christain
The Couple Who Fell to Earth by Michelle Bitting
Notes to the Beloved by Michelle Bitting